STEPHANIE FAZIO

HALVE HUMAN

BOOK II OF THE BISECTERSERIES

Syafant Press

Printed in the United States of America
First Printing: June 2019

Library of Congress Control Number: 2019902601

ISBN 978-1-7335929-3-2

To Mom and Dad, for your endless love and support

PROLOGUE

SOME DAYS EARLIER

Aunt Jadem and I stand back-to-back at the battle's center. My sling whips through the air as I release one stone after another. The tiny missiles cut across the sky, too fast to see, before embedding themselves in my enemy's throats. I turn, kicking a path through the Duskers. My aunt lets out a sharp breath as she cleaves a man in two with her sword.

I don't look down at the growing pile of bodies at my feet. All of my attention is on the few dots of blue in the sea of gray. Too few. Our army—my soldiers—are outnumbered at least ten to one.

"Go in darkness," Aunt Jadem grunts as she gives a Dusker's lifeless body a vicious kick.

We exchange a brief nod. Tanguro is *ours*. We defeated the Duskers here once. We'll do it again.

"Archers!"

I duck as a volley of arrows shoots out from the only lookout still standing. Shouts ring out across the courtyard. More soldiers fall, adding to the bodies scattered from the day's fighting.

In the few moments it takes for the Duskers to recover their positions, I spring forward, knocking two down with a flick of my wrist. I jump out of the way of their flailing limbs and sidestep a blade making a too-slow jab for my thigh.

Crunch. Bones shatter beneath my boot as the Dusker's scream cuts through the other battle sounds.

"Well done—"

Whatever else Aunt Jadem was about to say is drowned out by the harsh horn blasting across the courtyard.

More Duskers are cresting the hill overlooking what remains of our fortress. Fresh soldiers to replace the ones who have been fighting all day.

This can't be happening, my mind screams. *Do something, Hemera!*

But there's nothing I can do, nothing any of us can do. My soldiers have no replacements.

"We have to retreat," Jadem gasps as she duels two Duskers at once.

I look up to see another soldier in blue fall to his knees, a Dusker's sword poised for the killing blow.

There's nothing I can do.

The Dusker pulls his bloodied sword from flesh and bone. It takes all of my will and strength to keep from collapsing myself. My aunt is right.

I shout the order to retreat, ignoring the way my voice cracks and every part of me rebels against the idea of giving up. My soldiers hesitate, stare at each other, and then begin to flee. They head toward the mountains, to the caves we stocked months ago in case we ever needed to make a fast escape from Tanguro. But I never thought that time would come so soon. We've only had six months to make this place home—

"Hemera!"

Before I can react, a fiery pain slashes across the back of my head. My vision blurs. I try to turn, but my legs are rooted in place.

I've failed. We're all going to die.

It's my last thought before I slip into darkness.

CHAPTER 1

SOME DAYS LATER

The ringing in my ears blocks out every other sound and thought. I try to clap my hands over my ears to drown out the noise, but my arms won't obey the simple command.

I open one eye, expecting the harsh sunlight to blind me, but it's dark. The smell of damp earth raises the old feeling of suffocation, but I force down my panic.

My head feels like it was bashed against a stone.

My eyes fly open as my memory of the battle rushes back.

"Where am I? What happened? Where's Aunt Jadem?"

"So many questions," a cold, unfamiliar voice answers. "If I were you, I'd be more worried about my broken skull than about your dead comrades."

Shooting pain rips across the back of my head as I turn. I clench my jaw to keep from screaming. Metal chains clank together as I try to get my body into an upright position.

Chains…around my wrists and ankles.

The realization itself is little cause for worry. I could break the iron without much difficulty, but there's no point until I know what I'm dealing with. The pain in my head is making my vision too blurry to see anything.

"Where am I?" I ask again as I give up trying to stand. I gasp as the back of my head falls back against the ground. It's like hot iron being driven through my skull.

"You're in the tunnels of your own fortress," the same voice informs me.

I'm in Tanguro. The place we have been fortifying to become the new Solguard fortress since the Duskers discovered Solis, the fortress Aunt Jadem built. The place the rest of the Solguards would be coming to, expecting safety and—

"So you are the infamous Zeidan Harkibel's daughter. I wonder…is there any truth to the rumors about you?"

"She just looks like another dying rebel," another voice replies with a chuckle.

The mention of my father's name makes a cold fury pulse through my veins. My vision sharpens.

Shadowy figures lining the sides of the tunnel come into focus.

Even below ground and without their signature gray, hooded cloaks, I know they are Duskers from their too-white skin that is almost its own light source down here. There are at least ten of them, standing with their backs pressed against both sides of the narrow tunnel. They each hold a loaded crossbow.

Swallowing a wave of nausea, I tilt my head back to look at the man standing over me. He wears the black armband of the captains around his thick bicep. The white skin of his face is almost translucent in the lantern light.

"Is this all that's left of your army?" I meant the question to sound challenging, but it comes out as a squeak, my unused voice betraying me.

"Our army has returned to Malarusk to report your defeat." Another Dusker, this one a woman with a raspy voice, curls her lip in what could be a grin or a snarl. Her status as a Banished who betrayed her people for a life with the Duskers is written across her scarred face. The Dusker practice of breaking the faces of potential recruits to test their loyalty is visible in the misfitting lines of her jaw and jagged scar across her nose. She looks to her Captain for approval the way a dog would solicit its master.

Even though I'm stronger than five of them put together, the old habits bred into me since childhood, to fear and obey the Duskers without question, make me want to cower as the Dusker Captain leans over me. He grabs the shackles binding my wrists and hauls me to my feet.

"The Dusker Supreme has some questions for you." He gives me a shake, making the chains around my wrists and ankles rattle. "How long have you been in league with the Solguard leader?"

At the mention of my aunt, muttered curses ring through the tunnel. Aunt Jadem was once a high-ranking Dusker. She and Dayne, the older half-brother I discovered only a year ago, tried to infiltrate the Dusker citadel Malarusk. Their charade was discovered, and they were both thrown into the dungeon. They were the first—and only—ones to ever escape.

From the sound of it, these Duskers have not forgotten.

"I'm waiting." The Dusker rests a hand on the hilt of his sword.

I force a smile onto my face. Dried blood cracks around the corners of my mouth. "We have been *in league*," I sneer, "ever since I met her."

I hold up my right hand, displaying the Solguard sun emblazoned on my flesh.

Snarls echo down the tunnel, but the Captain's face remains impassive.

"You have lost the battle of Tanguro. The moment the Dusker Supreme gives the order, that pathetic Solguard fortress and all its rebels will be wiped off the map." He erases the lives of hundreds with a sweep of his hand. "The Solguards will soon be nothing but a memory."

His words should fill me with fear. Instead, relief washes through me. Solis used to be a secret known only to those who lived there, but then Gorgoran betrayed us and gave up the fortress' location. Jadem knew the fortress wouldn't survive an attack from the Duskers, so the Solguards living there were going to come to Tanguro.

For weeks, we've had no word from Wade and the rest of the Solguards. They should have been here by now, and every day that passed without word made us think….

"They're alive," I breathe.

"Only until the Dusker Supreme decides to punish them for their leader's lies. The Supreme does not take kindly to oath-breakers."

Lies? Oath-breakers?

"Look!" Another Dusker gestures with his crossbow. "That cut on her head…it's gone." He meets my black eyes for just a moment before a shudder visibly goes through his body.

"Ah, yes. Our spy told us about you."

Gorgoran.

My anger makes me forget about the dull ache in my head.

"Do you realize I could kill you all?"

There are a few nervous snickers, but the Captain doesn't blink.

"I wouldn't try anything if I were you," his lip quirks in a twisted grin, "since your friends would be the ones to pay for your foolishness."

My blood goes cold.

"Gorgoran told us which ones you care about most." The man taps his white cheek. "There was a scrawny barbarian child, an archer with a mess of red hair, and the *traitor.*"

All the air leaves my body. *Wokee, Ry, and Aunt Jadem.*

"Where are they?" I gasp. "What have you done with them?"

"They're alive…for now." The Captain's threat hangs between us. "Some of my soldiers are accompanying them back to Malarusk as we speak."

"If there's so much as a scratch on them…." I hate the way my voice trembles.

The man studies me for a moment. "What happens to them all depends on you."

"What do you want to know?" *I'll tell you anything. Just don't hurt them.*

"For starters," he taps the blade of his sword against his hand, "what are you, exactly?"

"A Bisecter," I say.

"How did you come to be?"

"Halve blood touched my mother while she was pregnant." I talk quickly. The sooner this interrogation ends, the sooner the Duskers will release my friends. "I absorbed the poison."

There is an angry murmur from the other Duskers.

"There have been reports you are stronger than even the Halves. Some say you can go on the Outside without a cloak, even during the high day." He eyes me. "Clearly, the rumors about your healing are true."

"I don't hear a question," I retort.

The Dusker Captain flexes his arms. "Is it all true?"

"Yes." I stare at him, even though he can't hold my black eyes with his pale gray ones.

"Are there any more of you?"

I think about the Zeroes, the creatures my father spawned in his experiments to recreate me.

"No."

"She's an abomination!" one of the Duskers calls.

"I've answered your questions," I say. "When will you release the others?"

"That will be up to the Dusker Supreme." The Captain's face takes on a dreamy expression that seems entirely at odds with the rest of him. When he blinks, his cold mask is back in place. "But if you cooperate, I don't see any reason why your friends can't become loyal servants of the Dark God."

Another wave of nausea surges through me.

"When the rest of my army returns, they'll find us." My throat feels like it's coated with sand, and the words ring hollow.

Raucous laughter fills the tunnel.

"There is no *rest of your army*," the Dusker smirks. "Our archers destroyed every last one of those cowards as they fled to the mountains."

"You're lying." My head turns back and forth, like my army might be just out of sight. They can't all be….

"I expect the Burn vultures are feeding on their rotting corpses as we speak," the Dusker says with a casual wave of his hand.

"Liar!"

I wrench my bound wrists apart. The iron links snap as if they were made of dried grass. I twist my legs to break the bindings around them. Free of chains, I'm on my feet before the Duskers can even raise their crossbows.

I wrap one arm around the Captain's throat and squeeze.

He gasps and writhes against my grip. I turn, using his body to shield mine in case any of the others decide to shoot. "The other prisoners…where are you keeping them?" I demand.

"There are…no others," the Captain gasps. His legs scrabble against the ground. "Only the three captives. The rest are dead."

My anger leaves me as quickly as it came. I hardly notice the arrows pointing at me from all sides. I release the Dusker, my shoulders collapsing in defeat.

All of them…dead?

"Stupid Halve bitch," the Dusker chokes out, holding his neck with one hand.

My army. My friends…who stood and fought beside me even as the Duskers closed in around us….

The Duskers are talking, but their voices are nothing more than a dull buzz in the corner of my mind.

Dead.

Jadem, Ry, and Wokee are still alive, but who knows for how long. As soon as the Duskers have gotten what they want from me….

The Duskers don't show mercy, especially not to people with the Solguard tattoo.

Everything we were working for…everything we dreamed of…none of it matters if the ones who built it are gone.

"You're all doomed," the Dusker woman says into the silence. "The Darkness is coming sooner than you can imagine."

The Duskers have prophesied about the darkness for years, but something about the way she says the words makes fear shiver down my spine.

"Quiet, soldier!" the Captain commands, his face purpling.

The woman hunches her shoulders and melts back against the wall.

I don't have time to wonder at the exchange. There is movement out of the corner of my eye, a blinding pain through my skull, and then my vision goes black.

CHAPTER 2

I'm dragged to my feet by rough hands. My feet, clumsy enough on their own, almost give out beneath me without the ability to use my arms for balance.

When I remember the Duskers are holding Wokee, Aunt Jadem, and Ry captive and that the rest of my army is dead, I double over and vomit.

The Dusker Captain scowls as he steps over the mess. "You can put your famed strength to the test today. It's a long way to the citadel."

"You're taking me to Malarusk?" Dread coils itself in the pit of my stomach. It's only a small comfort that at least I'll be heading to where Aunt Jadem, Ry, and Wokee were taken.

I'm not hopeful or foolish enough to think I could manage to free them once we're all in Malarusk. There are hundreds of guards in the citadel, and once they—or I—am in the dungeon, we'll never see the light of day again.

"You don't deserve to set foot in the Dusker territory. You are an abomination that could threaten the peace the Supreme has woven."

"Peace?" I scoff. "You just want to make sure I won't be able to end your tyranny."

"Careful," the Dusker breathes. "Or your three friends will pay the price for your traitorous words."

I stand very still as the Duskers make ready to leave. One of them tosses a nearly-empty waterskin at me. I swallow the few mouthfuls, unable to resist with the fiery ache in my throat. My stomach clenches with hunger.

The Duskers pull on their cloaks, hiding their ghostly skin beneath the hoods and thick gray fabric. Gloves are pulled over bone-white hands.

"There seems little point in binding you," the Dusker Captain says, "but if you try anything, your friends will be Burn vulture breakfast."

I clench my jaw. Blinding sunlight floods the tunnel as one of the men throws open the stone covering. I follow the Duskers up the steps cut into the upward sloping earth tunnel and emerge into the low day.

Blinking, I scour the haze of reds, greens, and blues of the landscape. We're facing the mountains south of the fortress that form a natural barrier separating the Wild Lands of Tanguro from the rest of civilization. I turn back to find the buildings—or what's left of them—engulfed in a roaring fire. The wood cracks and pops as flames lick up the sides.

The orchards Wokee spent months nurturing are now nothing more than smoking embers. The defensive wall we all labored on for weeks is in ruins.

I remember when Thutmose placed the final stone on the wall, he kissed it. I stood on that wall and watched the sun color the mountains from pink to orange to deep red. We were going to defeat the Duskers from behind those walls.

All the breath leaves my body when I see the beautiful golden tree that marks Brice's grave. It's on fire.

As the flames turn the tree to ash, I feel my heart crack into a thousand pieces.

The ground rumbles, and a plume of dust rises from the far end of the courtyard.

"Explosives in the tunnels," the Dusker Captain tells me. "Just to make sure no one gets the idea to mount a resistance from here again."

I wipe a sleeve across my nose but can't stop the tears from carving a path down the dirt on my face. "You're all monsters."

"*You* are the only monster here," the Captain says, pointing a gloved finger at me.

The thought of what the Duskers will do to Aunt Jadem and my two best friends if I don't go with them is all that keeps me from falling to my knees and refusing to move another inch.

The Captain signals his soldiers, and they begin to move.

"Walk." There is the sharp jab of an arrow at my back.

If they stabbed me, I think, *there would be nothing inside.* I'm hollow. *Empty.*

With the crackling of the inferno and the ground still rumbling from the tunnels' destruction, I let the enemy lead me out of Tanguro. The next time I look back, all I can see of the fortress is the smoke curling above the ruins.

"Captain, look." One of the Duskers waves his sword in the direction of the mountain. "Is that—?"

"Draw weapons," the Captain commands.

There is the sound of blades being pulled from scabbards and the click of arrows being fitted into crossbows.

"Halve!"

"Dark God protect us…."

"Form lines," the Captain snaps.

I crane my neck, but the taller Duskers in front make a shield of gray that blocks my view.

My heart pounds a rhythm of hope against my chest. I haven't heard from Ekil and the rest of the Halves since they left the fortress in search of their own lands. *Did Ekil somehow hear about the attack and come to help?*

"No mercy," the Dusker Captain is saying. "We will destroy it."

As the Duskers spread out, an opening in their ranks gives me a view of the incomer. I see the Halve they're talking about, but as it comes closer, I make out other smaller figures running behind.

My hope plummets. One Halve and three soldiers, no matter how skilled, are nothing against the Duskers. They'll be dead long before they reach us.

As they near, I can see the three humans running behind the Halve are wearing Solguard blue. I squint into the blinding sunlight, hardly daring to breathe. One of them is tiny—even compared to the other humans. *Wokee?*

Hope and fear rage inside me.

"Crossbows ready!"

A few more seconds pass before Ry's red, frizzy hair curling around the sides of her blue hood comes into view. The bow and arrow in her hands leaves no doubt in my mind. The third figure—my aunt—dwarfs the other two even though she lags behind.

Something almost like—but not quite—hope makes the fog in my brain begin to lift.

My sling is gone, taken by the Duskers, but that doesn't mean I'm weaponless. Before the guards can react, I grab the nearest Dusker's sword. I wrench it from his belt and slice straight through him in the way Wade and I practiced months ago. I grit my teeth against the feeling of the blade piercing through flesh and bone.

A gurgling sound of protest erupts from his throat.

"The Bisecter," someone shouts. "Kill the Bisecter!"

"No—the Supreme wants her alive."

I sweep the bloodied sword in an arc, felling two more men before they can even raise their crossbows. A snarl rips free from my throat as I hurl my body at the tightening circle of Duskers, carving a path through them in the direction of my friends.

"Mer, down!"

I would know Ry's voice anywhere. Without thinking, I drop to a crouch. Two arrows pass directly over my head and bury themselves into the Duskers behind me.

"You leave her alone!"

The sound of Wokee's shrill voice gives me a burst of energy. With one slash of the sword in my hand, two more Duskers fall. When I look up from my slaughter, Ekil is beside me, bludgeoning Duskers with a stone club. Ry's arrows are flying. I turn my attention on the Dusker Captain, who is standing behind his few remaining soldiers.

Aunt Jadem is yelling something, and it's not until my sword is poised at the Captain's throat that her words become clear.

"Stand down!" she's calling. "Hemera, don't."

When she reaches me, she's panting for breath and her face is red with exertion.

"Aunt Jadem, he—they—" I can't even bring myself to say what they've done.

Aunt Jadem holds up a finger as she gasps for air. "Enough blood has been spilled already. Killing them will only make things worse."

But they're Duskers. They would have killed every one of you without a thought.

My response is drowned out by the sound of—laughter. The Dusker Captain is laughing so hard tears are streaming down his face.

"Is he crazy?" Ry asks, looking from me to Aunt Jadem.

"Oh, that's rich," the Dusker says, wiping tears from his eyes as he stares unblinking at Aunt Jadem. "You trying to make amends, oath-breaker?"

My aunt's one good eye narrows.

"But you'll get what you deserve," the Captain continues. "The darkness is coming. The Supreme—"

Before I've even realized the sword has left my hand, Aunt Jadem slices the blade across the man's throat.

He crumples in a gray heap on the ground.

"I thought you said we needed to let him live," I say, raising an eyebrow.

"I changed my mind." Aunt Jadem wipes the Dusker's blade on the ground.

"What was he talking about?" Ry asks. "All that nonsense about making amends?"

"Just that." Aunt Jadem slides the Dusker's blade into the empty sheath on her belt. "Nonsense."

Her words are nonchalant, but worry lines pucker my aunt's brow, adding to the map of scars across her forehead.

"That Dusker said something about oath-breakers to me, too," I say. "He said that the Dusker Supreme would punish them. And there was something else." I squint into the sunlight, trying to remember. "One of them said the darkness was coming sooner than we thought."

"Please," Ry scoffs. "They've been saying that for about a hundred years now." She wipes sweat from her brow. "No darkness yet."

"This was different, though." I shake my head, trying to put words to the feeling. "The Captain got angry at the soldier who said it, like she wasn't supposed to talk about it."

"What else did he say?" Aunt Jadem's eye is intent on me. "Think hard, Hemera. I want to know every word."

I shrug. "He knocked me out after that."

At the look on my aunt's face, I hurry to say, "It probably meant nothing."

My aunt is silent for a moment, and then she shakes her head. "Ravings of a dead man."

She gives me a lopsided smile, but she seems lost in her own thoughts.

"Did you see Hemera kill one with just her fist?" Wokee breaks the silence. "That was awesome!"

A jolt of regret passes through me. Not for killing the Duskers, but because Wokee had to see it. If I could, I would shield him from everything unpleasant.

I look at Wokee, hardly daring to believe he is standing here…alive.

Even though he's grown since Dayne and I rescued him from the hilltop, Wokee's round eyes are still too big for his freckled face. His mop of blonde curls has grown past his ears, and he keeps tucking the stray pieces back into his hood. A layer of dust and grime coats his face and neck, but that isn't unusual for him.

Wokee's dimpled cheeks break into a grin as I study him. I pull him into my arms. Wokee returns my embrace for a fraction of a moment, and then squirms away, muttering something about girls and mushy emotions.

"That's right," Ry opens her arms to me. "Come give me some of that mush."

Ry lifts me off the ground in an embrace tight enough to hurt any normal person.

"I was so worried," I say. "I thought…." I swallow, unable to continue. I blink away the blurriness in my vision before anyone notices.

"Lucky Ekil found us when he did." Aunt Jadem nods at the Halve. "If it wasn't for him, we'd still be at the Duskers' mercy."

"Yeah," Wokee adds. "He," he points his dagger at the Halve, "broke into the traveling cave they were keeping us in. Probably would have killed us along with the Duskers if it—I mean, Ekil—hadn't recognized us." Wokee gives Ekil a sidelong glance. "He tried talking to us, but you know, it was all gibberish. But then he said your name. And he led us here."

"Hemera." Ekil says my name in the guttural language of the Halves, which, thanks to the blood I share with them, I understand.

After being surrounded by only humans for these past months, Ekil seems to loom even larger than I remember. When I take the gnarled, scaly hand he holds out to me, everything below my wrist is swallowed in his grip.

His posture is hunched, and the longer of his uneven arms reaches almost to the ground. He wears a new animal hide skirt, which doesn't hang in filthy tatters like the one he wore when he was my father's prisoner. His eyes, as black as mine, still have that intelligent gleam that first made me realize he was different from the other Halves. And yet, as familiar as he is, there's something different about him.

Ekil is still more than a foot taller than even the largest man, but he isn't as round as the last time I saw him. His rough skin hangs off him like he's lost a lot of weight quickly, and I can see his ribs protruding from his sunken chest. His back is more curved than I remember, and I can see the knobs of his spine under his skin.

"Thank you for rescuing us," I say to Ekil. "Again."

"Things very bad for Halves," Ekil says without acknowledging my gratitude. "Gray humans took our river."

"What's he saying?" Wokee asks.

"He says the Duskers took their river," I translate.

"How does someone take a river?" Wokee demands, wrinkling his nose. I repeat the question to Ekil.

"They dug new ditches. Made the river flow away."

"Why?"

Ekil blinks at me, like my stupidity is beyond his comprehension. "Duskers dug new streams. Made the river flow away. No water, no animals. No animals, no food. Halves starving."

"Why in the sun would the Duskers do that?" Ry asks after I have finished translating. "Why not just attack the Halves outright?"

"Perhaps they don't want to risk being poisoned by Halve blood," Aunt Jadem replies, "and think depriving them of their water to be a less risky way of destroying what they view to be a cursed species." She winces even as she says the words.

"But to go through the effort of re-coursing an entire river…?" Ry's question hangs in the air.

"We need help," Ekil states. "Humans have water but won't share. Halves and humans killing each other."

"You're living in the Banished Lands?" I ask Ekil.

The Banished Lands, where people expelled from the Subterrane Territory have lived for generations, are just south of the mountains. Until I met Wokee, I believed the Duskers' stories that all Banished people were criminals and barbarians. Now, I know better. The Banished don't associate with either the Dwellers or the Solguards; they live by their own laws.

"Nowhere else to go," he growls in reply.

I grimace, imagining the Banished people's reaction when a group of Halves decided to live among them. An image crystallizes in my mind. The Halves, desperate for food and water, invading the settlements. The people, terrified of the Halves and unable to understand them, defending their homes and families.

"We need help," Ekil says again.

"I'm sorry." I shake my head. "There's nothing I can do."

"You saved us from bad man. Save us from gray cloaks now."

"I couldn't even save my own people!" I gesture in the direction of the ruined fortress. "There's nothing, nothing, I can do." I sink to the ground, burying my face in my hands.

"Mer?" Aunt Jadem crouches beside me. "What's happened?"

It's only then that I realize the Duskers must have captured them before the end of the battle. Jadem, Ry, and Wokee don't know what happened to the rest of our army. I look at my aunt and feel my heart splinter.

"They're dead. They're all dead."

CHAPTER 3

y hands lift in a helpless gesture. The rebel sun, inked onto the back of my right hand, is now just a cruel reminder of my failure.

In broken sentences, I tell them what the Duskers said about the rest of our army. Ry wraps her arms around Wokee. For once, he doesn't try to stop her. Aunt Jadem's shoulders slump.

"I don't understand," Ry says. "The Duskers shouldn't have even been here. They were supposed to attack Solis first—"

"The Solguard fortress is still standing," I say before Ry can finish. "The Duskers said they were waiting until the Dusker Supreme was ready."

Momentary relief washes over Ry's face, but then her brow furrows. "Why?"

"It's a message," Aunt Jadem murmurs.

We all look at my aunt, but she seems lost in her own thoughts.

"Aunt Jadem?" I press.

"Nothing." She shakes her head. "But we need to get back to Solis. We have to warn them."

Aunt Jadem is already moving, like she's going to walk all the way back to the fortress right now.

"It'll take us weeks to get back," Ry protests. "Whatever the Duskers plan to do will be done by the time we get there."

"Hemera." Ekil raises a hand to get my attention. "Halves dying."

"I'm sorry," I say. "I can't help you." I turn my black eyes to the ground, unable to hold Ekil's gaze.

"I want to see Tanguro." Wokee's voice is quiet, but it cuts through Ry and Aunt Jadem's plans for returning to Solis.

I exchange a look with my aunt. There are a dozen things we need to do right now, and going back to the ruins of Tanguro will only slow us down. Still, I don't blame Wokee for wanting to see it one last time. I feel the same urge.

What would be the harm in taking a few extra minutes to say goodbye?

✳ ✳ ✳

No one speaks as we tramp past the huge chunks of stone littered across the ground, which used to be the wall surrounding Tanguro. The enormous white buildings we lived in are gone, turned into ash from the fires set by the Duskers. Trees from the orchard Wokee found in ruins and so carefully nurtured are dismembered. The bright pink and yellow fruits that had dragged at their boughs lay rotting on the ground.

But these details barely register in my consciousness. It's the blue cloaks dotting the ground between the fortress and the mountains that make my knees tremble. It is only Ry on my left and Aunt Jadem on my right who keep me standing.

The scattered black arrows, blue cloaks, and bones are all the Burn vultures left behind. There is no other evidence that nearly five-hundred soldiers and former prisoners fought here. Men and women who dreamed of a better life, who believed in my promises to give them that life.

A sob rips free from my throat.

"What happened here isn't your fault," Aunt Jadem tells me.

"We all knew the danger." Ry's voice hitches.

"They killed all the trees." Wokee's lip quivers.

Wokee spent his every waking moment learning about the unusual plants that grow only in Tanguro. He plied Aunt Jadem for her tricks for keeping trees alive in the heat of high day and her special recipe for plant food. Wokee spent half a day following me around, bragging about how Aunt Jadem had told him all her secrets about growing things.

It was because of Wokee's careful studies that we learned which plants would kill with a single touch, which fruits would stay fresh for weeks, and where to dig for the rare fungus that lured animals into our waiting traps. It was Wokee's labors that fed our people in this strange, unfamiliar land.

And it was all for nothing.

"Their ashes will go back into the land they sprung from." My aunt gives Wokee a sympathetic squeeze. "And from their ashes, new trees will grow."

"It won't be the same." Wokee swipes his gloved hand across his eyes.

Pain stabs through me like a hot knife.

"But that is your gift," Aunt Jadem tells Wokee, quirking her scarred lip at him. "The Duskers can never stop you from planting more. You are the most talented botanist I have ever met."

Wokee doesn't say anything, but I can tell the compliment means more to him than he'd ever admit.

I can't speak around the lump in my throat.

"Ahead."

I turn to see what Ekil is pointing at. A dark shape on the horizon is just visible through the bright orange haze of the sun.

"Burn vulture." Ry, whose trained archer eyes have already spotted the threat, has an arrow nocked in her bow. I reach for my sling before remembering I don't have it anymore.

"No, it isn't." Wokee tugs on Ry's arm to lower her bow. "It's Vlaz!"

"It can't be." Vlaz, the orphaned hyenair cub, is with Dayne.

"It's too big to be Vlaz." Ry raises her bow again. "It's a Burn vulture."

"I think I know the difference." Wokee stomps his foot.

The animal, whatever it is, has spotted us. It dives, hitting the ground with a spray of dirt. The moment the creature regains its footing and begins to run, its one flopped ear bouncing crazily while the other is pricked forward, I know Wokee is right.

The cub I remember is gone; in his place is a giant, winged hyenair I barely recognize. His wings, even folded on his back, are each the length of a full-grown man. He is as tall as three stags stacked one atop the other, except his body isn't sleek and delicate like a stag's. His thick, shaggy black fur hangs off his body in matted clumps. Thick cords of muscle wind around his haunches and down to his paws, each of which is bigger than my head. Two dagger-sharp fangs hang down from his upper lip.

There is something unfamiliar and vaguely terrifying about this massive creature. I shield Wokee with my body as Vlaz approaches.

Ekil's black eyes are darting between Vlaz and me. When he raises his club, I put up a hand. *Wait.*

"Unnatural creature." Ekil shakes his head.

I give him a wry smile. "That's what the Dwellers say about you." *About me.*

Ekil only blinks at me.

Darting around me, Wokee throws his arms around one of the giant forelegs that is as tall as he is. Vlaz utters little whimpers of excitement as he lowers his massive head to the boy. With a single nudge from the hyenair's nose, Wokee is sprawled on the ground, laughing as Vlaz bathes his face with his enormous purple tongue.

When his luminous yellow eyes spot me, Vlaz bounds over Wokee in one swift leap. I recoil. His fangs and claws are each as long as my entire hand, and they look like they could snap a person in two. Even his tail could kill with a single flick.

But as soon as Vlaz is beside me, my hesitation fades. *It's Vlaz.*

His huge purple tongue darts out to cover my entire face in sticky slobber. The force of it is enough to knock me over. Vlaz waits impatiently for me to right myself, and then he lowers his head to the ground so I can scratch his favorite spot underneath his flopped ear. I marvel at how his ears have grown the length of my forearm.

"Told you it was him," Wokee brags.

"You're nuts." Ry shakes her head as Wokee reaches up to scratch Vlaz's foreleg.

"Where is your brother?" Jadem asks me, echoing the question in my own mind.

"Something on the beast's neck." Ekil points up.

The blue collar Wokee made for Vlaz is gone—he must have outgrown it months ago—but in its place is a piece of blue fabric wound around the hyenair's thick neck.

"Down," Wokee commands, pointing his finger at the ground.

Without hesitation, Vlaz folds his legs until his enormous body is resting on the ground.

"Impressive," Ry murmurs.

Wokee gives us a superior grin. "I taught him that."

I reach up to the blue shred of cloth now just barely within my reach. On the fabric's tattered edge is a hastily drawn black sun, the symbol of the Solguards. A bit of yellowing script tree bark wedged between the fabric and Vlaz's fur falls to the ground.

My pulse quickens as I recognize the spidery text. I can feel the heat of everyone's gaze as I scan the note.

"Well?" Ry makes an impatient gesture.

"He did it." I swallow. "Dayne found my father."

CHAPTER 4

Is your father still alive?"

"Did Dayne capture him? Where are they?"

I pass the letter to Ry. She unrolls it and reads aloud.

Mer, I hope this beastly hyenair is as good at finding you as Wokee promised. I know where Zeidan is hiding. Meet me at Solis as soon as you are able.

-D

Ry lets out her breath in a low whistle. "How *did* the hyenair manage to find us?" She stares up at Vlaz, who is drooling as Wokee scratches his flopped ear.

Wokee grins. "I taught him to find his way back here."

"Dayne knows the Duskers are headed to the fortress next," Ry says. "Why didn't he just come back here?"

My brother never does anything without a reason, which leaves only one possible explanation. "The fortress must be near to where my father is hiding."

My words are met with silence. We all remember the catacombs where my father killed dozens in his effort to replicate me. We all remember his Zeroes.

What has my father been up to all this time?

"I hate mysteries," Ry grumbles.

"We need to get back to the fortress." Jadem paces back and forth. "Now."

I try not to think about how my father will have plenty of time to disappear again before we reach Solis. If I left the others behind, I could cover the distance in half the time. I know they would never agree to let me go after my father on my own, though.

"How do we know the Duskers won't attack the fortress before we get back?" Ry asks.

Aunt Jadem's face is grim. "We don't."

"We don't have—" Wokee begins, but Ry interrupts him.

"What's Ekil doing?"

We all look to where she's pointing. Ekil is squatting on the ground near the ruins of one of the buildings. He lifts up the wing of a dead Burn vulture and drags something from beneath it.

Not some*thing*, I realize. Some*one*.

"Oh suns, it can't be," Aunt Jadem breathes.

"Jarosh!" Ry takes off.

Jarosh, the first person to pledge his support to me as the leader of Tanguro, lies limp in Ekil's arms. His face is spattered with blood.

"He's alive!" Ry calls as she helps Ekil set him on the ground.

The rest of us run to them.

"Bastard tried to eat me," Jarosh rasps, gesturing at the Burn vulture's remains.

"Its wing kept him alive." Ekil nods his head up and down.

"You're bleeding!" Ry is already tearing off the shirt she's wearing beneath her cloak to use as a makeshift bandage.

Ekil holds the dead Burn vulture's wing over them, giving them shade while Ry kneels beside Jarosh.

"I have that effect on women," Jarosh whispers, eyeing the torn pieces of Ry's shirt.

"In your dreams," Ry mutters as she winds the fabric around Jarosh's stomach.

"You could do worse." Jarosh's attempt at a grin becomes more of a grimace as Ry knots the cloth.

Sweat pours down his temples as a tremor wracks his body.

"We need to find bandages, medical supplies, anything...." I look around, like they might just appear out of the ruins.

"He needs a healer," Wokee states the obvious.

"My fortress is too far." Aunt Jadem shakes her head. "And there are no settlements on this side of the mountain."

She doesn't mention that even if we could get him to Solis, there would be no healer to treat him. The Solguard healer, Gwendil, died from touching my blood when she was trying to help me.

A brokenness erases the hope we had all felt moments before.

"The Halves can save your friend."

I give Ekil a sharp look. "You can?"

Ekil nods. "There is one among our kind who can help him. If," Ekil's black eyes narrow, "you help the Halves."

Ekil and I stare at each other for a long moment. I have no idea what I could do get the Banished to stop attacking the Halves, and even less of an idea about how to get their river back. But Jarosh is alive. I can't do anything for the hundreds of others who fought and died here. I *won't* lose Jarosh, too.

"Okay," I say with a helpless shrug. "I'll try."

Ekil nods in agreement.

I translate our bargain for the others, and then I say, "We have to make a harness so I can carry Jarosh. And we'll need to stop by the traveling cave to get whatever supplies the Duskers didn't take."

For the first time since the Duskers told me my army was destroyed, I have a purpose. I'm going to save Jarosh.

"Mer." Aunt Jadem rests a gentle hand on my arm. "It's a seven-day walk to the Banished Lands." She looks pointedly at Jarosh, whose head is lolling.

"Hey guys," Wokee says.

"I can get there faster," I persist. "I'll run the whole way."

"Guys...."

"You'll still have to stop at high day," Aunt Jadem persists. "I know you want to help him, but it's too far."

"Hello!" Wokee waves his hands in front of us.

I shut my mouth and look at Wokee, whose face is red with exertion.

"We can get Jarosh to the Halves' lands before high day…today." Wokee gives us a sly look.

"Don't be ridiculous," Ry huffs. She looks at our shadows, which are growing shorter. The sun is already climbing back to an angle too deadly for any but me to withstand.

"We can," Wokee insists. "We can ride Vlaz."

Jarosh manages a weak snort from where he is propped against a pile of stones. "You trained the hyenair to carry people?"

"I did! While you were all doing boring grown-up stuff in the fortress, which you know, I'm not allowed to do," he pouts, "I taught him all kinds of stuff. Jadem showed me how to train the kynthia birds, and I figured if they could learn tricks, so could Vlaz."

I give my aunt an incredulous look, but she is too busy complimenting Wokee to notice. Wokee beams.

Ry crosses her arms. "So just to make sure I have this right, while we were talking about tunnels and walls, you were flying around on Vlaz?"

"Well, not exactly," Wokee admits. "He was too small back then to carry anyone, but I taught him the basics. I even made a man out of straw and put it on his back so he could get used to the feeling of—"

Ry puts up a hand to stop him. "You're telling me that you taught Vlaz how to fly with people on his back, but you've never actually put a person on his back?"

"Dayne took him to go find Hemera's dad before I could try," Wokee says.

"And now, you want us to *try him out*?"

"I don't see why it won't work." Wokee shrugs. "He seemed to like the straw man."

Jarosh makes an indistinct noise that might be a guffaw.

"Wokee, even if he could carry someone, and that's a serious *if*," I say, trying to keep my tone reasonable, "there are six of us."

"Have you seen how big he is?" Wokee opens his arms wide and bulges his eyes for emphasis.

"Well," Aunt Jadem gives Vlaz a considering look. "Technically, it should be possible for him to carry our weight."

Ry's jaw drops. "Tell me you aren't considering this."

Wokee smiles at my aunt, and then he turns to me. "See? Jadem says it's okay."

"Yeah, if okay means the same as a death wish, then I'd say this is the perfect plan." Ry rolls her eyes.

I agree with Ry.

"Does anyone have any better ideas for saving Jarosh?" Wokee challenges.

"When did you get so smart?" Ry counters, crossing her arms and frowning at Wokee.

He gives her a smug look before all eyes turn on me.

The thought of seeing the people I care about most climb on top of Vlaz and expect him to fly them where they need to go is absurd. It's suicide. But if there's a chance it could mean Jarosh lives….

"I guess if you both think it's safe," I begin, turning my attention on my aunt. "We can try it."

"You've all gone out of your minds," Ry mutters.

I just give her an apologetic shrug. *We can't lose Jarosh.*

Wokee is grinning and bouncing on his toes. "Down," he tells Vlaz.

The hyenair lowers his forepaws until his belly is in the dirt. Wokee grabs fistfuls of the hyenair's fur and scampers up Vlaz's side, like he's scaling a hairy boulder he's climbed a thousand times. He settles himself behind Vlaz's feathered wings.

Wokee looks ridiculously tiny on the hyenair's back.

"Changed my mind," I say. "There has to be some other way to get Jarosh there."

"There is no other way," Wokee insists.

"How's his steering coming?" Jadem asks Wokee.

"You knew about this?" I give my aunt an accusing look.

Of all of us, Jadem alone shares Wokee's love of animals and things that grow. But I never thought she would let Wokee do something so reckless.

"No one has had a tame hyenair before. I'll admit I was curious." Aunt Jadem lifts a shoulder. "Besides, the boy has a gift."

Wokee's chest is thrust out with pride.

"It's the only way we can make it back to the fortress in time," Aunt Jadem continues.

She doesn't say in time for what, but she doesn't have to. We all know it's just a matter of time before the Duskers do to Solis what they did to Tanguro.

"Won't be any help if we're dead," Jarosh mutters.

Every word seems to cost him, and he flops back against the rocks.

"If Ekil can show us the way," Jadem says, ignoring Jarosh, "Wokee can direct Vlaz."

"Can you show us how to find your lands?" I ask Ekil after I've explained the plan.

He gives Vlaz a dubious look, although he isn't as scared as the last time he saw Vlaz.

"Humans very stupid," Ekil says. "But I will try."

❋ ❋ ❋

While the others fashion a harness to keep Jarosh strapped onto Vlaz, I follow the magnetic pull to the place where Brice is buried. I pick my way through the rubble until I find the charred branches that are all that's left of the golden tree. I kneel next to the smooth stone, now the only marker of the remains buried here.

Brice. The man I loved. The man who lied and used me for his own gains. The man who died to save me.

I just wish—

"Ready, Mer?" Aunt Jadem sees where I'm kneeling, and she comes to stand beside me.

"I never told you about the reason why your mother married Zeidan."

I look at Aunt Jadem, distracted from my grief over Brice at her words. My hand moves unconsciously to the two necklaces I wear. Sal's Solguard pendant, the one Wade gave me when he left Tanguro, rests at the hollow of my throat. Underneath, on a delicate chain that reaches down to my heart, is the silver key my mother gave me. My hand finds the key and closes around it. *The key to my mother's heart.*

My aunt, with her almost masculine height and girth, looks nothing like my beautiful, slender mother. When I first met her months ago in Solis, I was sure Jadem was an enemy. But her fierce protectiveness of the Solguards and unwavering support of me reminds me my mother isn't truly gone, that a part of her still lives.

Aunt Jadem has told me many stories about my mother over the last few months, but there is so much I still want to know.

"Your mother was pregnant with Dayne," Aunt Jadem continues, "and she was also a Solguard sympathizer."

"She helped the Solguards?" It shouldn't surprise me given what Jadem has already told me about my mother, but still, I had no idea.

"Mhm." Aunt Jadem has that faraway look I know means she's reliving an old memory. "She gave it all up when she married Zeidan, of course. She thought by marrying him she could make life better for the Dwellers, and that she could influence him to be a better leader."

"That worked out well." I don't try to hide my sarcasm.

"It did, though. She made him kinder, tamed his hunger for power and dominance." Aunt Jadem shakes her head as if she can't believe it herself. "And over time, they really did come to love each other, in their own way."

"And now she's dead, and my father's a murderer."

"Hemera." Aunt Jadem's stern tone makes me look at her. "Your mother made a difficult choice because she wanted to make life better for her people. Even if the outcome was not what she wanted, it doesn't make her intentions any less wholesome." She stares out at the ruin of Tanguro. "There is nothing more powerful than a willing sacrifice. Nothing at all."

"I never meant for any of these people to be sacrifices," I manage, feeling a tightening at the back of my throat.

"And your mother never meant for Zeidan to do any of the things he did," Aunt Jadem replies.

"Yes, but she wasn't the reason why all of her people were killed," I counter.

"And neither are you." Aunt Jadem touches my chin. "You are more than the sum of your parts, Mer. I have no doubt we have only begun to see what you are capable of."

"Jadem, Mer!" Ry is waving to us from where she's perched on Vlaz. "Get back here before I come to my senses."

Aunt Jadem smiles at me; the lopsided grin that stretches her scars no longer seems repulsive or even strange to me. With an unsteady breath, I let Aunt Jadem lead me away from Brice's grave.

CHAPTER 5

When we get back to Vlaz, Ry is trying to haul Ekil onto the hyenair while Wokee yells encouragement.

"A little bit more," Wokee is saying. "Just use his fur as a handhold." He mimes the climbing action.

With me pushing him from behind, and loud grunting coming from Ekil, we finally manage to get the Halve onto Vlaz's back. Vlaz makes a rumbling *oof* sound as Ekil settles his weight behind Wokee.

I wince at the thought of Vlaz trying to take off with all of our weight bearing down on his back. Even with Aunt Jadem's confidence, I can't imagine how Vlaz is going to carry all of us. But it's not like we have any better options.

Wokee gathers the makeshift rope reins in one hand, and then turns back to tell Ekil to hold on tight.

"You next," I say, crouching next to Jarosh.

When I reach down to help him up, I see how ashen his face is. He's too weak even to grasp my outstretched hand.

Panic squeezes my chest.

Don't think about it, I command myself. *We're going to get Jarosh to the Halves' lands. He's going to be fine.*

"Son of a—" Jarosh growls as I lift him off the ground.

"Not in front of the children," Ry wags a finger at him.

"I'm not a child!" Wokee throws a wild punch behind his head that comes nowhere near Ry.

I brace myself against Vlaz's stomach as I lift Jarosh's body over my head. Ekil and Ry manage to pull him between them with only a few curses and groans from Jarosh.

I'm the last to climb on, and I can't help but notice how far away the ground is once I'm sitting on Vlaz's back. Ekil explains the directions for finding his lands, which I quickly translate for Wokee.

"You sure about this?" Ry asks Wokee.

"Positive," Wokee replies. "Just don't pull any of his feathers. He really hates that."

"We definitely wouldn't want to upset the hyenair," Ry mutters.

"Be careful," I warn as Wokee leans over Vlaz's side to say something into the hyenair's ear.

"Don't worry." Wokee pats Vlaz's neck. "Nothing to fear except mind blowing speed." He gives me a superior smile. "He might be even faster than you."

I can't help but grin back.

"Hang on, everyone!" Wokee calls.

Ekil turns back to look at me, and it is only when the fear in his black eyes meets mine that I realize what a terrible idea this is. *What were we thinking?* But before I can give voice to my concerns, Wokee lets out a single sharp whistle.

My stomach lurches into my throat as Vlaz rises from his crouch. I cling to the hyenair's sides with my legs, but he's too wide for me to wrap my legs around him, so I have to grab fistfuls of fur to keep from sliding off.

"We're all insane," I hear Ry mutter as Vlaz begins to move.

"It's been nice knowing you all," Jarosh says in a weak voice.

Aunt Jadem is saying something to Wokee, and Ekil is gesturing in the direction we need to fly. The cords of Vlaz's muscles ripple and churn beneath me. He begins to beat his wings, and Ry is thrust back against me.

We're too heavy. He'll never get off the ground.

Vlaz rears back, and it's all I can do to keep from sliding off as Vlaz lurches into the air. The ground drops away. Wokee whoops.

A ridiculous urge to shut my eyes comes over me. Instead, I stare down at the ruins of Tanguro below.

The fires the Duskers set are still smoldering. There is a crater between the two buildings where the Duskers' explosives collapsed the tunnels. The orderly grid of trees in the courtyard is now just a mess of charred, scattered branches. Somewhere below is Brice's grave and the bones of hundreds of soldiers who died for…what? Tanguro is destroyed, and we're no closer to freedom from the Duskers than when I was a scared little girl hiding in my father's Subterrane.

What made me think I could give the men and women who fought with me what they wanted? What made me think I could save them?

I look down at Tanguro, where I've left a part of myself. I look until Vlaz changes direction and the colors below start to melt into each other. Luminous greens, purples, golds, and pinks blend together and leave spots on my eyelids.

When I first entered the Wild Lands, the colors were too bright, the sun too strong. A flower with an intoxicating scent nearly lured me to my death. Even the insects wanted to kill us, and a fair number of them were large enough to do it.

In mere months, though, this place became more home to me than anywhere I have ever been. And now I'm leaving it all behind.

Wind crashes in my ears and lashes the strands of my hair across my cheeks. A scream sticks in my throat and my stomach drops as Vlaz rises.

If I had time to think about it, I would have expected riding a hyenair to feel the way it looks: fluid and graceful. But Vlaz's body pitches up and down with the invisible currents of the air. Every time he pumps his wings, the whole chain of our company is thrust backward onto my lap. Wokee shouts something, but I can't make out his words over the rushing wind. I grit my teeth and cling to Vlaz as we fly higher.

By the time I grow semi-used to the motion, the crest of the mountains is below us.

I echo Ry's scream when, without warning, Vlaz folds his wings and dives. I grab for a handhold and clutch Vlaz's fur until my knuckles turn white. Just when I'm sure we're about to crash nose-first, Vlaz's paws hit the ground with a jolt that rattles my bones. He gallops for a few paces, sending a spray of dust in our wake.

My body is shaking so violently I don't know for sure when we stop moving. I'm dimly aware of Wokee's shouts of *woohoo*, and Jadem congratulating him on getting us here alive.

I fall more than slide from Vlaz's back onto jellied legs. The others follow, looking more or less the way I feel. Ry's face is redder than her hair, which is sticking rebelliously out from the hood of her blue cloak.

Vlaz stands beside us. His purple tongue is hanging out of his mouth and his sides are matted with sweat, but he doesn't seem to be breathing nearly as hard as the rest of us.

Aunt Jadem passes down an unconscious Jarosh. It takes both Ekil and me, with our wobbling legs, to support his weight. Wokee slides to the ground and bows.

"See?" he gloats. "I told you."

"You're a marvel," Aunt Jadem agrees.

Wokee beams.

"Yeah," Ry grumbles. "Thanks for not letting us die."

"Any time," Wokee replies, giving Vlaz's leg a rub.

A crude wall of rocks marks the beginning of the Halves' lands. Just ahead, standing sentry at two shriveled, dust-covered trees, is a stooped Halve. The long wisps of black hair make me think this Halve is a female, but it's impossible to be sure. The Halve takes one look at Vlaz, shrieks, and runs away on all-fours.

"Flying beast stays away," Ekil says.

"Just a minute," Aunt Jadem raises a finger as soon as I have finished translating. "We need Vlaz to get back to the fortress."

"Don't worry," Wokee says. "He'll be back whenever I call for him."

"We don't have time to dally," Aunt Jadem presses.

Dally? I stare at my aunt. She couldn't possibly mean that stopping for Jarosh could be *dallying*, could she?

"But Jarosh…." Ry echoes my thoughts as she gestures to our friend's limp form. "We have to get him healed first."

"Of course, of course," Aunt Jadem says, but she isn't looking at Ry. Her attention is on the horizon to the south, in the direction of Solis.

Wokee whispers a few words into Vlaz's ear, and then the hyenair begins to pump his powerful wings. We shield our faces as a cyclone of dust threatens to engulf us. Vlaz rises higher and higher, until he's nothing more than a black speck against the bright sky.

"He might have gotten us here," Ry says rubbing her backside, "but I'm not getting back on him any time soon." She narrows her eyes at Wokee. "Unlike you, I value my life."

As soon as Vlaz is out of sight, Ekil puts two fingers in his mouth and makes a shrill whistling sound. In less than a minute, two Halves appear out of the haze of dust. Their bare feet stomp the ground with so much force I can feel the vibrations beneath my boots.

"They take your friend to our healer." Ekil gestures to Jarosh.

The two Halves reach to take Jarosh's limp body from me.

"That's alright," I say, shifting Jarosh away from them. "I'll take him."

"They take," Ekil insists. "You come with me."

"Where are we going?"

"Show you what humans have done to us."

"Um, Hemera?" Ry asks, giving the two Halves a pointed look. They're filthy and wear nothing but rags covering their lower body.

"Are you sure about this?" I ask Ekil.

The Halve nods. "They take care of him."

Reluctantly, I let the Halves take Jarosh from me. "Be gentle," I warn them, as one grabs Jarosh around his waist.

Jarosh looks too small and frail in the Halves' arms. He looks more like a child than the imposing soldier I know him to be. The sight of him like this makes my eyes sting with unshed tears.

When the Halves have vanished with Jarosh back the way they came, Ekil motions for us to follow. We fall into a line as a narrow footpath appears through the shriveled weeds.

After living in Tanguro for so long, the land on the other side of the mountains just looks…brown. There are hardly any trees, and the ones that have managed to grow in this parched land are thin and barren. There is an outcropping of rock not far away, but even the rocks are brown.

Divots in the earth that wind and curve across the dry land hold only the memory of water. We follow Ekil down a steep ravine, which used to be where the Banished River flowed. It's now bone dry.

"You weren't joking," I tell Ekil. "The Duskers really took away your water." Until now, I don't think I actually believed what he had said.

"What's joking?" is Ekil's only reply.

We pass the skeleton of some large animal beneath the shriveled remains of what must have been a towering script tree before the river went dry. Now, the tree is just a mass of leafless branches.

The twisting fury that has been building inside me since we left Tanguro roars to life. *The Duskers did this.*

"Do you think they have anything decent to eat?" Wokee asks as we walk.

"Judging from what we've seen so far," Ry says, "I wouldn't bet on it."

Wokee's next question is drowned out by raucous shouting.

At first, I can't see anything through the dust cloud hanging over whatever is making the noise. The cries get louder as we make our way closer. The path ends in front of what looks like a large wooden pen surrounded by dozens of Halves. Every movement sends a new plume of dust into the air. Ry, Aunt Jadem, and Wokee are all coughing and rubbing their eyes, but the Halves don't even seem to notice the pollution.

"It's because of the river," Aunt Jadem says between coughs. "Without the water and plant life, there's nothing to hold the dirt down anymore."

Ekil leads us through the mob of Halves, who are jeering as they stare transfixed at whatever is inside the ring. A chorus of rumbling, guttural calls erupts. The Halves stomp their bare feet with so much force the ground trembles. We're absorbed into the thick crowd, pushed and jostled from every side, until we find ourselves pressed up against the fence. There is a mob of Halves at our backs. Ry grabs my arm as one of the Halves nearly knocks her over with an excited wave of its arm. He's so much bigger than Ry, I doubt he even noticed her standing right beside him.

Inside the pen are two of the biggest Halves I've ever seen. Standing at my full height, I'd probably only reach their midsections. Their chests are broad and muscled, and each of their flexed biceps are as thick as my torso.

Their gnarled fists are clenched, and their crooked, yellow teeth are bared. Rust-colored blood streaks their faces and bare chests. They look every bit as savage as I grew up believing Halves to be.

The two Halves circle each other. One of them lunges, but it's too slow. The other pivots out of the way and lands a vicious kick at the first's kneecap. The Halve lets out a pained shriek, which is quickly drowned out by murderous shouts from the Halves surrounding the ring.

Before the injured Halve can recover, the other has him on the ground.

He presses one enormous foot on the other's chest. The Halve pinned to the ground writhes as he tries to free himself. Layers of muscle ripple across his bare, scaly chest as the winning Halve flexes his arm. Ry's gasp echoes my own as the Halve brings his fist down with a sickening crunch. The pinned Halve spasms.

My first reaction is a desperate urge to cover Wokee's eyes, but he's out of reach, and the Halves pressed all around us are making it impossible to move an inch.

The winning Halve raises his bare foot and brings it down on the other Halve's head. Brown blood flies through the air as the Halve's body jerks for several seconds before stilling.

We need to get out of here.

"What in the sun is happening?" Ry's voice is filled with revulsion. She fingers the feathered end of an arrow, even though there isn't enough space in this crowd for her to draw her bow.

The victorious Halve leaps out of the ring, almost landing on top of another Halve in the crowd. He doesn't even notice as we all scramble out of his way as he pumps his thick, scaly fists in the air. There is a feral look in his black eyes.

One of the Halves on the outermost edge of the circle shoves another. With a roar of anger, the offended Halve swings his fist in a wide arc, hitting two others on the way to his target. As more join the fray, a full-on brawl erupts. I shove the Halve beside me to keep it from barreling straight into Wokee.

A firm tap on my shoulder makes me whirl around.

"Ekil." I'm almost dizzy with relief. "What's happening?" I have to shout to be heard over the bedlam.

"They fight." Ekil nods.

"I see that." The little patience I had is fast waning as chaos explodes around us. "*Why* are they fighting?"

Ekil moves one of his shoulders in what might be a shrug as he carves a path for us out of the bedlam. "To practice."

The path takes us past a stagnant pool covered in a brown, oily substance that wafts a foul odor. Beside it, a Halve crouched on all fours is gnawing on a bone. With a shudder, it occurs to me the bone might not be an animal's. I swallow hard. *Have I sentenced Jarosh to death by bringing him here?*

From the looks on Aunt Jadem and Ry's faces, I know they're having similar thoughts.

"Practice for what?" I ask.

The look in Ekil's eye makes me cold with dread.

"Kill the humans," Ekil nods his head up and down, "and the land will be ours."

CHAPTER 6

The Halves are going to kill the Banished.

Pain gouges my stomach as I realize what the Duskers have done. By redirecting the river, they're forcing the Halves and Banished to kill each other over fast-dwindling resources. The Duskers won't need to come anywhere near here to do battle—their enemies are doing their work for them.

And I promised Ekil I would help.

"What am I supposed to do?"

I only realize I spoke the question aloud when Aunt Jadem answers.

"If you can convince the Halves to come back to the fortress, I could call a council with the Banished leaders." She purses her lips, making the scar across her mouth stand out in a thin, white line. "Perhaps we can help them see they have a common enemy, and it's not each other."

"Oh yeah," Ry rolls her eyes. "That will go really well. Tell the Banished they have to sit at the same table as the Halves who have been stealing from them and killing them."

"It's not their fault," I tell her.

"Of course it's not," my aunt says. "It's the Duskers'. And the sooner we can make both the Halves and the Banished realize that, the better for us all." She rubs at her one good eye, and for a moment, her exhaustion is obvious.

"We can't fight the Duskers on our own," my aunt continues. "We need the Banished and the Halves to help."

"The Halves will never agree to fight with the Banished," I say.

"And vice versa," adds Ry.

"If either wishes to survive, they may not have a choice."

Ry and I exchange a look before I turn back to Ekil. "Will you come with us to the rebel fortress?"

Ekil regards me with his black eyes. "We will not live with humans again." He shivers, and I know he's thinking about the time he spent as my father's prisoner.

"Tell them there's lots of good food at Jadem's," Wokee suggests, reading the expression on my face.

I translate Wokee's offer, which Ekil considers.

"They help destroy the gray cloaks?"

"Yes." My answer comes without hesitation.

Ekil nods once. "I will ask them."

"And you'll stop attacking the settlements until then?"

Ekil nods again. "If you will promise we get our land and river back."

I don't know if that's a promise I can make.

"I'll do my best," I tell him.

We follow Ekil away from the fight to an above-ground hut, which is the only structure the Halves built on the Outside aside from the fighting pen. The white specere leaves thatched around the hut's outside remind me of Tanguro. An ache I'm beginning to be familiar with nestles deeper into my gut.

By now, the pen where two new Halves are fighting is out of sight, but their jeering is still audible. Wokee's face is pale, and I know he must be thinking about the Halve crushing the other one's skull with his bare foot. A wave of guilt washes over me. *I never should have brought him here.*

Ekil pushes open the rickety door, which is taller and wider than any human door, and waves us inside.

"I hope we don't find Jarosh roasting over a spit in here," Ry mutters.

The grunts of the Halves still fighting fade as soon as we step into the hut.

The inside is more spacious than I would have guessed. It's also cleaner. The fat candles burning in each corner give off a strong, but not unpleasant, scent. Large, crudely-made earthen bowls filled with various powders and dried herbs are lined against the wall. Hammocks stitched from dried leaves hang between wooden poles on the far side of the hut.

Everything is twice as large as it would be in a human-made cave, from the earthen pots to the hammocks that could easily fit four humans on each. It makes me feel tiny and helpless, like I'm a little kid surrounded by grown-ups.

A Halve leans over the first hammock, where the blue hood of Jarosh's cloak is just visible over the top of the Halve's head. At the sound of the door creaking shut, the Halve stands up and turns to face us.

"Camike is our healer," Ekil says by way of introduction. "She will help your friend."

"This one looks different," Wokee observes.

Like Ekil, this Halve is much less stooped than the others. Her skin is still rough, but it glistens like she has covered it in some kind of oil. She is also smaller than the others, both shorter and less stout. She's easily the height and girth of a full-grown man, but standing beside Ekil, she looks almost dainty. She has made her hair look fuller by weaving brightly colored feathers among the strands. Instead of the filthy loincloth the others wear, she has an animal hide dress that covers one shoulder and is tied around her waist with a leather belt.

"You are the one who saved us from the bad man." The Halve's voice is less guttural than the others, with a note of femininity. She bows her head to me. "We owe you our lives."

My face flushes with the undeserved reverence.

"Can you save our friend?" I ask.

"His wounds are deep." She pads barefoot over to the hammock. "We will see."

"She likes humans," Ekil observes as Camike bustles around the hut, piling more animal hides on Jarosh and gathering bunches of dried plants from earthen shelves. There is a note of what sounds like disapproval in his voice.

Camike wafts a smoking bunch of herbs across Jarosh's face, which makes him go limp in his hammock. Then, she picks up a long bone needle and thread from one of her bowls.

There is a collective intake of breath as we all realize what she is about to do.

"Don't—" Wokee begins, but I clap a hand over his mouth, stifling whatever else he was going to say.

Jarosh moans and edges away from the needle.

"Hold him," Camike commands.

I jump when I realize she's talking to me.

I'm grateful for the distraction of holding Jarosh's shoulders steady so I don't have to look at the bright red blood beading up with every prick of the needle. Camike's hand is steady as she threads the bone in and out of his flesh, closing Jarosh's gaping wound. She ties off the thread with deft fingers.

"Well done," Aunt Jadem says, impressed.

"He must sleep now." Camike says. She waves a hand in the direction of the hammocks. "You too."

No sooner have I translated Camike's offer, Wokee is clambering into one of the hammocks. He is snoring before the rest of us can even discuss who will stay awake to watch Jarosh.

* * *

"Hey! What do you think you're doing?"

I jolt to my feet at the sound of Jarosh's voice.

"Where am I?" Jarosh tries to sit up. "What's going on? Who are you?"

"Relax," Ry is saying. "You'll tear out your stitches."

"Like hell I'll relax! I'm—" Jarosh's mouth goes slack as Camike waves a bundle of smoking herbs over his face.

"Hmmm," Jarosh murmurs. "Smells like waterfalls and rainbows." His eyes roll upward to regard Camike. "You're not half bad looking, you know that?" And then, after a pause, he starts to laugh. "Get it? You're not *Halve* bad looking?" He cracks himself up again. "But seriously. You're a regular hottie."

Ry raises her eyebrow. "What'd she give him?" She points at the bundle Camike is holding far away from her own face as she brings it over to a pot of water.

"Come here, Cutie." Jarosh crooks a finger at Camike.

Camike turns her head away, but not before I catch a blush darkening her cheeks.

"Camike," I tell him with an exasperated look. "Her name is Camike."

"Cutie." Jarosh insists. "You know something? I feel *great*." He opens and closes his mouth a few times, like he's just realizing he has it. "It's like that time I drank liquid fire and ate a whole pile of Thutmose's special mushrooms."

Wokee giggles. Aunt Jadem, who has been pacing around the hut since I woke up, shakes her head.

"Hey, watch yourself," Jarosh complains as Camike's hands sweep over his bare chest. "Normally I like to have dinner with a girl first, if you know what I mean."

Camike takes the last handful of berries from the largest of the earthen pots and smashes them against a flat stone. As I look at the supplies scattered around her, I notice most of the other bowls are empty, too. Probably whatever herbs they grew for healing dried up with the rest of the plants here. I would feel guiltier if I wasn't so desperate for Jarosh to live.

If Jarosh dies, after everything else that's happened, I don't think I could bear it.

Camike dumps the juice from the berries unceremoniously over Jarosh's wound. "He will live," she announces.

A lightness floods my insides. "Thank you." I look from Camike to Ekil. "How long until we can move him?"

"Some weeks," Camike replies.

"Weeks?" I gasp.

"He is safe here," Ekil says.

"I saw what was going on in that pen out there," I point out.

"We take good care of friend of Halve saver," Camike bows her head toward me. "Do not fear."

"Ahem." Ry clears her throat and raises an eyebrow at me.

I translate our conversation for the others.

"We can't leave him here." Ry looks horrified by the very thought.

"He seems to be in good hands, and we don't have any time to spare," Aunt Jadem says.

I give my aunt a surprised look. I would have expected her to side with Ry. The last time a Solguard was injured, she stayed by his bedside for two full days until he woke up. She never left him, not even to eat or sleep.

But my aunt is right about not having time to spare. We may not know exactly when the Duskers are going to attack the fortress, but there's no doubt it will be soon. It's a miracle they haven't already destroyed the fortress. We have to get back in time to warn the others and give what help we can.

"When your friend gets strong, I will bring him to you," Camike offers.

Already, the muscles in my legs twitch with the expectation of crossing the land that separates me from Solis.

"What do you think?" Ry asks me. "You're still our leader." She gives me a small smile.

I look from Jarosh's still form to my aunt, Ry, and Wokee. Their eyes are fixed expectantly on me.

"We leave as soon as it's low day."

✳ ✳ ✳

I wake up some time during the high day. Even though the specere leaves covering the building's exterior protect it from the sun, my internal clock tells me there are at least a few more hours before the sun is low enough for the rest of my companions to leave the hut. Ry is asleep in the hammock next to me, and I can hear Wokee's snoring from across the hut.

When my gaze shifts to Aunt Jadem's hammock, it's empty. I look around, panicked, until I see my aunt standing by the door.

"What are you doing?" I ask, rising to go stand with her.

"Oh, hello Mer." Aunt Jadem's scarred face is lined and has taken on an ashen hue. She looks exhausted. "Just keeping an eye out for low day."

Guilt washes over me. I should be the one counting down the seconds until we can leave. Dayne is waiting to give me news about my father. For months, I've waited for word from him. Now, all I can think about are the blue cloaks and bones scattered around Tanguro's ruined courtyard.

"You're really worried about them, aren't you?" I ask.

It's a stupid question—of course she's worried. We all are.

"What I don't understand," Aunt Jadem says, "is why the Solguards never made it to Tanguro. If the Duskers still haven't attacked, our people should have left like we planned."

"I've been wondering the same thing," I say. "And there hasn't been a single word from Wade."

I try to ignore the jumble of emotions I feel every time I think about him.

"Well, I suppose we'll find out what's going on soon enough," she says a little too brightly.

"I wish my mom was here." It's a childish thing to say, and I have no idea what made it come out of my mouth.

Aunt Jadem gives me a sympathetic look. "So do I." She runs a hand over my dark, wavy hair that is the only trait I inherited from my mother.

"I miss her stories," I continue when Aunt Jadem doesn't say anything else. "She used to tell me this story about magical caves with a crystal-clear river flowing through them…." I close my eyes, seeing the place so vividly it's almost like I can feel the clean water on my bare feet.

"The Crystal Caves," Aunt Jadem says, her voice far away. She looks like she's going to say more but then decides against it. She manages a small laugh. "Your mother was always making up the wildest stories. She had such an imagination."

I nod. I want to ask Jadem what she isn't telling me, but my aunt's face looks so drawn. I ask instead, "Are you sure you're alright?"

"Oh, I'm fine. Don't worry about me, Mer."

My aunt smiles, but it seems forced. She turns back to peer through the slit in the door. "Get some rest, dear niece."

✻ ✻ ✻

By the time we're ready to leave, Jarosh is already sitting up in the hammock. Camike, who has been bustling around him, lifts a steaming bowl to his lips.

"Jarosh!" Wokee runs to the hammock. "You're alive!"

Jarosh grins down at him. "What'd you expect? I'm a Solguard for sun's sake." He gives Camike a dazzling smile. "Turns out these Halves know a thing or two about putting a man back together."

Even though Camike can't understand a word he's saying, she makes a sound that *might* be a giggle.

"So, what now?" Jarosh looks at us, his gaze taking in the bags slung over our shoulders.

"Solis." Aunt Jadem says. "You're going to stay here and rest," she fixes him with her eye.

We're all poised for Jarosh to argue, but he doesn't.

"You all go along." He waves a hand at us before turning back to Camike, who is hovering beside his hammock. "As long as they don't go bleeding on me, we'll get along just fine."

Ry, Aunt Jadem, and I exchange a look.

"Alright then," Ry blows a drooping curl off her face. She goes over to the hammock and wraps her arms around Jarosh.

Jarosh winces. "You take care of yourselves," he says when Ry straightens back up.

"Just get better so you can hurry back to us," Ry replies.

Aunt Jadem and I have time for only a quick goodbye before Camike is ushering us toward the door.

"Hemera," Jarosh calls just before I step outside. All of the humor has faded from his face. "Make those Duskers pay for what they did."

CHAPTER 7

What's he doing here?" I demand.

The enormous, hulking brute we watched slaughter another Halve in the ring is glowering up at Vlaz, threatening him with his black eyes. Vlaz, who is still dripping wet from whichever river Wokee called him out of, is crunching happily on some poor forest creature and oblivious to the Halve's glares.

"Brogut is my second," Ekil says.

Brogut's knuckles are crusted with brown blood. The animal hide covering the lower part of his body is filthy and bloodstained. He has no supplies aside from a tree trunk the width of my torso, which is sharpened to a point at one end. It's the length of my entire body, but the Halve carries it with no more effort than it takes Ry to lift one of her arrows.

"You want to bring *him* to a meeting?" I ask Ekil. "With humans?"

Ekil looks at the other Halve, who is picking at his yellow teeth with a pointed claw.

"Don't tell me that Halve is coming with us," Ry groans.

"Look at the size of his arm." Wokee's eyes are wide with a combination of fear and fascination. "I bet just one of them weighs as much as I do."

"Brogut will protect," Ekil nods. "You saved him from Tanguro."

I shrug helplessly at my friends. To Ekil, I say, "He better behave himself."

Brogut lets out a low rumble, which doesn't make me feel more confident.

Vlaz, with Wokee, Ry, and Aunt Jadem on his back, paws the ground. The Halves and I, with our superior strength and speed, will follow on foot.

More than a small part of me is relieved I won't need to make my sore backside any worse. Ry, to her credit, gets back on Vlaz with only a small amount of grumbling and wincing.

Ekil convinced a fair number of his Halves to come with us, and they are waiting on either side of the footpath for us to go first. When I pass by them, they lower their heads in reverence.

They think I can save them.

A vague sense of dread descends on me as we make our way down the path to the edge of the Halves' lands.

Wokee keeps Vlaz on the ground, both to stay near to me and to conserve Vlaz's strength. Even with fewer people on his back, the sun beating down on Vlaz's black fur is making a frothy sweat appear on his sides.

I have to jog to keep pace with Vlaz, taking ten steps for every one of his. Jarosh's words echo in my head as I go. *Make those Duskers pay for what they did.*

✳ ✳ ✳

When Ekil and Brogut stop short, I almost run into them. They both cock their heads at something. Ekil turns his bulbous nose to the wind and sniffs deeply. Brogut growls.

"Bad humans," Ekil says.

At first, I think he's talking about my father, but then I realize he's referring to the Banished.

"A lot of them?" I ask.

"Not many," Ekil says.

"Humans smell very bad," Brogut adds.

I bite back a retort. Something tells me irony isn't something the Halves can appreciate.

I signal to Wokee to stop Vlaz. "The Halves say there are Banished ahead."

"Any Duskers?" Aunt Jadem asks, already sliding off Vlaz's back.

"Not sure." I shake my head.

Wokee pulls his small knife from his belt and starts to climb down.

"Stay with Vlaz," I tell him.

"But Hemera—"

"Stay here!"

"Draw weapons," Aunt Jadem says. "The Banished aren't usually fighters, but with all these Halves…."

A group of the Banished appears through the haze of sun and dust. Brogut snarls, lifting his tree trunk-sharpened-into-a-spear.

"Keep the Halves back behind Vlaz," I tell Ekil. "I'll signal you once we've explained things to the Banished." All we need right now is a battle.

Ry, Aunt Jadem, and I slink forward, as if we're approaching wild animals.

There are more than a dozen Banished. They're haggard, filthy, and have a desperate look in their eyes. They look like human versions of the Halves.

They carry no weapons, but the ones in front hold up their fists like they're ready to use them against us. Behind the adults is a small group of children, looking every bit as starved and desperate.

"Friends," Aunt Jadem holds up an appeasing hand. "We mean you no harm. If we can be of any assistance—"

"Get outta the way," the one in front shakes his fist. He's tall and bone-thin, and he's holding the frayed end of a rope. At the other end of the rope is another person, a girl who is so emaciated she's more wraith than human. Her wrists and legs are bound. She seems to be the only one who is tied, though.

"You're hungry," Jadem says. "I am the Banished leader of the South. If you come with us, you will find—"

"Malarusk," the one in front barks. "We're going to Malarusk."

Ry, Aunt Jadem, and I exchange puzzled looks.

"Malarusk?" Aunt Jadem repeats.

"Aye."

The others are nodding, like the man hasn't gone out of his mind.

Maybe the sun is making them delirious….

"We got waylaid by some Halves, and now we're turned around."

"Why are you trying to get to Malarusk?" Ry asks. There's none of my aunt's gentleness in her tone.

"For protection from the Halves."

"But—" Ry and I exchange an incredulous look. "The Duskers aren't going to protect you."

"If you recall," Ry says, her voice dripping with sarcasm, "the Duskers are the ones who banished you in the first place."

"They changed their minds, didn't they?" The man, clearly these people's leader, gives the girl on the end of the rope a savage tug. "Promised us protection in exchange for labor."

"There are only two types of people granted access into Malarusk," Aunt Jadem says. Her voice is calm, but when she moves her hand, it wavers. "Duskers and prisoners. The Duskers don't *change their minds*."

"Ack, we don't have time for you. I know what I know, and that's enough. Come on!" With that, the other Banished behind him begin to shuffle forward.

"How are you planning to get there if you don't know where the citadel is?" Ry asks.

"Got it all figured out," the man replies. "We'll go to Darkness Peak. The new initiates will be headed up the mountain at some point. We can do the ritual and return to Malarusk with them."

"That ritual is no small thing," my aunt says, turning to look at the towering mountain behind us.

I'm not even sure she notices how she reaches up to touch her scarred face as she speaks.

"You can't really be going to Darkness Peak," I say.

Darkness Peak, the highest mountain outside of the Wild Lands, is the place that's supposed to contain the Dark God's spirit. It's the mountain to which all Duskers and Subterrane Dwellers direct their prayers, and is the place where new Dusker recruits complete their initiation ritual. Those of pure Dusker blood are brought there when they die. They're set atop great pyres and burned so their spirit will mingle with the Dark God's. My own grandfather's body was cremated atop Darkness Peak.

"Aye," the man replies. "We go to join with them and offer our service to the Dark God."

"But the Duskers are the ones who made the Banished River go dry," I argue. "They're the reason for your suffering, not the Halves."

As if on cue, Ekil and Brogut appear out of the dust.

A chorus of bloodcurdling shrieks rise as the skeletal Banished clamber forward, their hands grasping like claws.

Brogut and Ekil answer with growls of their own. They raise their weapons.

"No!" Ry and I cry.

"There is no need for violence," my aunt is saying in a soothing voice.

No one listens. Both humans and Halves are crying out for the other's blood. If I thought the Banished seemed insane before, it's nothing compared to when they catch sight of the Halves.

Beside Ekil, Brogut is making hideous sounds as he brandishes his tree trunk spear.

"Ekil," I demand, "get that Halve under control."

For a moment, I think we might have averted a disaster. Brogut is still snarling, but at least he's lowered his weapon. And then the screams start.

"Hyenair!" one of the Banished yells.

Vlaz, still standing beside Wokee where we left them, is oblivious to his effect on the already-panicking Banished.

"It's okay, he's a friend!"

"Calm down!" Ry bellows.

No one listens.

At the sight of Vlaz, his fangs glinting in the sunlight, the Banished scatter.

"You're going the wrong way." Ry stops one of the women stumbling off to the east. "The Banished Lands are that way." She gestures in the opposite direction.

"Malarusk," the woman shouts in her hoarse voice. "We're going to Malarusk."

"You can't be serious." Ry smacks her gloved hand to her forehead.

"We can give you protection," Aunt Jadem pleads to the ragged bunch of children who can't be much older than Wokee. "You don't have to go to the Duskers."

None of them give her so much as a glance as they follow the others south, in the direction of the Dusker territory.

The leader lets out an animal-like cry and runs at Ekil. Brogut aims the pointed end of his tree trunk at the man, and Ekil raises his club.

"I'll stop them!" Wokee, appearing out of nowhere, leaps into the fray.

"Wokee," I gasp, but he's already darting under Brogut's raised arm.

The Banished man is already in motion. All of his momentum propels him forward. There's a murderous look in his eye as Wokee steps straight into his path. Too late, I see the glint of a dagger in the man's hand.

CHAPTER 8

I throw myself in front of Wokee, my only thought to protect him. The knife cuts through the place where his chest had been only a moment before. The blade slices into my stomach.

"Hemera!" Wokee screams.

Pain explodes through my body as I double over. Instinctively, I wrap my hands around the foreign object lodged inside me and pull it out. There is a horrible squelching sound as my flesh gives up the blade. Blood spatters my clothes as I fight to stay conscious.

Screams of agony pierce the air. At first, I think they're mine, but even when I put a hand over my mouth to stop the ear-splitting sound, the screams continue.

Through darkening vision, I see the Banished man. He's shrieking and ripping his cloak off to claw at his skin. I want to tell him he's going to get the Burn, that no one can be on the Outside without their cloaks except for me, but I can't summon the words.

"Demon blood!" the man howls.

I see him racing toward me, his knife held out, the blade still covered in my brown blood. Even from this distance, I can see the blisters racing up the man's bare arms. Whether they're from my blood or the sun, I'm not sure. But my body is too sluggish to do anything except stand there.

A familiar twang cuts through the air, and then the Banished man crumples to the ground. A single arrow sticks out of his neck.

I collapse, the weight of my own body too much to support any longer. My hands cover the gaping wound left in the blade's absence.

"Hemera," Wokee whimpers.

"Move aside," my aunt commands. And then to me, "Hemera, let me see."

The dark stain of wet blood covers the entire front of my cloak. But the wound itself is already beginning to heal. The searing pain is beginning to eb.

"I'm sorry," Wokee sobs as he wraps his arms around himself.

I pull aside the fabric of my cloak and lift the bottom of my blood-soaked shirt. The gash is already partially sealed. A trickle of brown blood oozes out, but the pain is fading.

"No permanent harm done." I give Wokee a weak smile.

"Greater than the sum of your parts, like I've always said." Aunt Jadem shakes her head. "You really are a wonder, Mer."

Wokee lets out a sound that is part hiccup-part sob before running to me.

"Careful!" Three voices yell at the same time before he can come within reach of my poisonous blood.

Wokee's lip trembles.

"Don't worry," I reassure him. "See?" I point to my stomach. "As good as new."

I look at the Banished man's corpse. A shudder runs down my spine at the sight of him. The blisters have spread over every visible part of him, making him look like some grotesque version of a person.

"Well," Ry clears her throat. "If this hasn't been the most bizarre day I've ever had…." She stops speaking, and we all follow the direction of her gaze.

The Banished have all disappeared…all except for the one who was being dragged by the leader. The rope lies in a heap on the ground, no longer attached to anyone or anything.

The girl regards us. Even though her face is shadowed by her hood, I can feel the intensity of her gaze. She's filthy and nothing but bones, and yet there's an air about her that's almost regal. Her spine is straight, and she doesn't look away or seem cowed when we all focus on her.

"What about you?" Ry asks, eyeing her.

"What about me?" the Banished girl counters.

Ry raises an eyebrow. "You're not going to go chasing after the rest of the crazies?"

"In case you hadn't noticed, I wasn't exactly going with them of my own free will."

Ry grins and jabs me in the side. "I think I like this one."

The girl is tall, like Ry. When she looks down at me, it's through gray eyes. I would guess she's around Ry's age, maybe a few years older than me, but she's too covered in grime and sweat to tell much more about her.

"Can you tell us what's really going on?" Aunt Jadem asks.

"It's as they say," the girl replies. "The Duskers promised safety in return for our labor in Malarusk."

A flash of understanding passes over my aunt's face before it's replaced by worry.

"Aunt Jadem?" I ask.

She clears her throat. "The Dusker Supreme is not prone to acts of generosity. Their offer does not bode well."

"That's what I said," the girl agrees. "But the leader of my settlement made me come. He thought if I stayed behind it would anger the Duskers, and then they would refuse the rest of our group."

"Well, I guess you better come with us," Ry tells the girl. She looks to Aunt Jadem and me for confirmation.

"Only if you want to," I say, thinking of the shrieking Banished racing toward Malarusk.

The girl takes a step closer to me. "You have Halve eyes."

A year ago, that comment would have made me want to bury my head in the sand. Now, all I say is, "and you have gray eyes."

Ry snorts.

"Alright," the girl says. She turns her attention on Jadem. "And you? A Dusker traveling with Solguards?"

I open my mouth, but Ry's faster.

"How do you know about the Solguards? Who are you? What's your business around here?"

The girl raises her chin. "Just because I live in a settlement, it doesn't mean I'm ignorant."

Ry starts to retort, but Aunt Jadem puts a hand on her shoulder.

"I may bear the mark of the Duskers," Aunt Jadem says, "but I assure you I am not one of them." She runs a hand across the place where her left eye should be. "This was a parting gift from the Dusker Supreme."

I start. My aunt never talks about her scars or her time in Malarusk. I didn't know the Dusker Supreme was the one to take away her eye. I want to ask her more about it, but I know now isn't the time.

"Jadem looks scary," Wokee pipes up, "because a long time ago, she pretended to be a Dusker to get information, and so they did the initiation ritual on her." Wokee looks at my aunt. "Jadem is the leader of the Solguards, you know." There is fierce pride in his voice, and I can't help but smile.

"What's your name?" Wokee asks.

"Dellin."

"It's nice to meet you, Dellin." My aunt holds out a hand to the girl.

The girl's gloved hand disappears as it's swallowed up in my aunt's handshake.

The girl turns a cold, piercing look on me. "I think it only fair to warn you…I'm the best archer you will ever meet—"

"I doubt that," Ry scoffs, running a hand lovingly over the curve of her bow.

Before Ry can protest, Dellin snatches Ry's bow out of her hands. She bends down and picks up a twisted stick from the ground. She breaks off the end so it bears a slight resemblance to an arrow. She threads the stick through the bow with quick fingers and takes aim.

"That tree," she says, already aiming her stick at the narrow target in the distance.

Ry rolls her eyes. "You couldn't hit that with a real arrow."

The girl's reply comes in the twang of the bowstring.

A laugh escapes me at the look on Ry's face as the stick lands its mark.

Ry whistles. "Oh, I definitely like this one." She gives the girl a once-over and nods in approval.

Dellin glares at Ekil and Brogut as she passes the bow back to Ry.

"They're with us," I say. "If that's a problem for you—"

"It's not a problem," Ry says, looping an arm through Dellin's as if they're already the best of friends.

Dellin looks at Aunt Jadem and me once more, and then she stares up at Vlaz. "Am I going to have to ride that?"

"Unless you'd rather walk." Ry shrugs.

Dellin takes one look in the direction where the other Banished disappeared, and then she steps over the rope coiled at her feet.

"Riding the hyenair it is."

* * *

Ekil, Brogut, and I wind through trees and leap over boulders in our path as we try to make up the distance between us and the others. Wokee keeps Vlaz's pace as slow as he can manage from the air, but the Halves are starving and dehydrated, and they're slower than I am.

It's just before high day when we reach the edge of the forest that shrouds Solis. Vlaz is already on the ground and the others are in the process of sliding off his back by the time we catch up.

Everyone except for Wokee looks stiff and exhausted. Wokee, on the other hand, leaps from Vlaz's back and does a little dance in place.

"We're almost there," Wokee says, waving his skinny arm ahead. "Do you think Dayne will be impressed when I tell him how we got here?"

"Very impressed," I assure him.

Wokee, his blonde curls spilling out of his hood as he hops around, can barely contain his euphoria.

Vlaz walks beside us, his great sides heaving, as we make our way into the dense trees.

At the first stream we pass, both Ekil and Brogut fall to their knees and plunge their entire heads into the shallow water. At the sight of the Halves with their heads fully submerged, and the gurgling sounds of pleasure they're making, I can't help but cringe. I can only imagine what the Solguards are going to think when this army of Halves comes tramping into the fortress.

When Brogut emerges from the stream, shaking the water off himself like an animal and drenching everything and everyone nearby, Wokee dissolves into giggles. Dellin is walking bow-legged when Ry helps her to the ground, but she doesn't complain.

Aunt Jadem inhales and stares up at the green canopy. "It's good to be back."

She doesn't say *home*, but it's obvious that's what she means.

A flash of guilt passes through me. It's my fault Jadem has been gone for so long. She stayed in Tanguro to help me create a new fortress for the rebels. And it was all for nothing.

"Here." Wokee offers Dellin what's left in his waterskin.

Ry stoops to the water, soaks a rag, and mops her face and neck. "Ah," she sighs. She dips the cloth again, wrings it out, and hands it to Dellin.

Dellin stands there with the rag in her hand. It drips onto the ground, but Dellin makes no motion to use it.

"Might want to wash up," Ry prompts her.

"I'm fine." Dellin hands her back the rag.

Ry doesn't take it. "You do realize you look like a true barbarian, right? I bet you're gorgeous under all that dirt."

"I'm *fine*," the girl insists.

"But don't you just want—"

"No!"

Dellin's shout makes the Halves near her flinch and back away. We all stare at her uncomprehending.

"I'm just not washing my face, alright?" Dellin's posture is too stiff, her chin raised.

"It's okay," Wokee says, breaking the tension. "I hate it when they make me wash, too."

Sighing, Ry starts to unload her pack.

"What do you think you're doing?" Aunt Jadem asks her.

"Aren't we near the travel cave?" Ry asks.

"We're not stopping," my aunt says.

"But—" Ry looks at her shadow. "Can we make it to the fortress before high day?"

"If we hurry." My aunt's face is set with determination. "Hemera, get the Halves moving. The rest of you, get back on Vlaz. There's no time for resting."

My companions are clearly feeling the effects of the rising sun. The skin on their faces is red and angry even though their hoods cast a protective shadow. Wokee and Ry scratch at their arms as though Burn blisters are forming under the thick material of their cloaks. Still, no one argues. There's a desperate, unfamiliar look in my aunt's eye.

The Halves move ahead of us, following the stream. They seem only too happy to put distance between themselves and Vlaz. Brogut, his animal hide skirt still dripping, swings his tree trunk spear back and forth. A fat, silver fish is spiked on the tip, its glassy eyes winking in the sunlight.

When the familiar break in the trees comes into sight, I hear the others heave a sigh of relief. A thrill goes through me as every step brings us nearer to my brother and the rest of the Solguards. But the feeling vanishes as soon as I hear the first scream.

CHAPTER 9

Two things happen at the same moment.

A volley of arrows flies through the trees. And Brogut hurls his tree trunk.

My aunt and I exchange a panicked look, and then we're all running.

"Get out of the way!" I yell to the Halves. Leaping straight into the air, I catch the tree trunk and pull it out of its deadly path.

Aunt Jadem is echoing my frantic yells for them—all of them—to stand down. I dart forward, trying to let the Solguards see me before they kill one of us.

A line of blue comes into focus.

I'm waving my hands, trying to make them see me, to keep them from releasing the next volley. There are at least ten archers, all with their arrows pointed straight at the Halves.

There have never been archers outside the fortress before….

"Stop," I yell.

"Fire at will!" one of the archers calls, ignoring me.

In a perfectly synchronized movement, they draw back their bowstrings.

"Hold your fire." My aunt's voice, tight with the effort of running, is still full of authority. The archers exchange looks with each other, and then slowly, they lower their weapons.

I want to weep with relief.

"What in the sun is going on up here?" Aunt Jadem demands. "Archers, report."

As my aunt and Ry talk with the archers, I go to the Halves, who are still lying motionless on the ground.

"It's safe now." I hand Brogut back his tree trunk spear, which he snatches from me.

"Filthy humans." He spits.

"You startled them." My heart is still thumping. "But everything is alright now."

Ekil shakes his head. "Coming here was bad."

"No," I shake my head. "You have to talk to the Banished leaders. Our only chance against the Duskers is if we fight them together."

The Halves still look unconvinced.

"I'll take them in," Wokee says, seeing the Halves' hesitation. "Come with me." He grabs Ekil's dangling hand with both of his and inclines his head at Brogut. "Jadem stocks her ponds with fish, you know," I hear him saying as he steers the Halves into the fortress. "As many as you can eat."

To my surprise and amusement, the Halves make an orderly line and follow Wokee through the stone archway.

"Hemera."

Even though a dozen people and Halves separate us, I somehow hear my brother's quiet voice through every other sound. I run to him.

Just before we collide, I see the bandages peeking up from the collar of his cloak. *Is that why he sent Vlaz to deliver his message rather than coming to Tanguro himself?* I stop short.

"What happened? Did he do this to you?"

Dayne's eyes flick up and down, scanning me for injuries. Trust my brother to be worried about me when he's the one covered in bandages.

"Zeidan," Dayne affirms. "Well, technically, it was his Zeroes."

My blood starts to boil as all of the old hatred rushes back. For everything my father did to the Halves, to our mother…what he tried to do to Dayne and me….

"Where is he?" I growl.

Dayne adjusts the cord that holds his lute around his neck. From the slowness of his movements, I can tell he is staving off bad news.

"Just tell me."

"He built a new place on the outskirts of the Dusker territory." Dayne looks at me, his eyes full of anger and regret. "He made more of his Zero hybrids with the blood he took from you and the Halves. He has ten now."

"*Ten?*" I almost died trying to fight a few of the Zeroes.

"They never leave his side," Dayne continues. "This happened," he motions to the bandages on his neck and the sling holding up his arm, "when I got too close."

"We'll go now."

Dayne looks at me, his eyes softening. My brother's blue eyes, the ones that are mirror images of our mother's, have deep shadows beneath them. His hair is pulled back in the same sleek plait as always, but there are more strands of gray than brown.

"I'm afraid it's not that easy." Dayne sighs.

The sheer exhaustion on my brother's face makes me feel something like desperation. He's been tracking my father all this time, and what have I been doing? Leading my army to slaughter and letting the place that was supposed to be the salvation of the Solguards be destroyed.

"Nephew." Aunt Jadem hesitates for just a moment before pulling Dayne into a one-armed hug.

"Jadem," he says, without returning the embrace.

There's a strained history between the two. It's partially because of the time they spent in the Malarusk dungeon, and also because of their shared feelings of blame for my mother's death.

"Alright, my turn!" Ry's grin stretches across her face as she wraps her arms around Dayne, taking care to avoid his bandages. She's nearly a head taller than my brother—two heads taller, counting her frizzy bun.

"This is Dellin." Ry motions to the girl, who is hovering at the edge of our group, looking out of place.

Dayne gives her a short nod. He doesn't ask any questions about who she is or where she came from.

"It's safe, I promise," Ry assures Dellin. She practically drags the other girl toward the fortress. "Not a single Dusker."

Aunt Jadem follows, already surrounded by a group of Solguards.

"And Stanly." Aunt Jadem looks over her shoulder at one of the archers. "Please be sure to feed Vlaz before he swipes every fish in my ponds. And help the Halves settle in to their quarters."

The unfortunate archer's face turns a little green as he looks at Vlaz, whose tongue is lolling out between his fangs as Dayne scratches his flopped ear.

"He's not here."

I hadn't even noticed Dayne watching me as I scanned the soldiers in blue.

A blush creeps up my neck. "Who?" I ask, fooling no one.

"Wade. He's not here." Dayne looks pointedly at the Solguard pendant hanging around my neck. "Went out with the scouts to track some Dusker recruits sniffing around the border."

"Oh." I turn away from my brother so he doesn't see my disappointment.

"Dayne!" Wokee darts between soldiers as he beelines for my brother.

"Be careful—" I begin, but it's too late.

Wokee leaps straight into Dayne's arms, oblivious to his injuries. Dayne winces, but he lifts Wokee off the ground. Hysterical laughter bubbles up from Wokee.

"I've gotten taller," Wokee says as soon as his feet touch the ground. "Did you notice?"

"I sure did," my brother replies, keeping a straight face. "You're becoming quite the young man."

Wokee puffs out his chest. "We rode Vlaz here. Did Jadem tell you?"

"Good boy," Dayne nods his approval. "You did a fine job training him."

"Quit fishing for compliments." Ry swats Wokee's backside.

"It's a good thing Jadem made these tunnels big enough," Wokee observes as Vlaz crouches to pass under the stone archway that leads into the fortress.

"Jadem did that on purpose, you know, in case a hyenair ever wanted to stop by for a visit," Ry says.

"Really?" Wokee's eyes widen.

Laughing, Ry ruffles Wokee's hair.

Dayne and I hang back to let the others go through first.

"It's good to see you, little sis," Dayne says.

"I missed you, big brother," I reply.

As soon as the words are out of my mouth, I feel the truth of them. An enormous weight I hadn't even known I was carrying lifts now that I'm with my brother.

The sun's oppressive heat fades as soon as we descend into the cavernous tunnels of Jadem's fortress. The waterfall pouring across the entire width of the tunnel bathes us with a delicious cool mist. I stop under the water and open my mouth, letting the water cleanse the dust coating my lips and tongue.

Unlike the dark and confining Subterrane tunnels where I grew up, these ones are wide enough for ten people to walk abreast. The tunnels are so tall that the beams of sunlight making their way through the pocked ceiling only reach the highest parts of the wall. It's enough to illuminate the space without any of the rays of sunlight filtering low enough to put anyone at risk of the Burn. The light filters through the waterfall mist and throws thousands of tiny rainbows onto the slick stone walls. Kynthia birds, the little black birds my mother loved so much, flutter overhead and serenade our company with their melodic chirping.

I sigh.

My brother gives me a tight smile. "That's why they wouldn't leave."

I turn to look at him. "What?"

"Wade tried to convince the Solguards to come to Tanguro, but they refused," Dayne explains. "Said they'd rather die fighting for their home, and that if they left, they'd be like the Banished."

With a sickening jolt, it occurs to me that Dayne doesn't know about Tanguro yet, and I'm going to have to tell him.

"Maybe it was wrong of us to think we could make a new rebel fortress," I say.

Dayne stops walking to regard me. "The Solguards are the fools," he says. "The Duskers are going to slaughter them if they stay here. This place wasn't made to withstand an attack." He shakes his head. "The Duskers will turn this place, and everyone in it, to rubble."

Just like they did to Tanguro.

"I've never seen anything like it." Dellin's voice is filled with awe as she stares around her.

"This place is one of a kind," Ry agrees. "Just wait until you see the rest of the fortress."

Having won Ry over with her skill with a bow, Dellin and Ry seem on their way to becoming inseparable. It makes a twinge of jealousy curl inside me.

"I don't trust that girl," I say. "She's hiding something."

"We all have our secrets." Dayne gives me a wan smile.

"The council leaders are on their way," Aunt Jadem announces. "Wade summoned them more than a week ago."

Instead of relief, annoyance pulses through me. "He sent messages to the Banished leaders, but he couldn't be bothered to tell us the Solguards weren't coming to Tanguro?"

"I have no doubt he tried," Aunt Jadem says. "My soldiers tell me our messengers have sustained heavy casualties."

My irritation evaporates.

Dayne nods, his expression grave. "Dusker recruits have been killing our scouts. Wade's had his hands full."

And now Wade is out there.

"We'll convene the council as soon as they all arrive." Aunt Jadem is already striding down the tunnel.

I hurry to catch up. "I'm going after my father."

"Not until after the council meeting." Aunt Jadem stops to face me. "You are the leader of Tanguro, and the others will need to hear from you." There is sympathy written into the lines of her face.

I have to tell the council what happened, I realize. In front of them all, I will need to explain why everyone I was supposed to protect is dead.

Dayne gives Aunt Jadem a questioning look, but she just says, "You'll hear everything at the meeting."

"What about my father?" I clear my throat. "If he disappears again...."

Dayne shakes his head. "He's not going anywhere."

The dozens of questions I have die on my lips at the sound of many pairs of boots coming down the tunnel.

Wade, followed by about ten others, tramp into the chamber.

CHAPTER 10

My heart lurches into my throat.

I had nearly forgotten—had tried to forget—how attractive Wade is. The tie at the top of his white shirt is undone, exposing smooth, coppery skin. The muscles of his arms and shoulders swell against the fabric of his shirt. His dark hair, longer than the last time I saw him, frames his face.

Wade comes to a screeching halt the moment his eyes land on me. His golden eyes widen.

His chest rises and falls as if he ran all the way up the thousand stairs from the lower tunnels.

Everything else, from the rush of the waterfall to the scrape of boots on stone, fades into the distance. Everything except for Wade blurs out of focus.

"Hemera."

The way he says my name makes a current run through my entire body. It's all I can do to keep from visibly shivering. I stand very still, knowing if I try to take even a step toward him, I'll probably trip and fall and humiliate myself.

Say something, I command myself. But my mouth can't form a single word. All I can do is stare.

"You're wounded." It's all I can think of, but it's true. There's a nasty-looking gash across Wade's forearm that is staining the shredded remains of his sleeve.

He doesn't even spare his wound a glance as he keeps his gaze fixed on me. His hands twitch at his sides, like if there weren't a dozen other people watching, he would wrap them around me.

Heat rises to my cheeks.

"Wade." Aunt Jadem gives me an apologetic look before turning her attention back to him. "What's the report?"

Like Dayne, Wade has shadows beneath his eyes. His sharp jawline is dark where he hasn't shaved. He's all bone and muscle, made of sharp angles like chiseled stone. There is something hard and dangerous about him that wasn't there before.

"Did you get my messages?" Wade asks.

At the look on our faces, he sighs. "I was afraid of that. Every scout I send out either doesn't return or comes back…" he struggles for the right word, "dying."

There is something about Wade I don't recognize. The smile I remember always playing at his lips is gone, replaced by something steely. There's no sign of the constant stream of chatter that is just so…*Wade.*

A soldier ducks through the waterfall.

"Beg pardon," his cheeks flush as his glance slides from Wade to Aunt Jadem. He looks between them like he doesn't know who he should be addressing. "Tulman just passed. If you'd like to see him before they take away the body, you'd best hurry."

Wade's face hardens into a grim mask I've never seen before. Without a word, he motions for us to follow as he strides from the chamber. The soldier remains behind, staring after us.

When we reach the glide at the end of the path, Wade swings himself inside in a single motion.

The glide looks like nothing more than a dark hole cut into the side of the fortress, but it's the fastest way down to the lower levels. I didn't truly appreciate the glide until I learned the only way back up was to climb the thousand steps.

"Fourth level," is all he says before he's gone.

After Aunt Jadem has disappeared into the darkness, Dayne nods to me to go next. With far less grace than either Wade or Jadem, I fold my body into the darkness. The metal sheet is narrow. I try not to think about the way the walls close around me as I reach for the lever.

I push the lever to the fourth notch. There is the sound of metal grating on stone, and then I'm flying.

My stomach lurches into my throat. I had forgotten the feeling of weightlessness, the complete lack of control, of the glide. A scream catches in my throat as my body shoots down, taking the curves at breakneck speed. A little gasp escapes me as I'm hurled against the metal sheet that will spin me into the right tunnel. I squeeze my eyes shut even though it's too dark to see anything.

I'm airborne for several seconds before I realize I'm no longer in the glide. My eyes open, and I'm filled with panic as the stone floor comes into focus.

I only stop rolling when the unforgiving stone wall turns my entire body into a jumble of limbs. Embarrassment, along with a rush of nerves and energy from the speed of the glide, makes it difficult to disentangle my arms and legs. By the time I finally manage to stand up, Wade and Aunt Jadem are already partway down the tunnel.

I run after them just as Dayne comes shooting out of the glide behind me. I scowl as he lands neatly on his feet.

When I step into the healing cave, the stinging scent of Burn ointment, healing herbs, and something else that is both unfamiliar and unpleasant makes acid churn in my stomach. Even if it wasn't for the terrible smell, this cave is the last place I would want to be. The last time I was here, it was because Gwendil was trying to save me from a knife wound in my shoulder. My poisonous blood killed her. Her death became even more senseless when I discovered my body could heal itself, and I didn't even need saving.

I suck in my breath as we step into the dimly lit chamber. The large cave is full. Tools, herbs, and bowls of frothing liquid are scattered over every available surface. Groans of pain echo throughout the room.

Wade scans the cave. He doesn't seem to notice the screams or reek of death, or maybe, it's just that he's grown too used to them to notice anymore. My heart swells with pity at the burden he's been carrying. All the anger and fear I've carried these last months because I hadn't heard from him is swept away.

I follow Wade over to a bed pushed against the wall.

"Oh, Tulman," Wade murmurs, bowing his head.

I step up beside Wade and look at the bed's occupant. I suck in a breath. Tulman's arms and face, the only parts visible above the sheet pulled over his body, are covered in something black and sticky. The unpleasant smell filling the air is coming from whatever substance is covering him. Reflexively, I reach out a hand.

"Don't!"

Wade grabs my hand and yanks it back.

"What is that?" I ask, trying not to think about how it's the first time Wade has touched me in months, and he's already letting go.

A soldier in blue comes up to the table and pulls the sheet up and over the man's head. Another soldier helps him roll the body up in the sheet and onto a stretcher. In a matter of moments, all that's left is the sticky black imprint of a man on the empty bed.

"Every soldier who gets anywhere close to the Dusker territory comes back here covered in that stuff." Wade nods in the direction of the others lying on beds. "Once it's on your skin, it doesn't come off." Wade leans back against the stone wall. "Whatever it is, it cooks them from the outside in."

Aunt Jadem leans closer to the bedsheets, inspecting the substance. When she straightens back up, she looks like she's going to be sick.

"It's started," Aunt Jadem breathes, her one eye roaming over the dying.

"What's started? Do you know something about all of this?" Wade pins my aunt with a stare so fierce he almost doesn't look like himself.

"I know the Duskers' assault has begun," Jadem says. "And if we don't stop them, they'll destroy us all."

"What do you think I've been trying to do all these months?" Wade demands, a muscle flexing at his jaw.

"I've never seen anything like that before," I say, partly because the way Wade is looking at Aunt Jadem is making me uncomfortable.

"No one has," Wade replies, anger making his voice rough. "And every scout I send to find answers comes back looking like this."

"Have any of them talked?" Aunt Jadem's voice is clinical, but her cheek is damp.

Wade shakes his head. His golden eyes are liquid fire, filled with the pain and anger that burn in my own chest.

An archer ducks his head into the cave. "The Banished leaders have arrived. The Council is waiting for you."

CHAPTER 11

Three guards, dressed in blue and with the rebel sun tattooed on their right hands, block the wide doorway to Aunt Jadem's meeting chamber. They step aside the moment we appear. A loud buzz from many people talking at once fills the tunnel as soon as the door swings open.

A long wooden table surrounded by high-backed chairs occupies the center of the room. Only four seats are filled, but from the noise they're making, there should be twice that number.

It takes only a moment to understand the gist of the conversation. Everyone is pointing and glaring at one seat…Ekil's.

Ekil is sitting in a chair that is too small for him. His black eyes stare straight ahead as the others around the table shout furious threats and grip their weapons.

One by one, the voices fall silent as Aunt Jadem enters the room, followed by Dayne, Wade, and me.

Aunt Jadem sits at the head of the table. Wade and Dayne take their seats. My face is on fire as I take another step into the chamber. A ridiculous urge to run in the opposite direction takes hold of me.

The room goes too quiet as I cross the room. I stare at my feet the whole time, hoping they don't stumble and betray me. The scraping of wood against stone as I pull back my chair is the only sound in the room.

I don't have time to be grateful I didn't trip and fall like I normally do whenever I'm trying to appear capable.

Everyone in the room is staring at me.

I force myself to meet the heated gazes of the strangers sitting at the table. I've never met the other Banished leaders before, but already, they're staring at me with open hostility.

"So *she* is the reason we must suffer a Halve on our council."

My eyes flick to the man at the other end of the table who has spoken. His ringleted hair is slicked back from his face, as is his goatee, which ends in a stiff point. He is wearing a golden cloak with gold tassels hanging off the bell-shaped sleeves, gold hoops through his earlobes, and a crown of golden leaves. Even his goatee is plaited with gold threads.

I remember hearing stories of the Northern settlement, and how they used to be rich from selling the gold they mined to the Subterranes. After the Duskers outlawed trade between the Dwellers and Banished, the Northern settlement fell into ruin along with the rest of the Banished.

I guess this leader wears the gold for lack of anything better to do with it, or perhaps it serves as a reminder of better times.

"I have already explained Ekil's presence," Aunt Jadem says. "The Halves are also Banished, in their own way, and they should have representation on the council."

The gold-clad man leans over the table to better stare at me. Even seated, I can tell he's tall—probably even as tall as Jadem. His skin hangs off him as it would for someone who used to be very fat. He even hovers one hand over the slight protrusion at his midsection as though he's resting it on the phantom of a potbelly.

There's something overbearing about this man's very presence. His chair is shoved back, and his legs are spread, making him take up more space than he needs. When he smiles at me in a way that is not at all friendly, his gold teeth flash.

"Hemera," Aunt Jadem says, "meet Tut, the Banished leader of the North."

"Ekil, Hemera," Tut grumbles. "Who *isn't* at this table?"

"Can we get down to business?" Dayne asks, resting his elbows on the table. "Given the nature of this meeting, I suggest we forego the usual formalities."

"Young people are always in such a hurry."

The hoarse, quavering voice belongs to an old man as small and frail as Tut is imposing. White hair springs up in unkempt tufts across his scalp. He sits on three cushions piled atop each other to reach the level of the table. His eyes are red and watery.

"Tut is right, though," the old man continues. "It's a *Halve*. It can't talk," he points a gnarled, quavering finger at Ekil. "It can't help. Toss it out, I say."

The old man reaches under the table and produces a small silver flask. He takes a quick, furtive gulp. Whatever is inside the flask makes him cough. His already-watering eyes spill over.

"Hemera will translate on Ekil's behalf." Aunt Jadem crosses her arms.

"That's Valior, Banished leader of the East," Dayne leans over to whisper to me, pointing to the old man. "And that's Liglette," he nods at the third Banished leader, a woman wearing an animal hide dress. "She's the Banished leader of the West."

Liglette's plaited hair is so long it hangs over the back of her chair and sweeps the floor. She has warm brown eyes and a round, friendly face. I can already tell that of the three, I'm going to like her best.

"Let us vote on whether the Halve can stay," Liglette says.

"This topic is not up for a vote." Aunt Jadem's voice is all authority. "Hemera, go ahead and tell Ekil to speak. It'll help clear the air."

Valior raises a bushy white eyebrow. "Your niece speaks the language of the Halves?"

Aunt Jadem quirks her lip. "See for yourself."

I feel more self-conscious than ever as I translate for Ekil, aware of every grunt and snarl and how it must make me look to the Banished leaders.

As he speaks, Ekil's nostrils flare. He points a long finger at the Banished leaders. "Stupid humans waste what they have. Never share. Kill us when they can. They are enemies."

"What's it saying, Halve girl?" Tut demands.

I ignore the barb.

"He says the Halves are starving since the Duskers took away their water," I lie.

Translator's prerogative.

"And that's supposed to be our problem now?" Tut growls, spit flying from his mouth.

"The Duskers are intentionally sowing fear and dissent among you," Aunt Jadem says. "Your quarrels with the Halves are meant to weaken you both."

Ekil nods his head up and down when I repeat this last part. "Halves will fight to kill gray cloaks," he says, "if they," he points at the Banished again, "stop attacking us."

"There, you see?" Aunt Jadem says, when I have repeated Ekil's words for the rest of the council. "We're all on the same side."

Valior huffs, but no one argues.

"Now that that's settled," Wade says with undisguised impatience, "can we discuss the matter of our impending doom?"

"Very well." My aunt steeples her hands before her on the table. "Who wants to start?"

"I called the council," Wade says. "I'll go first." His gold eyes sweep the room and then settle on the other Banished leaders. "As you know, our position in this fortress is precarious. We know the Duskers are preparing to attack."

Authority radiates off Wade. I've never seen him like this before. I don't know what to think about it, but I find I can't take my eyes off him.

"The question is," Dayne interjects, "what are they waiting for?"

"They've got a new weapon." Valior, who has taken another sip from his silver flask, is coughing too hard to continue.

"We've gotten word the Duskers are working on a weapon," Liglette says, when it's clear Valior is in no state to finish his thought. "Rumor has it they're waiting to attack the Solguards until it's ready."

"That would make sense." Dayne nods.

"Whether that's true or not," Wade makes eye contact with each of the Banished leaders, "we can't survive separated anymore." He pauses to let his words sink in. "Which is why we need you to join forces with the Solguards."

"With the Halves and the Banished added to our numbers," Dayne adds, "we'll be a true match for the Duskers. We can defeat them, together."

Liglette and Valior exchange a glance. Tut twirls his goatee.

"Your people are starving," Wade says. "You need to either join forces or die." The look he gives Tut makes it clear he would add something like *you idiot* if it weren't for Jadem's warning glance.

"Which is why we have decided to join forces," Tut says.

We all shift forward in our seats.

Tut holds up a hand. "Just not with you."

CHAPTER 12

The table erupts.

"What?!" Wade is on his feet, understanding something I've clearly missed.

"Sit down, boy," Valior chides.

"Tut speaks the truth," Liglette says. She turns to Jadem, an apology in her eyes. "The Dusker Supreme made us an offer—protection in exchange for our labor. Our people will be saved."

Aunt Jadem looks at me. We heard those same words from Dellin and the rest of the Banished on their way to Malarusk, but until now, I don't think either of us really believed them.

"You do recall that the Duskers are your oppressors?" Dayne raises his eyebrows.

"We can't afford to hold grudges any longer," Valior says. "The smaller settlements have already pledged their support. Most of them are already safe in Malarusk."

"There is no *safe* in Malarusk." There's a bitter edge to Aunt Jadem's words.

"Times change, Jadem," Valior replies.

"So, you're going to put your trust in the ones who dried up your river and are making your people starve?" I ask.

Wade smirks in satisfaction.

"The Duskers' quarrel is with the Halves," Liglette says.

When I translate this part for Ekil, the Halve shakes his head. "Banished and Halves share the river," he says. "Duskers trying to kill us both."

"They've set you against each other," I tell the Banished leaders. "If you joined forces—"

"Hah!" Tut laughs. "I'd rather be at the mercy of the Duskers than the Halves."

"But," I begin, but Valior cuts me off.

"We've got a history," he nods to Jadem, "and the sun knows I'd rather throw in my lot with you than the Duskers. But we," he gestures at the two other Banished leaders, "have an obligation to keep our people alive. And this is a war that can't be won."

"You old cowards." Wade turns his fury from Valior onto Tut and Liglette. "All of you!"

Aunt Jadem puts up a hand, and the table goes silent. "I would have thought," she says, looking at Valior, "that I wouldn't need to remind you that Crowe does not give something for nothing."

Crowe? I've never heard that name before.

At the confused look on my face, Jadem adds, "The Dusker Supreme."

No one except for me seems surprised my aunt is on a first name basis with the Dusker Supreme.

"You deaf?" Tut asks my aunt. "He said we were trading our labor."

Aunt Jadem shakes her head. "They've never allowed anyone but their own into the citadel before, and now, when they're stronger than ever, they invite the Banished into their realm? Use your head, Tut."

The way my aunt says it, I think she must know something she isn't saying out loud, but I can't imagine what it might be.

"Well, maybe," Liglette offers, but my aunt cuts her off.

"Crowe is always ten steps ahead, and she does nothing unless it will further her own gains."

The Dusker Supreme is a woman? Again, I'm the only one who seems surprised.

"She's the first woman to be Dusker Supreme," Dayne says, noticing my expression.

"Not only that," Aunt Jadem adds. "But she's the only Dusker Supreme to win her title through battle rather than birth."

"How do you know so much about her?" I ask. I've only ever heard about the Dusker Supreme in reverent whispers, and never anything specific.

"Because I helped her depose the previous Supreme."

I assume she's joking, but when I look at her, my aunt is serious.

Valior grins his toothless grin. "They got on rather well. That is, until Crowe found out Jadem was a Solguard and took her eye."

A million questions are on the tip of my tongue, but Aunt Jadem shakes her head as if to say *not now*.

"What about all the Dwellers in the Subterrane territory?" I ask.

I can't believe I hadn't thought of it before. I spent almost my whole life in Subterrane Harkibel, and when it was destroyed by the Halves, it meant the end of everything and everyone I had ever known.

Still, there were five other Subterranes. For all I know, they could be in as bad shape as the Banished and be waiting for someone to make them a better offer than the Duskers. I know it's a longshot—the Dwellers live and die by the Duskers' laws—but maybe, if we could offer them something in return, they could be persuaded to join forces with us.

"Never going to happen." Tut waves a dismissive hand.

"Most of the Subterranes have been abandoned," Liglette says. "After the Halves ravished their Subterranes, the surviving Dwellers fled to Malarusk."

The three leaders glare at Ekil, but I know the real reason the Halves attacked the Subterranes. I feel my cheeks flame as I think about how my own father used the Halves' fear of the Zeroes to force them to attack the Subterranes.

"No, the Dwellers wouldn't help us, even if they could," Aunt Jadem says, crushing my hopes.

"What we need," Dayne's quiet voice somehow captures the room, "is to return to our original plan." He faces Aunt Jadem. "Now that you're back, you can convince the Solguards to go to Tanguro. It's farther from the Dusker territory and more defensible than this place. It's big enough to offer refuge to all the Banished." He looks at Tut, Valior, and Liglette. "We can fight the Duskers from there, together."

"No, we can't." Once the words are out of my mouth, I can't take them back.

Everyone looks to me for an explanation. I can't meet Dayne or Wade's questioning gazes. They've each done what they promised; Dayne found my father, and Wade kept Solis alive. I alone have failed.

"There is no Tanguro," I say, forcing the words out one by one. "The Duskers destroyed everything and killed everyone."

"Everyone?" Wade's face has gone ashen.

"Ry and Wokee are alive," I say, "and Jarosh. But the rest…." I trail off, unable to finish the thought.

"We did not expect them to come for us so soon and strike with such a large force," Aunt Jadem says.

"You see?" Tut points at my aunt, a note of triumph in his voice. "Our only option is surrendering to the Duskers before Crowe does to us what she did to Tanguro."

"Now that the location of this fortress has been compromised," Liglette says, "you have no choice but to do the same."

The silence in the chamber is deafening. And then everyone begins to speak at once.

"There might be a way."

I think I'm the only one who hears my aunt, who has been brooding while the rest of the council argued.

"Council members," her voice is loud enough to make the others quiet down. "We've been talking about advantages in terms of numbers of swords, but there are other kinds of strength." She looks at me and gives me a small smile before turning back to the others. "Your concern," she looks at Valior, Tut, and Liglette, "is that the Duskers are a more formidable enemy than the Solguards."

The Banished leaders nod.

"What if I could find a way to put Crowe at our mercy, rather than the other way around?"

"Bah," Tut says.

Valior grins, showing his missing front tooth. "Only way I can see to do that is to kidnap Crowe and force her to give up Malarusk to us." He scratches his stubbled chin with a trembling hand. "Now, why didn't I think of that before?"

"Crowe never leaves the citadel," Dayne says. "And she's always surrounded by a hundred soldiers, besides. We wouldn't get within a mile of her."

"It was a joke, dear boy," Valior says with a wheezing laugh.

"We're not kidnapping Crowe," Jadem says. "But there is someone just as valuable who we might be able to secure."

"Jadem—no—" Dayne's face reddens.

Some kind of silent argument rages between them. After a moment, Aunt Jadem turns back to the rest of us. "Hendrix, Crowe's second. He has fewer soldiers guarding him."

"Crowe wouldn't care about losing one soldier, even if he is her second," Liglette says.

"She does care about this one." Aunt Jadem looks down at her clasped hands and then up at us. "Hendrix is Crowe's lover and the father of her only child."

Valior pauses with his flask partway to his lips.

Everyone around the table sits in stunned silence. Only Dayne doesn't look surprised.

"You're going to steal the Dusker Supreme's lover?" Tut asks.

"If he were to fall into our possession," Jadem says, "I am quite certain Crowe would be willing to bargain with us to get him back. Would that be sufficient leverage for you to pledge your troops to our side?"

The three Banished leaders exchange a look. Slowly, they begin to nod their assent.

"Why didn't you mention this before?" Wade demands. "We could have—"

"I made promises." Aunt Jadem looks at my brother as she says it. "But we have run out of options."

She's too kind to say it, but with a jolt in my gut, I realize that the other option was Tanguro. Because of me, we now have to do something far more dangerous.

"Well then, we better get moving." Wade stands up. "I'll have a team ready by low day."

"It is not that simple, I'm afraid." Aunt Jadem shakes her head.

"It never is," Tut grumbles.

"If we are going to kidnap Hendrix," Aunt Jadem makes eye contact with each of us, "then we're going to have to break into Malarusk."

CHAPTER 13

Once Hendrix goes missing, they'll seal all the tunnel exits,"
Liglette says. "You'll have no way out."

"There's still one way out," Aunt Jadem replies.

"I don't believe it." Wade looks from Dayne to Aunt Jadem. "You're
going to do it again, aren't you? You're going to escape like you did the last
time." He's grinning, a sight that reminds me of the Wade I knew before
the weight of the entire fortress and all the Solguards rested on his
shoulders.

The first time I met Wade, he was trying to convince Dayne to reveal
how he and Aunt Jadem had escaped from the Malarusk dungeon. The
memory makes the ghost of a smile cross my lips.

"No." Dayne is shaking his head. "We swore we would never—"

"It was my own damn brother." Valior cradles his flask in both hands,
as though its solidity gives him comfort. "I know the risks as well as you."

Aunt Jadem, Dayne, and Valior stare at each other, locked in a silent
debate.

"Are you going to speak in riddles or tell us how the hell you managed it
last time?" Tut demands.

The three exchange a final look. Dayne hangs his head.

"There are deep tunnels that run beneath the dungeon," Aunt Jadem
begins. She looks from Dayne to Valior, silently asking their permission to
reveal this secret before continuing. "They're the only tunnels where there
won't be a single Dusker, either inside or guarding the entrances. And one
of them leads straight to the Outside."

"What makes me think it's not as easy as it sounds?" Tut asks with a roll of his eyes.

"The tunnels are for the wormkill."

Liglette and Wade gasp. Tut waves a dismissive hand. "Stuff of legends, that is."

"My people tell a story about the wormkill," Liglette begins.

"Your people have a story about everything," Tut snaps.

Liglette tosses her long braid over her shoulder, ignoring Tut. "It's about a greedy Subterrane Captain who thought he could rule the world if only he made a big enough Subterrane. He dug deeper than anyone had ever thought to go, hoping to claim all the land beneath the surface as his own. But he unearthed a giant flesh-eating worm. The wormkill, as it came to be known, ate the Captain and every Dweller in the Subterrane."

Tut snorts.

"I can't speak to their origins, but I assure you the wormkill are quite real," Dayne says, as Valior takes another sip from his flask and shudders. "And one resides in the bowels of Malarusk."

"That is the only way out of the dungeon," Aunt Jadem says. "Through the wormkill tunnel."

"So, how do you get past it?" Tut asks.

"The creatures are blind but have an uncanny ability to smell human flesh," Liglette says. "According to the stories—"

"There's only one way to get past it." Dayne's face has gone pale and his eyes have taken on a faraway look.

"A sacrifice." Valior reaches inside the folds of his cloak for a dirty-looking handkerchief. "Someone to sate its appetite long enough to let the others escape." He mops his eyes with the handkerchief.

"Your brother was a good man," Aunt Jadem says to Valior, bowing her head. "My nephew and I owe him our lives."

Valior grips his flask.

"Even if we had a willing sacrifice, our survival wouldn't be assured," Dayne argues. "The wormkill is not easily sated. Jadem and I barely escaped last time."

"Let me get this straight." Tut holds up a hand, the gold bangles on his wrist clinking together with the motion. "You're going to break into Malarusk, steal Crowe's lover, and then throw some unsuspecting dolt to the wormkill to make your escape?"

"That's about how it works," Dayne says dryly.

"Well then," Tut shrugs. "Seems like all we need to do is find someone willing to be wormkill grub, and all our problems will be solved." He flashes a gold-toothed grin. "Not that I'm volunteering, of course."

"I must go since I'm the only one who can recognize Hendrix," Jadem says, "but I can't go alone."

No one speaks.

"I'll do it." My voice sounds too loud in the now-silent chamber.

"Absolutely not."

I recoil at the fury purpling my brother's face.

When Aunt Jadem turns to face me, there is an emotion on her face I've never seen before. *Fear, maybe? Uncertainty?* The sight of it makes my blood run cold.

"If I can outrun Vlaz, I can outrun this wormkill creature," I point out. "I'll lure it away from you, and then I'll get past it."

"The tunnel was made by the wormkill." Dayne pounds his fist on the table. "You can't outrun it because there is no way to get *past* it."

"Then, I'll fight it," I argue.

"No one has ever fought the wormkill and lived." Dayne's voice cracks from the fury he's barely containing.

"I've seen Hemera fight," Wade says. He stares at the table, like he's wrestling with some decision. "If there's anyone who can best the wormkill, it's her."

"She's a Bisecter," Dayne explodes. "The Duskers won't put her in the dungeon. They'll execute her on sight."

"There may be a way around that." Jadem rubs her scar again.

"I'll do it," Dayne says. "I won't have my little sister sacrificing herself to a man-eating worm."

"I wouldn't be a sacrifice," I argue. "And I'm not a man." I cross my arms in a show of confidence I don't feel.

"I don't like it," Aunt Jadem says. "But Wade's right. If there's anyone who can get past the wormkill, it's Hemera." She says my name with a tenderness that pulls at my heart.

"Do you have no conscience?" Dayne rounds on her. "She's your niece, for sun's sake."

"I understand that," Aunt Jadem says, "but we must get into Malarusk. And Hemera is our best chance for getting back out again."

I didn't expect my aunt to give in so readily, but I'm grateful to her for not fighting me on this. If capturing the Dusker Supreme's second will gain us the Banished people's support, then the Solguards will have a fighting chance against the Duskers. I might be able to stop what happened at Tanguro from happening here.

"I'll do it." I look at my brother, silently pleading with him to stop arguing.

Dayne glares at me for a long moment.

Ekil sits perfectly still. He understands some important decision hangs in the balance, even if he can't decipher our words.

"Please let me do this," I beg my brother. "I couldn't save the army at Tanguro. I need to do this."

When I look at Dayne again, his eyes are brimming with unshed tears. "No one escapes Malarusk without a sacrifice."

His words hang in the air like some kind of premonition.

"You do understand," Valior lifts his head to peer at me, "no one has ever met with the wormkill and lived?"

"I'm a Bisecter," I reply. "If anyone can survive this thing, it's me."

"Very brave or very stupid," Valior muses. "Reminds me of her mother."

I want to ask Valior what he knows about my mother, but I know now isn't the time.

Dayne's shoulders slump in defeat. "What about Zeidan?"

"We don't care a lick about your miscreant stepfather," Tut tells him.

"What Tut means to say," Liglette gives him a stern look before focusing on Dayne, "is that the sun won't stop rising and falling while you attend to other matters."

Tut gives a grumble of assent.

Liglette continues, "I'm afraid the Banished can only give you a week's time to get Hendrix."

A week?

I think I must have heard her wrong, but then Tut says, "If you haven't kidnapped Hendrix by then, we're pledging our allegiance to the Duskers." He crosses his arms, making it clear there will be no negotiations.

I want to go after my father, to make him answer for all the suffering he has caused. But saving the lives of the Solguards and protecting this fortress, the one refuge we have left, is more important.

I look at my brother. "As soon as we have Hendrix, we'll go after my father."

Please say yes. Please. I stare at Dayne, willing him to understand how much I need to do this.

A muscle in my brother's jaw works. "Fine. But you're not going without me."

"Or me," Wade says.

"Not you," Aunt Jadem shakes her head. "You're the Solguard leader in my absence."

Wade leaps to his feet with so much force his chair topples over backward. "Why don't you stay and command you own damn army?"

I've never seen Wade so angry. It makes tears prick at my eyes…for what he's been forced to become…for the way I'm at least in some part the reason for his pain….

"You know why." Jadem's hand goes to touch the jagged scar across her face. "I'm the only one who can get us into Malarusk."

"Then let Dayne stay behind." Wade's voice is desperate now.

"You have pledged yourself to the Solguards." There is a note of finality in my aunt's voice.

"Let me at least bring the Solguards to back you up. If anything goes wrong, we can storm the gate."

"That's impossible," Tut scoffs. "The Dusker archers would pick you off one-by-one before you could even reach the gate."

Aunt Jadem nods her agreement. "You're needed here."

Wade glares at her. When he kicks aside his fallen chair and storms out of the chamber, my aunt doesn't try to stop him.

I translate our conversation for Ekil, partly to fill the heavy silence left in Wade's absence.

"Brogut and I help," Ekil nods his head.

"Thank you." I put a hand over my heart the way Camike did when she was thanking me.

"Then it's decided." Valior points a gnarled finger at Aunt Jadem. "You capture Crowe's lover, and the Banished will fight with you. But if you fail," Valior looks straight at me, "then we belong to the Duskers."

"Agreed." Aunt Jadem rises from her seat. "I must find Ry and that new friend of hers," she says, almost to herself. "We'll be needing their skills."

Jadem walks to the door, her footsteps heavier than usual. She ducks under the low archway before turning back. "I'll have the cooks serve up something special for supper." She doesn't look at anyone in particular. "We should have a celebration of sorts before…." She looks up, like she just realized she's in a room full of people rather than by herself.

My aunt scans the room, and then her gaze settles on me. For just a second, I see an apology in her eye. But then she shakes her head and lets out a small laugh. "Well, it's good to cherish this time together, at any rate."

CHAPTER 14

A clean blue cloak, not torn or bloodstained like my current one, is laid out on the mound of pillows on my bed. A large copper tub filled with steaming water is set in the corner of the small chamber.

I stand there, looking around the room. In Tanguro, we bathed quickly in the river while an archer kept watch for Burn vultures. Still, it makes me miss the familiarity of Tanguro. *My fortress.*

When the door to my chamber bangs open, I nearly fall out of the tub.

"Still bathing? You'll miss the feast." A woman barges in, oblivious to my attempts to maintain at least a shred of modesty.

"No time for that, love." She holds up a long blue dress and matching slippers in one hand, offering me a towel with the other.

The woman motions for me to sit on the edge of the bed as she sets to work with a comb and perfumed oil.

"Our fortress might be on the edge of annihilation," she says as she works, "but we won't have our soldiers looking like savages."

She helps me into the feather-light blue dress and then dusts my cheeks and bare shoulders with shimmery gold powder. I try to object when she sets about winding blue and white flowers in my hair, but she bats my hand away.

"You'll be so pretty no one will even notice your eyes." She says it so kindly I don't take offense.

"Besides," she gives me a wink. "It's no secret the Captain fancies you. Think of what he'll say when he sees you in *this.*"

It takes me a second to realize *the Captain* is Wade. I feel my cheeks heat.

"Ah," the woman says, laughter in her voice. "I see the feeling's mutual."

By the time she's finished *making me look civilized, not like that poor half-starved Banished girl we brought with us*, everyone else is already at the feast.

I hurry down the tunnel, trying my hardest not to trip over the delicate train of my dress, as I follow the merry sounds and smells coming from the dining cave.

Garlands of blue and white flowers wind around the tall marble columns and spill out of bowls on the edges of each long table, giving off a scent nearly as rich and sweet as the food.

There isn't as much food as there was the last time I was at the fortress; instead of platters laid out on every surface, there is a single sideboard with roasted meats, bread, and bowls of fat, round rupyberries. Still, no one seems to notice. Musicians are playing a lively tune on their windpipes. A few couples are even dancing. Nowhere is there any hint that this fortress, and all who defend it, could soon cease to exist.

Aunt Jadem is sitting at the small table elevated on a platform in the center of the great hall. The other Banished leaders fill the rest of her table. To my annoyance, I see my aunt is wearing the same blue cloak she always wears. I look down at my dress and feel foolish.

"Mer, you look ravishing." Aunt Jadem smiles at me, but it doesn't mask the exhaustion that is plain on her face. "Go on," she waves me toward the table where Dayne, Wokee, Ry, and the Halves are already tucking into the feast. "Have some fun."

Ry, her arm draped over the back of Dellin's chair, whistles at me in approval. Her frizzy curls have been wetted and tamed into tight ringlets. Her eyes, lined with kohl, seem to smolder. The slinky black dress she's wearing dips low in both the front and back. It's so sheer it's almost see-through.

"Looking good, Bisecter!" she calls, raising a goblet in my direction.

Dellin is the only one at our table still wearing a cloak, albeit it a clean one. Her hood is thrown back, revealing shining, golden locks that are almost white in the candlelight. But while her hair and the rest of her is clean, Dellin's face is still covered in grime. Ry was right—if she bothered to clean her face, she would probably be very pretty. Her gray eyes and light hair give the impression of elegance and toughness. The dirt she still hasn't washed away just makes her look like every rumor of the Banished the Duskers have ever spread.

I turn away when Dellin returns my regard with a sour expression.

"Look at you, little sis." The corners of Dayne's eyes crease as his face breaks into one of his rare smiles. "You look like her."

I don't have to ask to know he means our mother. His compliment warms me to my core.

Dayne takes out his lute and strums a light tune. I'm happy to see he looks almost relaxed.

"You look different." Wokee, who has a meat pie in one hand and a berry tart in the other, looks me up and down. He sniffs the air and wrinkles his nose. "You smell different, too."

"And you're clean." I raise an eyebrow at him. "How many people did it take to wrestle you into a bath?"

"Four." Wokee crosses his arms, pouting.

Wokee's curls, brushed to a sheen, are free from leaves and twigs for once. His perpetually dirt-encrusted fingernails have been scrubbed pink.

"I almost didn't recognize you."

He sticks his tongue out at me before turning to Ekil, who is sitting beside him. "Aren't baths the worst?" He makes a motion of washing himself and screws up his face in disgust. Ekil nods.

The Halves, taking up several long tables, have no plates or goblets. Instead, there's a pile of bones in front of each of them. Brogut, who is sitting beside Ekil, has taken to carrying around a large pitcher meant for washing, which he fills up at every waterfall and takes periodic swigs from.

Earlier in the day, I saw him tip over the pitcher and splash the contents over his head. He drenched the Solguards in the vicinity and didn't even notice their angry exclamations.

When Wokee's goblet is filled with water rather than wine, he makes a pouting face. Dayne pours a few drops of his own wine into Wokee's goblet, putting his finger to his lips as he gives Wokee a wink.

"Where's Wade?" I ask, eyeing the empty spot on the bench beside Dayne, trying to sound casual.

Wokee pauses with the berry tart partway to his mouth and peers at me. "You *like* him, don't you? Like *like* him, like him."

My face flushes as I feel the heat of everyone's gaze. Dellin gives me a curious look.

"Keep your voice down," I hiss.

"I knew it!" Wokee does a little dance in his chair.

I shake my head before raising my goblet to hide the blush spreading across my face.

Dellin scooches closer to Ry and whispers something into her ear that makes Ry laugh. Ry raises her goblet to Dellin and then drains it in a single gulp. For no reason I can name, I scowl at Dellin.

A young girl, dressed in a pale pink dress, scampers past our table. "Hi Wokee," she says, a grin lighting up her freckled face. "I made this for you." She hands Wokee a blue ribbon with tassels hanging off either end.

Wokee, seeing everyone watching him, mutters something incoherent before turning away from the girl. She sighs in disappointment before running off again.

"What?" Wokee asks when he sees we're all looking at him. "She's a *girl*."

When I see him carefully fold up the ribbon and put it in his pocket, I don't say anything.

I feel Wade enter the dining cave before I see him. Off-duty scouts and guards call to him, raising their goblets in drunken salutes. They gesture for him to join them, but Wade shakes his head. My heart lurches into my throat as he makes his way over to us.

I take a sip of my wine, allowing the goblet and my long hair to shield my face. When I dare a glance up, Wade is standing behind Wokee and staring at me.

"Wow." He breathes the word.

I look up at him, and the noise in the hall fades to a distant buzz.

"Hey." Dayne pounds the table. "That's my sister you're drooling over."

"I never drool." Wade spares Dayne an affronted look.

"Just remember I could crush you," Dayne grumbles.

"Or tell Vlaz to eat you," Wokee adds. "I could do that, you know."

Wade grins. As he passes behind me on his way to the empty spot on the bench, I feel a gentle tug on my hair. As Wade sits down, he's twirling one of the blue flowers from my hair between his fingers.

Ekil points to Wade. "Will you mate with that one?"

I choke, feeling the burn of wine come back through my nose. Wokee thumps me on the back.

"What did Ekil say?" Ry asks, her clever eyes resting on my burning cheeks.

When I finally stop choking, I say, "He thinks the berry tarts are delicious."

✳ ✳ ✳

When the wine flagons are empty and all that's left of the berry tarts are the crumbs, Aunt Jadem makes her way over to our table.

"You all better get to bed. We leave at low day, and I want you in top condition."

"Yes, madam!" Ry shouts, a little too loudly, as she raises her cup to my aunt.

Aunt Jadem bends to say something in Ry's ear. She gives something to Ry, which looks like a small key. Jadem also gives her a sealed roll of script tree bark. Ry slips both into her pocket before I can get a better look. Aunt Jadem whispers something else before going to speak with Wade.

I'm about to ask what that was all about when Ry gets up and excuses herself from the table.

Wokee, who has spent the last hour trying to teach the Halves how to hold a fork and knife, turns to me. "You're going somewhere?"

I swallow.

"I want to come," he says, panic widening his eyes.

"Oh no you don't," Jadem cuts in, backtracking to Wokee's side of the table. "With me gone, who will be here to tend the orchards?"

Wokee pauses.

"You know there's no one else I can trust to care for my fruits." She frowns. "And believe me when I tell you, you don't want to see a hungry Solguard."

Wokee looks from me to Aunt Jadem, a torn expression on his face. Finally, he says, "Okay, okay. If you can't do without me, I'll stay."

I give my aunt a grateful look.

Wokee eyes me. "Will you be back soon?"

My heart gives a painful squeeze. "We'll be back as soon as we can."

When I stand up, Wade does too. Even though he doesn't say anything, the look he gives me is obvious. He wants me to follow him.

CHAPTER 15

As soon as I step out of the dining cave, Wade is there. He's so handsome it takes my breath away. The hard planes of his chest and back are accentuated by his tight-fitting cotton shirt. The edges of his hair just brush the sharp angles of his jaw.

My cheeks flush as I see his eyes roaming over me in the same way.

"Hemera." My name rumbles from deep in his throat. He takes a step toward me, and my heart leaps.

Before he can get any closer, there is the sound of boots tramping down the tunnel. Wade takes my hand, and before I can protest, he's tugging me down the tunnel away from the sound of voices.

I've never been to Wade's sleeping chamber before, but I know that's where he's taking me. There are no laws here about separate caves for men and women as there had been in the Subterrane, but it doesn't stop me from feeling like I'm doing something I shouldn't. Still, the feeling isn't enough for me to pull away. Wade's hand wrapped around mine feels too good.

The blue flowers growing in tangled cords along the walls give off a heady perfume. The scent, or maybe it's the wine I drank earlier, makes my head spin. Even the waterfall mist falling across on my face is like tiny pinpricks on my hot cheeks.

When we reach the threshold of Wade's chambers, I begin to panic.

Why did I come? What do I expect from Wade? What does he expect from me?

I swallow as Wade turns to face me.

The intensity of his gaze only makes me more nervous. *It's just Wade,* I try to tell myself. But it's no use. My heart continues its increasing efforts to pound straight out of my chest.

Wade takes another step toward me. Almost of their own accord, my feet match his, step for step, until we're close enough to touch. Wade closes the remaining distance between us with the fluid motion that is so familiar to me from our time training together.

We're still standing in the tunnel outside his chamber, but as Wade's arms wrap around me and pull me close, I stop caring whether someone will walk by and see us. My face is pressed to the hollow between his neck and collarbone, and I breathe in the salt and heat of his skin. I wrap my arms around his waist, as much to steady myself as to return his embrace.

Wade's hands move to both sides of my face. His calloused fingertips brush lightly against my cheeks. He steps back just enough to look directly into my eyes. I think he's going to say something, but instead, he leans down and presses his mouth to mine.

The last time we kissed it was gentle, sad…a goodbye. But this—this kiss is a fire in my chest.

He fumbles at the door handle behind him and pushes it open without moving his mouth from mine.

We stare at each other for a moment, dazed, before Wade breaks our embrace to step into the room.

My gaze flicks to the unmade bed wedged in the corner of the room. My heart thuds in my chest. The only sound is our ragged breathing as Wade steps back to reclaim my hands.

"What's all that?" I nod to the rolls of script tree bark, trying to pretend I'm not standing inside Wade's bedroom with my every nerve on fire.

Wade looks confused for a moment, and then, taking a breath, follows my gaze.

"Oh, you know. Just maps of Dusker troops, reports on raids in the Banished Lands, stuff to keep me busy while you all are at Malarusk." His face darkens.

"Wade…."

"I don't know how Jadem can expect me to stay behind while the people I love are going to the most dangerous place imaginable."

Love. He looks away from me when he says the word. When his gaze returns to me, it comes to rest on the Solguard pendant hanging around my neck.

"You're still wearing it." There's something like awe in his voice.

"I never took it off."

A shiver of pleasure goes through me as Wade traces the intricately curving spirals with his finger, following them out to the skin of my chest.

"You should have it back now," I say, a little breathless, as I reach up to untie the cord.

Wade shakes his head. "I want you to have it." He gazes at the pendant with a faraway look, and I know he's thinking of Sal, its original owner.

I reach up to touch the pendant, but instead, my fingers find my mother's silver key.

"I wish he were here," Wade says. "He would have known how to protect this fortress. He wouldn't be stumbling around like a blind man the way I am."

"I know the feeling." I look down, unable to meet his gaze. "But you've kept them alive. You haven't failed." *Like me,* I want to add.

Wade takes my face in both his hands.

"Hemera," he murmurs.

With that one word, I can hear a thousand more he doesn't say.

He looks into my eyes, unflinching, before our mouths find each other again. An intense heat flows from his lips to mine, from every place his hands touch my skin.

All of my longing for him, a longing I didn't even know I had, makes me cling to him.

I'm drowning in Wade, in the smell of waterfall mist and the heat of the sun and the taste of his lips. All that keeps me upright is the solid wall at my back and Wade's body pressed against mine.

His lips move to my neck, tracing a line across the place where the silk collar of my dress meets my bare skin. He pins my arms against the wall above my head with one of his. Even though I could break free from his grasp with barely a thought, I don't resist. My lips are just as eager, just as desperate, for his.

I'm dizzy from the pounding of his heart against mine. When he releases my arms to slide his hands over my hips and up my back, I reach beneath his shirt to feel his bare skin. My fingers trace over the scars across his ribs and backbone, feeling the heat of his skin against my hand. I barely know what I'm doing as I pull the fabric of his shirt over his head. In response, Wade makes a sound deep in his throat.

He lifts me off the ground and wraps my legs around him. I feel his hand on my bare thigh. I gasp.

There is such a certainty to his movements, a confidence to his touch. In spite of my desire, my need for him, I can't help but wonder how many times he has done…*this*.

It's been more than a year since Wade told me he loved me. *How many women has he been with since?*

Still, it's not like I've never kissed another man, never been with someone else.

Brice.

Like a punch to the gut, memories of Brice take hold of me even as Wade holds me in his arms. Images of our secret cave behind the waterfall come unbidden into my mind. The promises we made to each other. Brice's betrayal. His choice to die so I could live.

"What's wrong?"

Wade is still holding me, but he's pulled back. His eyes search my face. "Did I do something—?"

"No," I shake my head. We're both breathing hard as I struggle to clear my mind enough to make sense of my jumbled thoughts.

"It's just," I swallow, trying to find the right words for feelings I'm not sure I understand myself. "I thought I could forget…that I had moved on since…everything."

Wade steps back so quickly I almost fall over without the weight of his body pressed against me.

"You're still in love with him." The look on his face tears at my insides.

"No." I shake my head. "I mean, I don't know."

Even though Wade is mere inches from me, it feels like a vast chasm has opened between us. I want to pull him back to me. Instead, I stay rooted to the spot, hating myself for being the cause of his pain.

Wade turns his head away from me for a long moment. When he looks back, his face is a mask. His eyes, so unguarded and like liquid fire only moments ago, are expressionless. *Say something,* I want to beg him. *Yell, storm out, do* something. Anything would be better than this…nothingness.

"Wade," I say. "I just need some time…just to figure everything out."

His face doesn't betray any emotion. He looks not so much at me but through me when he says, "Take as much time as you need." He's far away, even though I can still feel the warmth radiating from his body.

"Oops. I guess we'll just come back later."

I let out a strangled scream as a voice—not Wade's—comes from the doorway.

Wade stumbles back from where our bodies are still almost—but not quite—touching, revealing Ry and Dellin standing just inside the room. Ry's unfocused gaze moves from Wade's bare chest to me as I hurry to pull my twisted dress back into place.

"I'm sorry." Ry takes a step forward before tripping over the hem of Dellin's cloak. Dellin reaches out a hand to steady her.

"What are you doing here?" I'm too surprised to feel embarrassed.

When Ry's gaze shifts to me, it's the saddest look I've ever seen.

A few moments ago, I hadn't thought my heart could sink any lower. But seeing the look in her eyes….

Ry is in love with Wade.

It strikes me like a blow to the chest. Wade and Ry have been friends for longer than I have known either of them, but they always seemed more like a brother and sister, like Dayne and me. I never thought, never once suspected, that Ry felt something more.

"I just wanted to say…." Ry gives a short, forced laugh. "You know, since there's a good chance we'll all be dead by next high day…." She laughs again, which turns into a hiccup.

"You're drunk." Wade turns away from us both, grabbing his shirt off the floor and pulling it over his head so violently the material tears.

Ry turns her face into Dellin's chest. The muffled sob is unmistakable.

"I'm sorry, I didn't mean—" Wade reaches out a hesitant hand in Ry's direction.

At the same time, I start toward her, but Dellin moves to shield Ry with her body, keeping one arm wrapped protectively around the other girl.

"Don't you think you've hurt her enough?" Dellin glares at me, her gray eyes sharp and accusing.

"I'm sorry," I say, echoing Wade.

Dellin keeps her body angled between me and Ry, like I'm some kind of threat she needs protection against.

"Come on Ry," she says with a gentleness I wouldn't have thought possible from someone with such a murderous glare. "Let's get you out of here."

"Glad to know you're already such an expert on what she needs, since you've known her for all of about two seconds," I snap.

Ry's face is tearstained when she looks at me.

"Ry—" Wade murmurs, but she just shakes her head and gives him a little smile.

"You're right." She hiccups. "I just need to sleep it off."

"I'll take you." I go to her, silently daring Dellin with my black eyes to try to stop me. I take Ry's other arm and lead her from Wade's chambers. I know Wade is still standing there, watching us, but I don't look back.

A part of me is relieved as soon as we're down the tunnel. I can breathe now without the heat of Wade's eyes, the press of his body against mine. The other part of me aches to run back, to take back everything I just said, to say those three little words I know he wants to hear.

But it's too late.

"Can you forgive me?" Ry asks as I help her into bed.

"I'm the one who should be sorry. I didn't know you felt that way about him."

Unbidden, an image of Ry locked in Wade's arms, the way I had been only a little while ago, flashes across my mind. My heart gives a small, painful jolt.

Dellin scoffs. "You really are as dumb as you look, aren't you?"

"What?"

"Dell," Ry gives her a warning look.

Dellin throws up her hands and stomps out of the chamber.

"What's her problem?" I demand, not even bothering to keep my voice down.

Ry doesn't respond. She's already asleep.

CHAPTER 16

Vlaz, who is standing beside Wokee, bounds over to me when I emerge from the fortress. He gives me a lick that has enough force behind it to send me sprawling. As soon as I'm on my feet, he lowers his head so I can scratch his flopped ear.

Aunt Jadem is tying the last of our supplies around the hyenair's neck while Wokee is talking, to no one in particular, about all of the commands he's taught Vlaz.

"Stop worrying," Ry is saying to Jadem. "We know the plan."

Ry gives me a distracted smile as she inspects the arrows being packed into her and Dellin's quivers. There doesn't seem to be any evidence of her breakdown during the high day, or any resentment she might be feeling for what she saw in Wade's chamber.

"Tell me again." Aunt Jadem puts her hands on her hips, the strain evident in her too-stiff posture.

Ry rolls her eyes. "In two low days, Vlaz will come back here for me and Dellin. We'll meet up with the Halves in the clearing beyond the citadel and wait for your signal. When it's time, we'll use Vlaz to give you cover from the air. Once Crowe's lover is past the iron gate, the Halves will snatch him and we'll get Dayne and Hemera. We'll all rendezvous back in the clearing."

"Wait," Dellin holds up a slender hand. "You said we would be staying in the woods. You promised we wouldn't enter the Dusker territory—you said—" Dellin's eyes are wide. She yanks at her hair beneath her hood and clenches her gloved fists.

"We'll be on Vlaz," Ry says. "You won't be in any danger."

"You don't understand." Dellin wraps her arms around herself as if she's trying to get warm, even though it's as stifling as ever out here. "I just can't…go there…ever." She's breathing too fast. Even from where I'm standing, I can see her too-quick pulse fluttering at the base of her throat.

"Shh, just breathe." Ry wraps her arms around the other girl. "You're going to make yourself pass out." She says something else to Dellin, but it's too quiet for me to hear.

Dellin's dirt-streaked face is still contorted in worry, but by the time Ry has finished speaking, she seems to have regained her composure.

I feel a moment of sympathy for Dellin, imagining what it must be like to be dragged almost all the way to Malarusk before escaping, and then to be asked to go there with people she's only just met.

"What about you?" I ask Aunt Jadem. "Where will you be?"

"With you and Dayne, of course." She turns to fiddle with a supply pack tied around Vlaz. It seems like she's trying not to look at me.

"How do you know you'll recognize Hendrix after all this time?" Ry asks.

"Because of his eyes." Valior, who has limped up to our group, has his flask in one hand and a cane in the other. "Hendrix is the only pure-blooded Dusker with green eyes."

"And," Aunt Jadem says, "because I worked by his side for eight years."

"Like emeralds," Valior continues as if my aunt hadn't spoken. "Can't miss 'em."

I try to look busy as I scan the tree line, hoping and fearing Wade will step into the clearing. He doesn't.

When Dayne comes out of the fortress, Aunt Jadem looks up from where she's stuffing supplies into a pack. "Do you have it?" she asks.

Her shoulders sag with relief when my brother holds up a pile of gray fabric.

Dayne's face has taken on a greenish hue, and he looks like he's going to be sick. His anger from the council meeting seems to have been replaced by a resigned silence.

Liglette and Tut emerge into the sunlight, their cloaks pulled tight around them. Liglette wears a smile on her face; Tut looks like he regrets the wine he drank at the feast.

"I hope, for your sake," Tut belches, "you're as strong as you think you are."

"I am," I assure him. *I have to be.*

"You'll be back soon, right? Wokee pulls on the sleeve of my cloak to get my attention.

"As soon as we can," I promise. I pull him against me, as much to comfort myself as him.

Valior moves his cane to the hand holding his flask and extends his free hand to me. His grip is stronger than I would have guessed. "Succeed, and the Banished will fight alongside you. Fail, and you're on your own."

Tut and Liglette nod.

"We'll do our best," Dayne says acidly.

Wokee holds a rope attached to Vlaz's neck to keep him still while Aunt Jadem climbs on his back.

Ry doesn't look at me as she arranges the arrows in her quiver for about the hundredth time. I should say something to her, but I have no idea what. At the same moment, Dellin catches my eye. A scowl twists her dirty face.

"We'll see you in the clearing," I say to Ry, mostly for an excuse to look away from Dellin.

"Take care of them," I tell Ekil and Brogut. They alone seem completely at ease.

We all watch as the two Halves head off into the trees. Brogut stomps through the underbrush, heedless of the noise he's making, which can still be heard long after he's disappeared from view. I bite my lip as I listen to his punishing footsteps, wondering if it was a mistake to rest so much of our plan on the Halves. I trust Ekil completely, but Brogut is a different story.

"Don't be so obvious about your worries," Dayne whispers to me. "The Banished leaders are watching."

Straightening my spine, I force myself to turn away from the Halves' receding figures. The Banished leaders are already skeptical enough without me giving them greater cause to distrust us.

"Shall we?" my aunt asks, when the other members of our party have disappeared from view.

Aunt Jadem, Dayne, and I climb onto Vlaz.

"Don't forget to give him time to hunt," Wokee says as he frets with the rope around Vlaz's neck. "And don't worry when he disappears during the high day. He'll come back."

I tap the roll of script tree bark peeking out of the top of my pack, the one Wokee filled with his scratchy, mostly illegible handwriting to explain the commands he trained Vlaz to obey. "We'll take good care of him."

Wokee gives me one of his dimpled grins, but I can see the worry lurking beneath.

"We'll see you soon," I tell him.

Once the three of us are settled on Vlaz, Aunt Jadem, who is sitting in the front of the makeshift saddle, whistles. Everyone else scatters as the hyenair begins to pump his wings.

I scramble to clutch at Vlaz's fur, belatedly remembering the way each movement propels me backward. I'm still fighting for balance as the ground, and everyone on it, drops away.

Wind crashes in my ears and whips the strands of loose hair about my face. For a few blessed minutes, all my other thoughts are lost. My body rocks as Vlaz shifts up and down with the invisible air currents. The sun makes orange spots dance across my eyelids.

It feels too soon when Vlaz starts to descend. When I look over his side, I can see the huge stone wall that rings the side of Malarusk that isn't bordered by the mountains. Lookouts are staggered every hundred feet or so, and even though we're too far away for me to see them, I remember Dayne saying there are two Duskers with loaded crossbows in each. From here, the iron gate marking the front entrance of the citadel just looks like a dark hole in the space between the mountains.

Vlaz hits the ground with an earth-shattering force, and I bite down hard on the inside of my cheek. I suck in my breath as Vlaz narrowly avoids a giant script tree and comes to a skidding halt. His sides are lathered in foamy sweat, and he's breathing fast.

Vlaz sinks his belly down onto the ground; he's probably as eager to get us off him as we are.

"Good boy." Aunt Jadem gives Vlaz a pat before sliding to the ground. She takes a large, round fruit out of her cloak pocket and offers it to Vlaz. He laps it up with a single flick of his purple tongue and nuzzles her. "I'm going to miss having you around," she tells the hyenair.

My aunt shifts back and forth on the balls of her feet, restless and uncomfortable. I've never seen her like this before.

"We'll see him again in a few days," I tell her, as much to reassure myself as Aunt Jadem.

She gives me a brief smile before turning back to Vlaz. She reaches up to give him a smack on his flank and says, "Go on, go find a river to cool off in, and then it's back to the fortress for the others."

As if he understands her every word, Vlaz gives each of us a final, sticky lick before trotting off into the trees.

"We're about an hour's walk due south." Aunt Jadem points through a gap in the trees.

We have to cover the rest of the distance on foot since we couldn't risk the Duskers seeing Vlaz. But that means we'll have to walk right up to the iron gate without any protection. This will be our first test.

CHAPTER 17

A cold feeling grips my insides in spite of the relentless sun and sweat gathering along my brow. After a lifetime of hiding from the Duskers, of constant fear of drawing their attention, I'm now walking straight into their territory. For some reason, it feels like surrender.

"Take this." Aunt Jadem hands me a thick, sand-colored cloak that is identical to the one I used to wear as a Dweller of Subterrane Harkibel.

I strip off my blue silk cloak and replace it with the drab one. I had forgotten how cumbersome the protective cloaks are…the ones every normal human must wear. The heavy, unbreathable material pulls my shoulders into a hunch. Sweat immediately begins to stream down my face and back.

Aunt Jadem chuckles at whatever expression is on my face. "You must play the part of a lowly human for a while."

We review the plan until the iron gate comes into view through the trees.

I thought the wooden gate outside Tanguro was big, but this one is so much more formidable. The iron is thick and unyielding. The mountains on either side make the gate appear more, rather than less, imposing.

"How are you going to get Hendrix alone?" I ask, mostly to distract myself from guessing at the number of Duskers waiting just inside the gate.

"Just leave it to me," is all Aunt Jadem says.

We all stop walking when the trees thin. Once we step onto the open plain, we'll be in view of the Duskers posted in the lookouts. Just the thought of their crossbows aimed at us makes my breathing shallow.

"You don't have to do this," Dayne tells me. "We can find another way."

I look straight ahead, but it's not the gate of Malarusk I see. The faces of the people killed at Tanguro fill my mind until I can think of nothing else.

"I have to do this."

"Did I ever tell you it was because of your mother I joined the Solguards?" Aunt Jadem asks.

Dayne and I exchange a look.

"I'm not really sure this is the best time for reminiscing," Dayne begins.

"She was going to run away to the Banished Lands," Aunt Jadem continues, as though Dayne hadn't spoken. "She'd heard the Solguards were gathering there and was going to try and find them." Aunt Jadem has a faraway look on her face. "Our parents discovered her intentions and kept her under constant watch. There was no chance of her getting away after that. So, I told her I would go in her place."

Aunt Jadem looks at me. "It was your mother who taught me to believe in something better, something more." She puts a hand to my cheek. "Now, when I look at you, I see that same spirit." She gives me a small, crooked smile. "You're going to save us all, Mer."

My throat burns and I have no words with which to respond, but it doesn't matter. Aunt Jadem draws me to her in a suffocating hug. Dayne makes a sound of protest but doesn't pull away as Jadem reaches for him with her other hand.

"Now, then." Aunt Jadem releases us and reaches into her pack, businesslike again. She pulls out the gray Dusker cloak Dayne gave her back at the fortress. I don't ask where he got it.

Protected by a tree's shade, Jadem strips off her blue cloak and quickly replaces it with the gray one. When she pulls the gray hood up, a feeling of dread passes through me. She looks like one of them, scarred face and all.

Dayne begins dumping the few things left in his pack—a wad of bandages, his waterskin, and finally, his lute. He runs a loving hand along its polished wood before setting it at the base of a script tree.

"We'll be back for it in a few days," I tell Dayne, hoping if I say the words out loud enough, I'll believe them.

My brother gives me a brief nod.

"Dayne, if you please." Aunt Jadem pulls on a pair of gray gloves, covering her Solguard tattoo.

Before I can register what he's doing, Dayne pulls back his arm and punches Aunt Jadem in the jaw.

There is a sickening thud as his knuckles connect with flesh. Aunt Jadem stumbles backward.

"Are you insane?" I gasp.

Aunt Jadem holds up a hand to stop me. "Again," she says.

Dayne hits her again. Blood sprays from her mouth as she falls to her knees. But then she stands, and faster than I would have thought her capable of, she punches Dayne back.

"Stop it!" I grab her hand, slick with blood, to keep her from hitting Dayne again. "Have you lost your minds?"

"The Duskers will need to think you put up a struggle." Aunt Jadem spits out a mouthful of blood. "Your wounds would heal before we reach the citadel, so you'll need to cover yourself with dirt."

"What?"

"And tear your cloak. Not enough that you'd have gotten the Burn, but enough to look the part of a prisoner."

Hands shaking, I rub the silty earth all over my face and cloak. I wince at the way the dirt clings to my hair, and try not to wonder if coming here is the dumbest thing I've ever done.

Once she deems me filthy and Dayne bloody enough, Aunt Jadem winds thick, coarse ropes around our wrists. She ties them tightly enough to cut into our flesh. I grit my teeth.

Dayne looks at me through bruised, swollen eyes. "You still want to do this, little sis?"

I take a deep breath, willing my feet to take me forward, straight to the most dangerous place in the world.

"Let's go."

✳ ✳ ✳

Aunt Jadem and four Dusker guards, each with a sword pointed at our backs, walk us from the iron gate to the citadel's entrance. Every nerve in my body screams danger.

A strange sucking at my boots temporarily draws my attention away from the iron gate looming ahead. The ground is…muddy.

When I look closer, I notice there are dozens—no, hundreds—of tiny rivulets curling through the mud in the direction of the citadel. Ekil was right. It looks like the Duskers have somehow made all of the surrounding bodies of water flow straight to them. *But why would they go to all that trouble?*

I crane my head to see more and stumble on an upturned root.

"Move your feet, idiot!" Aunt Jadem screeches in a voice I've never heard before. She gives me a great shove, and I fall to my knees. The mud slurps around the fabric of my cloak.

"You too, swine!" She pushes Dayne into the mud beside me. "Do you think I have all day?"

The other Duskers laugh. One of them gives Dayne a swift kick to the back. I sneak a glance at my brother, but his eyes are downturned and his shoulders slumped.

After we're searched for weapons, the guards allow Aunt Jadem to push us into the darkness.

"These ones go straight to the dungeon," Jadem, who barely sounds like my aunt anymore, says.

One of the Duskers grabs my chin with a gloved hand. "Might be worth something under all that dirt." I can picture the nasty smirk on his face even though my eyes are squeezed shut. "Might be a good companion for my men."

He laughs as my body is wracked with a shudder.

A slap rings out. I glance up just in time to see the Dusker stumbling backward and Aunt Jadem lowering her hand. "My orders come from the top. Now move aside!"

The Dusker stands back as Aunt Jadem yanks Dayne and me forward.

"We come in darkness," she barks as we reach the two Dark God statues marking the tunnel's entrance. On either side are twelve guards. They each hold a crossbow aimed at us.

"Just a minute, soldier."

There is someone standing in front of us, but I don't dare to look up.

"All prisoners go to the trees. No exceptions." He puts a gloved hand on the ropes between Dayne and me.

Trees? Perspiration drips down my face and stings my eyes. It's all I can do to keep from turning my panicked gaze on Dayne.

"These ones *are* an exception," Aunt Jadem shoots back. "The Solguards are getting too bold." She rips Dayne's glove off, exposing his tattoo in the dim light of the tunnel. "We're making an example."

The Dusker keeps his hand on our rope.

"Perhaps you'd like to tell the Supreme you disapprove of her orders," Aunt Jadem suggests, her voice low and deadly.

"Didn't know your orders came from Her." There is both surprise and reverence in the Dusker's voice.

Aunt Jadem reaches around and pulls the rope out of the man's grip. "Go in darkness."

And then, with a vicious tug, Dayne and I are drawn down into the darkness of Malarusk.

CHAPTER 18

Guards with crossbows are posted at every branch of the tunnel. Even if I could keep track of the labyrinthine paths, there would be no way to sneak past the guards. Their suspicious gazes track our every step.

Even though it's high day, when most people are asleep, the citadel is abuzz with activity. Scouts, laden down with armfuls of maps and messages on pieces of script tree bark, run past us on their way to deliver their reports. Captains, their black Dark God armbands prominently displayed, stride past us with a dozen or so armed soldiers marching in their wake.

At every check point, Aunt Jadem is questioned.

The farther down the tunnels take us, the hotter it gets. I'm drenched in sweat beneath my cloak. Even though we pass a well on each level, Aunt Jadem doesn't let us stop.

The tunnel narrows, and the lanterns lighting the way get farther apart.

"Welcome to hell," a voice laughs.

It takes me a moment to recognize it as my aunt's.

I look up to see a metal grate blocking us from moving farther down the tunnel. Two guards stand at either side.

"We've had no orders about new prisoners," one of the guards says, consulting a long roll of script tree bark. He keeps his crossbow aimed at Dayne's chest.

"My orders come from the top, fool," Aunt Jadem barks. "Move your feet, or I'll report you."

A long pause follows, during which I force myself to keep staring at the ground. Sheer terror sets my teeth to chattering.

"Open the passage," one of the guards orders.

A creaking fills the tunnel as the grate rolls back on its hinges.

"Look at her, shaking like a little leaf," one of the guards chuckles as Aunt Jadem pulls off our rope and shoves Dayne inside. Before my wrists are even untied, Aunt Jadem strides away without a backward glance.

"No one's going to save you now, little leaf," I hear as I'm shoved into the darkness. There is the sound of creaking as the grate clanks shut behind us.

"Happy travels, little leaf." The guard's laughter fills the tunnel as I stumble my way after Dayne.

"Come on." Dayne's voice sounds too loud in the empty tunnel.

My stomach turns at the fetid stench of the air. Images of decomposing bodies fill my mind, and I almost scream when I trip over a rock on the path.

The tunnel ends in a large, circular chamber. The ceiling is so low I need to hunch my shoulders to keep from scraping my head. The candle stubs lining the outer wall are blinding compared to the blackness of the tunnel.

"Stay close," Dayne mutters.

I can see the outline of people approaching us through the gloom.

"Welcome to the dungeon, friends."

The voice comes from my left elbow. I jump back, knocking into Dayne.

Two more men, all skin and bones, appear in front of us. They move as silently as ghosts. Each one holds a long, rusted nail that looks like it was pulled from one of the support beams that keep the rest of the fortress from collapsing on top of us. They hold the nails out in front of them as they would a dagger or sword.

I guess that without access to real weapons, the prisoners make use of whatever they can find down here.

"Ah, fresh meat," one of them says, sidling up to Dayne.

I force myself to loosen my grip on Dayne's arm before I break it.

The prisoner at my elbow glides around until he's facing me. "A girl." He throws back his head and laughs maniacally. The candlelight reflects off his bare chest, exposing the individual bones of his ribs. He looks more skeleton than human. "I've just been saying how all's we need is a bit of fun, ain't that right, Morey?"

"Back off," Dayne growls as he steps in front of me.

"What you causin' trouble for, fresh meat?" The one called Morey jabs his rusted nail in my brother's face. "You ain't plannin' to deprive us of a last bit of entertainment, are ya?"

It's then that I notice it's no longer just the four of us. Other prisoners, dozens of them, have surrounded us. Their eyes gleam like orbs in their sunken faces.

"We don't want trouble," Dayne says. "But if you make a move on me or my sister, it'll be the last thing you do."

From the way the other prisoners look at Morey, it's obvious he's the one who gives orders down here…at least when the Duskers aren't around.

Morey laughs again. "I'ma leave it all to Wormy. 'E's about due for 'is next feedin'." He pokes Dayne's chest with the rusted nail. "Since ye have more meat on ye than the rest of us, you's is gonna go down the hole."

"When is the next feeding?" There is no hint of fear in Dayne's voice.

"You know about the feedin'?" Morey sounds impressed.

"Word travels far," my brother replies.

The other prisoner turns his mouth in an imitation of a smile. "Wormy will 'preciate hearing it, I'm sure."

The two prisoners standing before us exchange a look. Quick as a lizard darting out its tongue, Morey thrusts his nail at my brother's neck.

In one fluid move, Dayne grabs the man's wrist just before the metal pierces his skin, and twists.

Morey screams. The nail falls from his grasp.

The other man lunges for me, but Dayne told me to expect this, and I'm ready. I step to the side so the man's fist sails past my cheek. While he's off balance, I shove him with just enough force to send his body hurling in a perfect arc through the air. There's a dull thud as he hits the far end of the chamber and slides to the ground. He gets back up—slowly—whimpering like a wounded animal.

Morey hisses low in his throat. "Bad move, fresh meat."

The other prisoners, moving as silently as though they really are ghosts, tighten the circle around us. They all carry some kind of makeshift weapon, and the cold, dead look in their eyes says it all: they have nothing to lose.

Dayne and I stand back-to-back. I try to count them, but there are too many. *We can't fight them all.*

A harsh clanging cuts through the quiet. Before the ringing ends, the prisoners dissolve into weeping, whimpering shells. They drop to the ground and curl into themselves. Some of them tear out their hair.

Dayne grabs my arm and pushes me into the crowd of prisoners who, just moments ago, were about to kill us.

"Stay down," he murmurs in my ear as he pushes me to the ground.

A bright light bounces off the walls as the echo of boots ricochets through the chamber. I can just make out the beefy outlines of two Dusker guards as they step through the mouth of the tunnel.

"Anyone know what time it is?" The Dusker's voice fills the chamber.

"It's lunchtime," the other guard sings.

They stomp toward us, pausing to inspect a prisoner here, give another prisoner a shove there….

"Look at these weaklings," one guard tsks. His pale skin glows in the dark. "We'll have to throw down double the usual number to satisfy Wormy."

A cry goes up from the prisoners, but that only makes the guards laugh.

When the heavy boots stomp over to our side of the chamber, I train my black eyes on the ground. The footsteps still. I stop breathing.

The reeking smell of urine becomes almost unbearable as a small puddle trickles out from beneath the prisoner curled beside me. One of the guards reaches a gloved hand down. I feel the displacement of air as he reaches for me.

Not yet, a voice in my head screams.

Almost too quick to see, Dayne shoves the prisoner beside me into the guard's legs.

There is a squeak, and then a howl, as the guard's gloved hand drags the other man to his feet.

"You'll be the appetizer," the guard announces.

"No, p-p-please," the prisoner begs.

"I got the entrée," the other guard announces farther down the wall. He holds another weeping, struggling prisoner like a fish dangling from a line.

"And what about some dessert?" The guard nearest me swoops down and grabs the man beside Dayne by his armpits.

"I've already pledged allegiance to the Dark God!" the man shrieks.

"Well then, say your prayers," the Dusker replies. "Because you'll be meeting Him for judgment soon enough."

"No!" The prisoner reaches out his bony fingers, grasping at nothing. "I know where to find the Solguard leader. I can lead you straight to her."

Fear flashes through me. *Who is this man?* I look at Dayne, but he just puts a finger to his lips and shakes his head.

"Shut your trap." There is a dull thud as the guard's boot connects with the prisoner's ribs. "The Supreme doesn't need filthy scum telling her what she already knows."

I don't have time to worry about what any of this might mean for Aunt Jadem.

As the three prisoners twist and turn in their captors' grips—pleading, threatening, and sobbing—the rest of the prisoners follow the guards, pulling Dayne and me with them. Someone pushes me from behind, and I find myself at the front of the crowd. A rickety wooden balustrade is all that separates me from the endless darkness beyond.

Instinct tells me to keep back from the edge, even though it's impossible to tell how far the fall might be. One of the guards plucks a candle stub from the ground. As he holds it up over the fence, the prisoners around me erupt into raucous shouts. They stomp the ground with their bare feet and begin to chant.

"Wormy! Wormy! Wormy!"

"Up and over," a guard says.

The chanting stops, and it's as if every person in the cave is holding his breath.

The guards toss the prisoners over the fence one by one like they're nothing more than empty sacks.

I clap a hand over my mouth to silence my cry. The wood groans as everyone presses forward.

There are splashes as the men hit the bottom. I can hear the scraping and whimpering as they try to claw their way back up to the top. There is the sound of loose dirt and gravel sliding down. For a moment, everything goes quiet.

And then there's another sound, this one unfamiliar. It's a great sucking, like the belly of an enormous snake is ploughing its way through a muddy riverbank.

Something white cuts through the darkness below.

"'E's here!"

I grip the rail to still my shaking hands. That *thing*, the wormkill, is as tall as Vlaz and many times longer. The giant, shapeless white blob moves slowly, lazily. It stops, swiveling what must be its head back and forth on its fleshy body.

And then it lunges.

The wormkill's maw is open, displaying a set of double fangs that shine luminous in the darkness. There is a cry that sounds like "help," and then the beast's fangs slam shut. All three of the men disappear.

There's a sigh as the prisoners around me release a collective breath.

The wormkill slithers backward, making the same disgusting, sucking noise as its belly cuts through the filth beneath it.

"Well, then." One of the guards rubs his hands together. "Same time, same place, tomorrow, shall we say?"

The other guard laughs as they stomp out of the chamber. Almost as an afterthought, one of them unslings a bag from his shoulder, opens the drawstring, and overturns it on the ground. The smell of rank meat mingles with the stench of body odor. My stomach turns even as the other prisoners race for the food.

The guards amuse themselves by watching as the prisoners rip and tear at each other for their share. Dayne and I hang back. When I glance at my brother, I see his face is as gray as the Duskers' cloaks. With a pang, I realize he's living through this madness for the second time.

Eight years. My brother was down here for eight years.

I try not to think about Dayne being forced to fight for his share of the rotten meat. I don't want to know what he had to do to avoid the wormkill for eight years. When I look at him again, I realize I can't possibly imagine what it must have meant for my brother to agree to come back here.

If I had known, I never would have pushed for it. *How could Aunt Jadem have let him come, knowing what it would be like for him?*

Barely a minute goes by before the meat is gone and the prisoners have slunk back into their shadowed corners. Two prisoners are left behind, their bodies contorted and crumpled next to the empty food sack.

The heavy metal grate clangs shut behind the guards.

CHAPTER 19

"Wake up, Hemera."

My throat feels like a thousand tiny fires have been lit inside. I had been dreaming about a man-eating worm in a black tunnel. When I realize where I am, and that my dream was far too close to my reality, I sit up so fast my head spins. I grab instinctively for my sling before remembering I'm weaponless.

Dayne is standing between me and the other prisoners, a living shield. Overwhelmed by guilt, I jump to my feet. He should have been the one resting.

Before I can say anything, the sound of metal screeching against stone cuts through the eerie quiet. The other prisoners are already pushing and shoving each other to get as far away as possible from the wooden fence.

There isn't enough time for me to steady my shaking limbs before the light of the Duskers' lantern floods the tunnel.

The whimpering begins as the two guards tramp into the chamber.

They walk slowly, probably to prolong the anticipation and misery. But as they come closer, it's obvious something is wrong with one of them. He's leaning against the other, who is dragging him across the dirt. The Duskers make their way into the center of the chamber, and then the taller of the guards, the one holding up the other, does something no Dusker guard would ever do in the presence of a non-Dusker. He takes off his hood.

Her hood.

Aunt Jadem, sweat beading across her temple, shifts her arm to better support the Dusker's dead weight.

A sob of relief is cut short partway through my lips.

"We have to go. Right now." Aunt Jadem's free hand makes an urgent gesture.

"What's happened?" Dayne demands, finding his voice first.

Aunt Jadem's mouth is pressed in a tight line. "He's already been missed."

"Were you exposed?" Dayne pulls me to my feet.

"Just help me with him," is her only reply.

Aunt Jadem drags Hendrix to the fence.

The other prisoners, who have been gawking at Aunt Jadem and the bound and gagged Dusker, awaken from their stupor. Moving as stealthily as they had when Dayne and I were first brought to the dungeon, they surround us. The prisoners clutch their makeshift weapons. Their hollow eyes gleam with desperation.

"What the 'ell you doin'?"

Morey, the one who threatened Dayne and me when we were first brought to the dungeon, stands in front of Aunt Jadem. A dozen or more of the prisoners gather behind him. They look like some kind of skeleton army.

"I'm the Solguard leader and friend of all who oppose the Duskers." Aunt Jadem's eye shifts to the dark tunnel once, twice. Her meaning is plain: we have to get out of here. But Morey has planted his feet and shows no sign of backing down.

"If you're our frien'," Morey waves a bony hand at the other Dusker, "then who the 'ell is tha'?"

"Hendrix." Jadem pulls the hood off the man. "The Dusker Supreme's second-in-command."

Even with the gag stuffed in his mouth and the trickle of blood that has smeared and dried across his forehead, it would be impossible not to notice how *perfect* he is.

Hendrix's pale, muscled body looks like it was cut from marble rather than made of bone and flesh. His hair, a rich brown, falls in perfect, silky ringlets down to his shoulders. And his eyes really do look like glowing emeralds.

Aunt Jadem looks back at the tunnel again. This time, I hear movement near the grate.

"We have to go." Aunt Jadem tries to drag Hendrix through the mass of prisoners standing between us and the fence. "The exits have already been sealed. This is the only way out."

"They'll punish us," an especially bone-thin man points an unsteady finger at us. "They'll throw us all to Wormy at once."

The metal grate creaks to life, followed by the unmistakable sound of boots clomping down the tunnel.

"They're coming," Dayne says. "Make your choice."

For a moment, no one moves. The prisoners remain poised with their pathetic weapons. I don't dare to breathe.

"Go," Morey says. "We'll hold 'em off as long as we can."

He makes a complicated hand gesture at the prisoners. They move their bodies to create a makeshift shield between us and the entrance to the chamber.

"Thank you." Aunt Jadem puts her right hand over her heart. "We are in your debt."

"Then build me a palace an' fill it with meat pies an' pretty girls," Morey calls to our backs.

"We can't just leave them," I say as Dayne grasps my elbow. "The Duskers will know they helped us."

"No one leaves the dungeon without a sacrifice," comes my brother's grim reply.

I don't have time to say anything else, because we're standing at the chamber's edge. The blackness beyond the fence looks endless.

"The wormkill is blind, so it will sense you by sound and smell," Aunt Jadem reminds me. "Make sure to stay clear of its fangs."

I grip the railing as I stare down into nothingness.

Except it's not nothing…the wormkill is down there.

"The slime coating its belly is poisonous," my aunt adds. "Its touch acts faster than the Burn."

"You sure about this?" Dayne asks, turning my shoulders so I face him.

"It's a bit late for that now." I clear my throat to cover the waver in my voice.

The rhythmic click of the Duskers' crossbows, followed by screams, fills the chamber behind us.

For a moment, it's not Morey and his army of ghostlike prisoners, but my own army that's crying out. *I have to save them. I have to help.*

But it's too late for the army at Tanguro.

"The mission, Hemera," my aunt says. "Too much depends on our success."

Even though every part of me screams to go back, to fight alongside these defenseless prisoners, I know it would only serve to get me—and probably Dayne and Jadem—killed.

But if we can get Hendrix out, if we can use him as leverage against Crowe, then we might be able to save hundreds…thousands….

Not trusting myself to speak, I duck between the slats of the wooden balustrade. The sounds of fighting grow louder.

I step off the ledge.

CHAPTER 20

My body hits the bottom. My ankle twists and I go down elbows-first. Before I can catch my breath, I'm being sucked into a pool of reeking mud.

A horrible squelching sound sucks all around me as I try to stand. The bones in my leg click back into place, and I have to bite down hard to keep from screaming.

As soon as I'm on my feet, the stench hits me full force. I turn to the side and retch. My every step is weighed down as I sludge through wormkill refuse. My stomach convulses.

There is a heavy splash somewhere nearby, although it's too dark to see much of anything.

I take a step forward and stumble over something beneath the sludge's surface. I kick my foot out, raising whatever is stuck at the bottom. It bobs to the top, visible for a moment, before sinking back down.

A human skull.

What I had imagined to be rocks making the ground uneven beneath my feet are bones…thousands of them. As the muck thins out, bones crack and crunch under my every step.

I take a shallow breath, trying to steady my racing heart. I have to move deeper into the wormkill's den so Jadem and Dayne will have a clear path to the Outside. I know this—I remember the drawing Aunt Jadem made on a piece of script tree bark, and the amount of time I'll need to distract the wormkill to give the others enough time to make it out—and yet my feet protest every step that takes me deeper into the darkness.

I hear the plunk and a muffled grunt as either Jadem or Dayne lands in the tunnel behind me. My instincts scream for me to go still and be silent so the wormkill won't be able to find me. Instead, I force myself to make extra noise as I move away from the others…away from any chance of an easy escape.

Don't look down. Don't look down. Don't—

A squelching sound that doesn't match my footsteps comes from somewhere nearby. I stop moving. My heart stutters in my chest as something enormous and white fills the mouth of the tunnel.

The wormkill.

If I thought it looked big when I was staring down at it from the fence, it's nothing compared to the enormity of the beast making its way toward me now. It slurps and sucks its way through the mud, moving with all of the slowness of a predator that knows its prey is trapped.

Jadem and Dayne had told me the wormkill's body took up all the space in the tunnel and that I wouldn't be able to simply skirt around it, but until this moment, I hadn't really understood what that meant.

The tunnel is molded to the wormkill; I hear the scraping and sucking as its flesh pulls along the rim of the circular tunnel. I won't be able to run past the beast. I have to keep it here, in this part of the tunnel, until enough time has passed for the others to make it out.

That panicky feeling I used to get in the Subterrane takes hold of me again. My breathing constricts. *What made me think that even with my abilities, I'd be able to take on a creature like this?*

I can't fight something this huge.

But if I fail, Jadem and Dayne will die. And it's not just them. If we don't take Hendrix captive, the Banished will surrender to the Duskers, and it will mean the end of the Solguards. I can't let that happen. I won't.

I bend, fumbling through the sludge, until my hand closes around something solid. I grasp a bone and throw it at the eyeless head of the beast.

The wormkill lets out a sharp hiss that sets my teeth on edge. It stops moving. I had thought the sucking and scraping sounds were bad, but this silence is worse. I stand rooted in place, waiting for the creature to move again.

The wormkill thrusts its head forward so fast it blurs. My body reacts before my mind has even registered what is happening. I fall to the ground on my back, barely avoiding being knocked out by the force of the wormkill's strike.

When I lift my head from the mud, the beast's great maw is already open, displaying double sets of rotten fangs. A wave of hot breath fills the air with the smell of corpses.

Jaws clamp shut on the edge of my cloak as I dive out of the way.

Run, Hemera! my brain screams.

But I can't. It's too soon for the others to have made it out of the tunnel. I have to stall the wormkill. Just a little longer….

As the beast descends on me again, I'm forced to take several steps back down the tunnel, in the direction of the Outside.

Too fast. The wormkill is forcing me to retreat too fast for any human to outpace, even if they were running flat out and weren't dragging a hostage's dead weight.

I have to stop it.

The wormkill slides back, like it's getting ready to lunge at me. Instead of backing away from it, I hold my ground.

My hands search the waste at my feet until I find a jagged bone. This time, I hold it like a spear. When I see the flash of the wormkill's teeth, I throw the bone with all of my strength.

The bone disappears into the darkness of the creature's throat.

Elation is replaced by terror as the wormkill rears up its great head, breaking straight through the ceiling above. Dirt rains down, filling my mouth, choking and blinding me. I hurl myself against the wall as a thick, mucousy strand of slime drops down from the wormkill's swiveling neck. Before I can move, the beast snaps its head down, pinning my body to the ground with what I imagine to be its snout.

My eyes sting at the fetid breath rushing out of its flaring nostrils. Thick mucus wavers just above my head. Terror paralyzes me.

Move, I command myself.

I manage to free one of my hands and swing it around to strike the side of the wormkill's head. It roars, an earsplitting sound that shakes the ground, and releases me.

I scream as a fiery pain rushes from my fist up my arm. The wormkill slime has already burned through my clothes and skin. It feels like my bones are melting. For all I can tell, they are.

But if the wormkill gets past me, Jadem and Dayne will be next.

The wormkill continues to rear its head, taking out whole chunks of the ceiling and wall. We'll all be buried alive if this keeps up. I force myself to a standing position, ducking the wormkill's next strike. *I'm not finished yet, beast.*

I back up just enough to give myself some space. With a running start, I use the banked base of the tunnel to climb up the wall. I jump at the last moment, swinging my hand around to strike the side of the wormkill's head. It shrieks as it's hurled backward, cutting through earth and bedrock.

But without any bones in its body to break, the beast recovers and is lunging at me again in seconds.

The wormkill's jaws click together in anticipation. I let out a frustrated scream. All I've managed to do is whet its appetite.

This is it, I think. *This is how I'm going to die.*

A noise far down the tunnel makes the wormkill pause. My brother's voice…calling…*taunting* the wormkill.

Why are you still here? I want to scream at him. *Get out of here!*

The wormkill is already in motion. It slams me into one of the newly-made craters in the wall as it hurls its enormous bulk down the tunnel past me…in the direction of Aunt Jadem and Dayne.

"Come back!"

I scramble to my feet, my right arm hanging useless by my side. It takes me precious seconds to catch up. Even when I do, my sweaty hand can't find purchase on the fat, slimy tail. My wild punches and kicks are useless; the wormkill's spongy flesh just absorbs the blows. The acid of its slime burns into my skin.

Some natural light is making its way in from the Outside. I can hear the scrabbling of human steps ahead. *Move,* I silently beg my aunt and brother. *Please.*

The wormkill is between me and the Outside. If I can't stop it, there will be nothing to keep it from devouring the others. I jump onto the creature's flailing tail and rain down blows. The beast wriggles its body, flinging poisonous slime in every direction.

More dirt and stones crash down from above.

Fresh waves of panic steal my breath away. I grab the wormkill's tail, digging my nails into its flesh to get a hold on it. I don't try to stifle my screams as the poison races through my fingertips and up my arms. As soon as I have a grip on the slime-covered tail, I yank it backward with all of my strength.

A gurgling protest erupts from the wormkill as its body is launched up through the ceiling. I hear screams overhead, and then the wormkill is crashing back down. I sprint underneath it, managing to position myself between the creature and the Outside before it hits the ground in a heap of white flesh, slime, and debris.

The wormkill snarls, and then it slithers toward me on its venomous belly. Its approach is slower this time—more calculated, like it knows I'm not the prey it's used to.

Both of my arms are numb, useless. I back away from the wormkill, moving in the direction of the Outside as fast as I dare.

I've lost track of how much time has passed, but Jadem, Dayne, and Hendrix have to be on the Outside by now. I strain my ears for any sound of them, but all I hear is the click of the wormkill's fangs.

I give Aunt Jadem and the others a few more precious seconds, waiting until the wormkill is a mere snap of its fangs away from me. Then, I run.

CHAPTER 21

"Come on!"

Aunt Jadem and Dayne are standing just outside the tunnel and waving frantically at me.

I throw myself out of the tunnel's opening.

The wormkill shrieks in protest when its teeth clamp shut on empty air. Its hideous roars fill my ears as we run, but it doesn't leave the darkness of the tunnel.

Too close, I think, as my heart thuds against my ribcage.

We stumble away from the tunnel before I collapse in a heap of nerves left over from my encounter with the wormkill. Feeling is coming back into my arms, and with it, a fiery pain.

"You did it!" Dayne sinks to his knees and pulls me to him. "Thank the sun."

My brother's grip on me is almost violent. It's like he expects someone to come and throw me back into the wormkill tunnel. My face is pressed into his cloak so I can't see his expression, but I can hear the relief and emotion in his voice.

"You did it," he says again.

"I never had a single doubt," Aunt Jadem says.

Dayne finally releases me. When I look at my aunt, I see the pride shining in her eyes as she regards me.

"Darling niece. Our savior."

I swallow, not wanting them to know how much my skin is burning from contact with the wormkill slime…how close I came to failing them.

My aunt continues to look at me in a way that makes me uncomfortable. It's like she thinks I'm invincible. She thinks I can fix everything that's wrong and broken. She thinks I can control the fate of the Solguards.

I already failed our people at Tanguro. *What if I fail again?*

I manage a smile. "It was nothing," I say with a forced lightness.

Dayne lets out a bark of laughter.

My thoughts are drowned out by the sound of a blaring horn.

"Second alarm," Aunt Jadem says, offering me a hand. "Archers on the way."

Sure enough, before the horn's echo has died, I see figures in gray appear in the distance. I don't think they've spotted us yet, but then an arrow hits the ground only a few feet from us.

Dayne curses.

There's yelling, and then more arrows strike the ground all around us. "Take him!"

I let out a surprised *oof* as Aunt Jadem shoves Hendrix at me. I don't ask questions. I just lift up the man's limp form in my arms without missing a step.

There are more Duskers now, and they're running straight for us.

We just need to get to the gate.

The iron gate is ahead of us, looking somehow even taller and more imposing from this side. It's still open, at least, just as Aunt Jadem said it would be.

No sooner has the thought entered my mind, the gate gives a squeal of protest as it begins to crank shut.

I turn back to my aunt.

"Run!" she screams.

We do. I match my pace to Dayne's, making sure not to outrun him.

Faster, I want to yell, but I know they're running as fast as they can. The thought of the iron gate sliding closed and locking us in with our enemies is worse than the thought of facing the wormkill again.

The horn continues its incessant cry as Duskers stream out of the citadel.

The muddy ground slurps and sucks at our feet, slowing us down. We're so close. Just beyond the iron gate, I can see Ekil and Brogut hurling stones the size of my head through the opening, taking out the Duskers nearest to us and scattering the others. Still, they won't be able to help us if we get trapped on this side.

The gate is more than halfway closed. Duskers are churning the crank with every ounce of strength they possess.

When Dayne stumbles in the mud, I shift Hendrix's dead weight and use my free hand to haul my brother up.

"Come on!" I yell.

The gate is almost closed.

A shadow crosses overhead. I look up to see Vlaz, with Ry and Dellin on his back. Arrows rain down from the air like there are a dozen archers riding Vlaz instead of just two. The Duskers scatter, giving us a clear path out.

I yank Hendrix through the gate behind me and then shove him at Ekil.

"Get him out of here," I tell the Halves.

Dayne races through the narrow opening just behind me. We turn back at the same time, looking for Aunt Jadem.

The gate is still open, wide enough to allow one more person to get out, but Aunt Jadem isn't here.

"Where is she?" I gasp, searching for my aunt in the crowd of Duskers scrambling to avoid Ry and Dellin's arrows.

"She was right behind us—"

The rest of Dayne's words are cut off as the iron gate shudders into place against the mountains hemming it in.

"No!"

"Hemera." Dayne's voice is hoarse. "We have to get out of range."

"Aunt Jadem. We have to get her. She's still inside." My words trip over themselves. I can barely think beyond the panic.

Aunt Jadem is still in there.

"Above you," Dayne calls.

I look up just in time to see a rope dangling over my head. Terror makes my movements sluggish as I reach up a hand.

"Grab it!" Ry yells, motioning to me to take the rope. I let my hands close around it, taking some comfort from the feel of something solid in my grasp.

The rope yanks upward, and my arms almost comes out of their sockets as Ry hauls me onto Vlaz's back. As she does the same for Dayne, I watch the Dusker archers in the lookouts. They're trying to aim their crossbows at us, but Dellin's relentless attack forces them to duck rather than take their own shots.

"Jadem," I begin, but Ry cuts me off.

"We'll get her."

At the look of determination on my friend's face, I want to weep with gratitude. Once the four of us are settled enough that we're not going to fall off, Ry steers Vlaz lower.

My heart drops away as my gaze finds Aunt Jadem. She's surrounded by a ring of Duskers.

"Crowe!" Dayne calls, his voice somehow breaking through the shouting from below. "We have Hendrix. If anyone harms Jadem, he dies."

Almost as soon as he's finished speaking, the Duskers part to reveal a single person in gray striding up to Jadem. I can't make out much about her from this height, but I can see the precise, unhurried steps she takes to approach my aunt. Her movements are not those of a leader who is worried about what might happen next.

But that's ridiculous, I tell myself. *We just kidnapped her lover and second-in-command. She has to be as desperate to get him back as we are for Jadem.*

Hendrix is in the woods with the Halves. The Duskers were too focused on the rest of us to follow them, and now the soldiers are stuck inside the iron gate with Jadem. By the time they could crank the gate back open and start searching for Hendrix, it might be too late for their second-in-command. They have no choice but to return Jadem to us unharmed if they ever want to see him again.

"Go lower," I demand.

Maybe, if we're quick, we can get the rope to Jadem and sweep her out of there before the Duskers can grasp her.

The reasoning is solid, but it doesn't stop my stomach from tying itself into knots.

Vlaz howls and pitches to the side. We lose altitude. I can hear Ry yelling and feel Vlaz's flailing attempts to right himself. And then I see two Duskers on the ground, operating what looks to be a giant crossbow. It's anchored in the mud, and they're fitting a second arrow into the wooden frame.

I watch in horror as the Duskers work in tandem to release the missile. "No!" I scream, just as Vlaz lets out a deafening roar.

CHAPTER 22

Vlaz's body pitches again, and I see the arrow shaft protruding from his neck.

Vlaz flaps his wings spasmodically as he tries to stay airborne. Bloody froth coats the fur on his sides.

"Get him past the gate before he falls," Dayne yells.

There's the creak of metal as Vlaz's belly scrapes against the top of the gate, and then we're falling.

Vlaz strikes the ground hard, sending the rest of us hurtling through the air. We fall in a heap of limbs and groans just past the trees.

"Is everyone alright?" Dayne demands.

My arms ache with the reminiscent heat of the wormkill's slime. Still, I take that as a good sign I'm healing. Ry and Dellin seem fine, too. Dayne inspects Vlaz, who is growling as he tries to reach around and bite at the shafts protruding from his neck and side.

"Steady boy," Dayne murmurs as he wraps his hand around the first shaft.

Vlaz yelps and shies away from Dayne. When Ry moves to block his escape, Vlaz's yellow eyes go wide with terror. He snaps his fangs once—not an attack, but a warning. Then, he flees.

By the time it occurs to me to run after Vlaz, the hyenair is gone.

"We have to go back for Aunt Jadem," I say, already starting back toward the iron gate. "They'll kill her if we don't do something."

"I'm sorry, I can't." Dellin gives Ry a fleeting look of apology, and then she's running into the forest, away from the citadel.

"Dellin!" Ry calls after her.

The other girl looks back once, but then she's swallowed up by the trees.

Coward.

"Forget about her," I say.

Aunt Jadem is on the wrong side of the gate, and without Vlaz, we have no way to get back in.

"What are we going to do?"

From here, I can see the Duskers in the lookouts, their crossbows aimed at us. The moment we come in range, they'll shoot.

"We're not getting anywhere near the gate without Hendrix," Dayne says, his eyes on the Duskers in the lookouts.

"Ekil, Brogut!" I scream, praying they haven't made it too deep into the forest to hear me.

After a few breathless moments, the Halves emerge with Hendrix in Ekil's grip.

"Thank the sun," Ry breathes.

"We need to get Hendrix to the gate," Dayne says. "When Crowe sees him, she'll call off her archers and let Jadem go."

Ry looks back at the trees once, but Dellin is nowhere to be seen.

Ekil, his arms wrapped around our prisoner, pushes him forward. Brogut follows, crouching to make himself a smaller target. We all cluster behind Hendrix, using his body as a shield as we approach the iron gate.

"We have your second-in-command," Dayne calls up to the Duskers in the lookouts as soon as we're within range. "If you even point a weapon at any one of us, he dies."

A part of me understands we'll need to trade Hendrix for Jadem and that this whole mission will have been a waste, but right now, I don't care. All I care about is getting my aunt back.

My brother pulls back Hendrix's hood enough for the archers to see his face, but not so much he's at risk of the Burn.

I barely notice when the archers exchange looks with each other and then lower their weapons. All of my attention is on the slight gap between the gate's hinges and the mountain, which gives me a view of what's happening on the other side. Aunt Jadem is standing unarmed in front of the Dusker Supreme.

There must be hundreds of Duskers just inside the gate. They're standing in two columns on either side of their Supreme and her prisoner. They all hold a sword and crossbow.

Even though I've never seen Crowe before, it would be impossible not to know who she is from the way the other Duskers keep their attention fixed on her. Still, she looks nothing like the brutish, hulking leader of the Duskers I pictured. The woman standing opposite Jadem is small and delicate-looking. She reminds me of a doll my mother gave me when I was a child.

The doll was beautiful, with silky hair and perfectly-chiseled features. Its glazed clay skin cracked at even the slightest pressure, though, so I stopped playing with it for fear it would break. I put it on a shelf next to my bed where it would be safe. Eventually, one of the other Dweller children stole the doll, and I found it smashed to pieces on the ground outside my sleeping chamber.

Something tells me that even though the Dusker Supreme looks like that doll, she's neither delicate nor breakable. Her steely eyes are locked on my aunt in a way that promises death and destruction. I wrap my hands around the iron hinge and clutch at it until my hands turn white, like I can will the gate open through sheer force of will.

"Hemera, get behind Hendrix," Dayne hisses. His lips are white with anger. Or fear.

A retort is on the tip of my tongue, but I hold back because I know he's right. The Duskers won't touch us as long as they're afraid they might hit one of their leaders.

"What are they talking about?" Ry murmurs, peeking around Hendrix to squint through the gap between the gate and the mountain.

It's clear Crowe and Jadem are talking, although we're too far to tell what they're saying.

If the situation were different, it might be comical. Crowe barely comes up to Aunt Jadem's shoulder and has to tip her head almost all the way back to look my aunt in the eye. She's so narrow that when my aunt shifts her body, Crowe disappears from view.

I try to imagine her face beneath the gray hood, but all I can conjure up is pale skin. Crowe makes a gesture in our general direction. It's then that I see the long sword sheathed at her hip.

Crowe steps up to my aunt until there's no space left between them. Aunt Jadem lowers her head, and I see Crowe whisper something in her ear. When she steps back, Crowe puts her hand on the pommel of her sword and unsheathes it.

I gasp.

Crowe turns her attention on us for the first time. Even at this distance, the steel of her gaze makes my blood run cold. Her lips quirk in the barest hint of a smile. Before I can even take a breath, Crowe's focus is back on Jadem as she offers my aunt the naked blade.

"What in the sun?" Ry whispers.

Crowe turns to the soldier standing nearest to her and unsheathes the sword at his belt. More words are exchanged between them, and then Aunt Jadem raises her sword.

"What's she doing?" Panic flutters in my stomach like a caged bird. *Crowe should be opening the gate to exchange our prisoners.*

"This isn't supposed to be happening," Ry says. She turns to Dayne and me. "Is this supposed to be happening?"

Even though I can't hear it, I imagine the ringing of swords as Aunt Jadem strikes the first blow. She moves fast, but Crowe blocks her. My aunt swings again. Crowe pivots, staying just out of range as she dances on the points of her toes. She reminds me of the insects in Tanguro that used to buzz around Vlaz's snout.

But the next time Jadem strikes, Crowe doesn't move back. She lunges.

CHAPTER 23

My scream is lost in my own ears as the Dusker soldiers shout and pump their fists, egging their leader on.

Somehow, despite their height difference, Crowe manages to grab Jadem's sword arm. My aunt's mouth opens in what I'm sure is a cry of pain as Crowe wrenches her arm behind her back. My aunt's weapon falls to the ground. Crowe kicks it away, even as she tightens her hold on Jadem with one hand and raises her sword with the other.

It's as if time has slowed and everything around me has faded away. There is nothing except for Crowe's sword. When I blink, it's no longer my aunt, but my mother. Then, Crowe and her sword disappear, too. In her place is a Halve with a wooden club.

I stay hidden in the tree as the Halve's club bludgeons my mother's head. A flock of kynthia birds—my mother's favorites—scatter from a nearby tree as she falls to the ground. Dark red blood streams down her face.

But Crowe's blade doesn't fall.

Time stands still as Aunt Jadem kneels on the ground with Crowe's sword at her throat. Everything has gone quiet. Even the Duskers have stopped their shouting and stamping.

Crowe turns, looking right at me. She raises her sword, and then, still holding my gaze, lets it fall to the ground beside her. A second later, as if on cue, someone begins to laugh.

Hendrix struggles in Ekil's grip. When he turns his head to the side, I see fat tears rolling down his pale cheeks as he continues to laugh.

Ekil gives me a small shrug as if to ask if this human is insane. For all I know, he could be.

Dayne grabs the sleeve of Hendrix's cloak in case he somehow manages to wriggle free from Ekil. But Hendrix doesn't seem like he's trying to escape.

"Something funny?" Dayne growls. His voice is quiet and dangerous.

"If your precious leader had half the brain of the Supreme," he pauses to wipe a tear from his eyes as he continues to chuckle, "she would have known the real Hendrix wouldn't be so easy to snatch."

The real Hendrix…?

Dayne searches his face. Whatever he sees makes him let go of Hendrix's sleeve and bury his face in his hands.

I grab the collar of Hendrix's cloak, heedless of the archers who have their weapons loaded and are just waiting for a clear shot at one of us. I shake him until his bones rattle and his laughter quiets. "What are you talking about?"

It's then that he looks straight at me.

Immediately, I understand what Dayne saw. Hendrix's brilliant green eyes, the ones that proved he was Crowe's lover, are no longer green. They're a dull brown. The curls peeking out from his gray hood have transformed from rich brown to ashy gray.

"How?" I ask.

The man—whoever he is—cocks his head, regarding me. "Dyes that cover up the true color beneath." He smirks. "For a little while, anyway."

With an effort, Dayne raises his head from his hands. He wipes one of his gloved hands across Hendrix's face. When he turns up his palm, Ry and I let out simultaneous gasps. His glove is covered in a white residue. The red-brown of the man's real skin peeks out from whatever paint had been used to mask it.

We all stare at each other in horror as the truth of what we're seeing comes into focus. I can hardly breathe.

"So, if this isn't real Hendrix," Ry says, "then that means we have—"

"Nothing," Fake Hendrix says with a twisted smile.

"No one leaves Malarusk without a sacrifice," Dayne murmurs.

We all look back at Aunt Jadem, who is still kneeling in the mud. Crowe stands over her.

Everything that comes next happens very fast. Crowe lets go of Jadem's arms. And then, using both her hands, she grasps my aunt's neck and twists.

I am powerless to stop it, powerless to help, as Aunt Jadem's lifeless body collapses.

"NO!" My legs are already moving.

Dayne calls to me, but his words are nothing more than background noise. He could be speaking in a different language for how little meaning they hold.

Jadem. I need to get to Jadem.

But before I can think about how I'm going to get inside the citadel, the iron gate is creaking open. I pause for a fraction of an instant, confused. And then the Duskers start to pour out.

CHAPTER 24

Ekil and Brogut are yelling for us to retreat.

We run for the trees. I keep one hand tight on Fake Hendrix's wrist. I know he' worthless to us now, but we risked so much to capture him….

Before we even get close to the forest, Duskers flood around the sides. They're penning us in.

There must have been more of them hiding out in the trees, because they're running at us from the direction of the forest, too. Everywhere I look, there are soldiers in gray closing in on us. We're trapped.

We stop running. Ry and Dayne stand on either side of me; the Halves are back-to-back. Ry's arrows are long gone, and Dayne and I have nothing to fight with. Vlaz and Dellin have disappeared, and in spite of Ry's constant looks in the direction where they disappeared, I know they won't be back to save us. Ekil has his club and Brogut his tree trunk, but what good are those against a hundred Duskers?

I raise my fists.

"Don't let them take you alive." My brother's voice is hoarse and defeated. "Hemera, don't let them take you alive."

I don't have a chance to process the meaning of his words. The perfectly-forming ring of Duskers stops advancing.

Their lines start to disintegrate as the soldiers are thrown into confusion. The Duskers nearest the trees turn away from us to fight someone—or something—else. At first, I think Vlaz and Dellin must have returned, after all. But there's no sign of either of them.

When the Duskers in the back of the circle fall, and their attackers cut a path toward us, I get my first glimpse of our saviors. At first, I don't even know what I'm looking at.

They are both like and unlike humans….They're tall, taller than any person or Halve I've ever seen. Their long black hair hangs down in greasy strands. They don't wear cloaks; instead, they have skirts made of woven metal links. The metal must be heavy and burning hot from the sun, but the creatures don't seem phased. Their inhumanly muscled chests are bare and covered in blisters oozing a black fluid.

When the Duskers give way before them and the creatures approach, I see their eyes are as black as mine.

Zeroes. These creatures could be nothing other than the new race my father made when he combined my blood with that of the Halves. They are the result of his experiments to blend a new race of Bisecters.

Except the Zeroes I fought in Tanguro were mangled, monstrous creatures. They looked and moved like they were put together from the parts of too many different bodies. These Zeroes, the ones driving terror into the fearless Dusker army, look and move in a way that is far more human than Halve.

One of them turns its ashy gray face toward me, pinning me with empty, pitiless black eyes. A new kind of dread rises in my stomach.

Our small company huddles together as the Zeroes, ten of them in all, advance. They each hold a scythe in their right hand. The sickle blades, dripping with blood and twinkling in the low day sun, look thin enough to slice between ribs and sturdy enough to cleave through metal. They carve a path to us through the Duskers.

"Hemera, come on!" A voice, different from any in my company and yet familiar, calls over the sounds of fighting. The face that accompanies the voice makes my insides turn over.

The Zeroes part, leaving room for their master to fill the space between them.

My father. Captain Harkibel. The man I've been hunting for months.

"Hurry," he says. "If you want to live, come with me."

I have time to exchange one quick glance with my brother. "Aunt Jadem—" I begin, my voice breaking.

"She's dead, Hemera." My brother's voice is gentle, even with madness threatening to engulf us.

"The Zeroes can hold them off, but not forever," the Captain warns.

The Duskers are already reforming their lines and advancing.

"We have to go." Ry's voice breaks.

There's no choice. We follow my father through the gap his Zeroes keep open long enough for us to pass through. I grab Fake Hendrix's arm and drag him with us.

I look back once, but I can't even glimpse my aunt's body through the crush of Dusker soldiers separating us. With every step I take, I feel my heart splinter.

✳ ✳ ✳

When Vlaz and Dellin appear from deep in the woods, they fall into step with our company. They both look chastened. I hate Dellin for the way her eyes roam all around us, like she's ready to bolt if she sees even a hint of a gray cloak. A dark pleasure ripples through me when the cowardly girl goes to put her hand on Ry's arm, and Ry pulls away.

Vlaz tries to nuzzle Dayne and me, his yellow eyes mournful. It's stupid to expect him to have stayed after he got shot, to think he might have been able to save Aunt Jadem…but I still shove his snout away and ignore his whimpering.

We push on for what feels like hours, putting distance between us and Malarusk. The Zeroes caught up to us some time ago, and from the complicated hand gestures they make, Zeidan tells us the Duskers aren't far behind.

We stop moving at the sound of rushing water. The Darkness River, swollen from the Banished River that has been redirected into its path, flows with a strong current.

I let go of Fake Hendrix, who I've been dragging with us, and he collapses in exhaustion.

Ry, Dayne, and Dellin clutch their sides, gasping for air. Before I understand what's happening, Brogut, his hands and tree trunk stained red from human blood, lets out a roar. He raises his weapon and aims it directly at my father. Ekil is right behind him, his club clutched between two scaly fists.

Brogut throws his tree trunk.

In a blur of motion, the Zeroes step in front of my father and close him off from view. A Zero catches Brogut's weapon with one hand before slamming it onto the ground. It cracks into three separate pieces.

The Zeroes grip their scythes. The curved blades are pointed outward, ready to slice through Ekil and Brogut.

"Stop," I cry.

Before I can take a step, the Zeroes are already parting at a word from the Captain.

Brogut lunges again, but this time, I wrap both my arms around his bulk and force him back.

"Kill now," Brogut growls, pushing against the force of my arms.

"This human tortured our kind." Ekil tightens his grip around the club, moving to step past me.

"Don't be stupid," I tell the Halves. "These beasts will kill you." *And I have no strength left to fight them.*

The Zeroes' empty black eyes are fixed straight ahead. Every muscle in their bodies is taut, ready to destroy the Halves at a single command from my father.

"Hemera."

The Zeroes crowd around my father as he walks toward me.

"Tell your Halves there is a place for them by my side, too. There's no need for us to be enemies."

"They'll be flattered by the offer, I'm sure," I reply, still wrestling with Brogut. "You locked them in your catacombs and tortured them."

A shudder visibly wracks my brother's body before he composes himself again. The Halves aren't the only ones who remember their torture at Captain Harkibel's hands.

My father nods at the Halves, undeterred by their murderous glares.

"What's the snake-tongue saying?" Ekil demands.

When I translate his words, Brogut tries to launch himself at my father again. He wrestles against me, trying to break free from my grip.

"He'll make slaves of us," Ekil growls.

"I won't let that happen," I tell him.

A voice in the back of my head wonders whether this is yet another promise I won't be able to keep.

"Besides," I say, "we don't have a lot of options right now. We can either go with my father or wait for the Duskers to catch up to us."

Ekil grunts in what I take to be grudging acceptance.

A muffled sob makes me turn. Ry is kneeling on the ground, her face buried in her hands. I go to her, kneeling so I can wrap my arms around my friend. Tears burn the back of my throat as Ry trembles in my arms.

"Hemera," my father says. "We need to keep moving."

"Give us a minute," I manage, my words coming out strangled.

This might be our last chance to say goodbye to my aunt while we're still on the same side of the river.

Zcidan looks like he's going to argue, but then he gestures for his Zeroes to make a protective ring around us. Dellin and the Halves stand off to the side, trying to keep some distance from both Vlaz and the Zeroes. The Zeroes prowl back and forth, their faces tilted up like wild beasts as they scent the air.

Dayne, Ry, and I huddle together. The look in their eyes mirrors my own grief. *Aunt Jadem.* She's gone.

"I don't understand." Ry's voice is small. "Jadem seemed so sure of what she was doing." Her gloved hand tightens around something, but I can't see what. "I never would have let her…if I thought…if I thought…." Ry shoves her hand in the pocket of her cloak and lets out a low, keening, cry.

She leans into me, her whole body convulsing with her sobs.

Ry is right. Aunt Jadem was the one who came up with the plan to kidnap Hendrix…she is the one who insisted we come here. She seemed so sure it would work.

How could she have misjudged Crowe so completely?

I shake my head. My aunt was a warrior, the leader of the Solguards. She was the one who fooled the Dusker Supreme into thinking she was one of them for eight years.

How did everything go so wrong?

The fact that I'll never know widens the hole in my heart. All the questions I need to ask her, all the stories she promised to tell me about my mother….

She's gone. Aunt Jadem is gone.

All the *what ifs* and *if onlys* strike me like blows to the chest. Aunt Jadem is dead, and for what?

It was all for nothing.

I think about my aunt's still body, left in a crumpled heap to be devoured by Burn vultures or to rot on the wrong side of the iron gate. I can't stand it.

"We couldn't even bury her," I say, covering my face with my hands.

"I know." Dayne's voice is hoarse. He looks as dazed as I feel. His arms wrap around me as hot tears course down my cheeks.

"I failed—" I begin, but my brother cuts me off.

"This was not your fault." He gives me a little shake when I don't respond. "Do you hear me? This wasn't your fault!"

The Captain clears his throat. "My Zeroes smell the Duskers getting close. We need to be on the move."

CHAPTER 25

Since when do you care about our safety?" Ry demands, swiping at her eyes.

My father gives us a hard look. "My interests are unchanged. My daughter's safety is of the utmost importance."

One of the Zeroes motions with its scythe.

"The Duskers are nearly upon us. Come with me, and we can discuss the rest once we are inside."

"Inside where?" My voice sounds distant and detached.

"I call it the Lair," my father replies.

I follow the direction of his gaze. The Darkness River is in front of us. Directly across the roiling water is the base of Darkness Peak.

"Don't tell me you expect us to climb that." Ry has to practically yell to be heard over the churning water below.

We all look up to where the mountain's peak scrapes the sky. The mountain's sides are sheer, without footholds. The rocks are a sleek, glistening gray. There is no way up the mountain except for the path the Duskers carved for their own use.

Vaguely, I wonder whether that group of crazed Banished made it to the mountain, and whether the Duskers accepted them.

"His lair is *inside* the mountain," Dayne replies. "I couldn't get him without you because—"

"No human is strong enough to swim against the current," the Captain finishes his sentence. "And the entrance to the Lair can only be accessed by swimming under the mountain."

Ry's jaw goes slack. Dayne gives me a short nod, confirming what the Captain has said.

My father is keeping his Zeroes inside Darkness Peak. The irony isn't lost on me.

"You're mad," Ry says as we all stare up at the mountain.

My father lifts a shoulder. "I have found there to be a thin line between madness and brilliance."

"Yeah?" Ry plants a hand on her hip. "I happen to know you crossed that line a long time ago."

My father meets her challenging stare. "Only time will tell."

"If we go with you," Dellin says, her voice stronger and less panicked than it had been before the Duskers' attack, "what's to keep you from making us all your prisoners?"

My father's eyes come to rest on me. "I have something to offer you. If what I propose is not to your liking, you'll all be free to leave."

"You'll let us go, just like that?" I ask, not believing a single word out of his mouth.

"I'm confident that when I have laid out my plan for you, you won't want to leave."

When I don't reply, he continues, "But if I'm wrong, I give you my word I won't try to stop you from leaving."

The Zero gestures again.

Brogut says, "Lots of gray cloaks coming."

I exchange a look with Dayne and Ry.

"How do we get in?" I ask.

My father's mouth twists as he glances at Dayne, and then at the others in our ragtag group. But he knows enough not to suggest I leave them behind.

"The hyenair and Halves should be able to make the swim on their own, but the Zeroes will have to help the others," he says. There is undisguised disdain in his voice for the other members of my company.

"Like hell I will," Ry says. "Hemera can help me if I need it."

Zeidan shrugs. "Suit yourself."

He motions to the Zeroes. In a perfectly-synchronized motion, they dive into the frothing river. Nine of them cut graceful strokes through the powerful current and then hover partway between the bank and the mountain's base. The last one waits until my father jumps off the bank, treading water just past the edge.

The Zero catches my father in one arm, its other holding its scythe, and uses its powerful legs to cut through the water.

"We better go after them," I say.

I take another step toward the edge. My boots disrupt some loose stones, which tumble down the bank and are swallowed up by the churning blue-black water.

"You first." I shove Fake Hendrix into the water without giving him a chance to react.

A Zero returns for him. The creature takes hold of the man, and I feel some satisfaction at the way the Dusker strains against the Zero's iron grip.

Brogut jumps in next.

"Dellin, go with him," Ry says. She still won't look the other girl in the eye. "Ekil can take Dayne, and I'll go with Hemera."

No one argues. Dellin jumps in, and I can see her eyes widen as the churning water threatens to swallow her. Brogut wraps an enormous arm around Dellin's waist and paddles after the Zeroes. His strokes are far less graceful. He splashes and splutters as he tries to swim and keep Dellin's head above water.

Ekil and Dayne are next. Vlaz, pacing along the river bank, whines and jumps in after them. He grasps Dayne's cloak between his fangs, helping to keep him above water as Ekil strains against the current.

The moment my feet break the water's surface, I'm dragged down. My clothes and boots suck me beneath the surface. Silt and pebbles swirls around me, getting inside my clothes and scratching at my skin.

Before I've gotten used to the roiling current, Ry is in the water. She immediately sinks, having no power to withstand the water's downward pull. It's only because of her flame-red hair I'm able to find her and yank her back up.

I kick out in the direction where the others disappeared, fighting the current that is trying to sweep us downriver and away from the mountain.

Kick and drag. When I turn my head to the side, I'm met with Ry's wide, panic-stricken eyes. I lift her even farther out of the water, giving her a chance to breathe. She coughs and splutters as I kick on.

Ekil, whose trailing bubbles I've been following, disappears. It's like he swam underneath the mountain itself.

"Hold your breath," I yell to Ry. I hope she's heard me over the roar of the water. I plunge under the surface, dragging Ry with me.

I try to follow the bubbles trailing Ekil and Dayne, but there is so much silt and muck being churned up from the bottom I can barely see. I dive deeper, silently begging Ry to hang on, as I pull her under a stone ledge.

Darkness envelops us. There is no space, no breathable air, between the water and the rock overhead.

I blink, sand stinging my eyes and blurring my vision. The faint outline of movement catches my eye, and I kick toward it.

A trail of bubbles escapes from my lips as I let out a choking cough. Panic begins to squeeze around me as no light, and no end to the stone above us, appears. We've gone too far to turn back now. Instinct tells me the fastest path to fresh air is on the other side of this ledge.

Don't breathe. Don't breathe. Don't breathe.

Black spots dance across my vision. My chest aches with the need for oxygen. The rock scraping against the top of my head is a constant reminder we're trapped. Every second is a fight…a fight to cover more distance…a fight against my body's need to breathe….

The water's color changes ahead. I kick forward with a frantic urgency, putting every bit of will and strength I have left into reaching the light.

With a final, desperate kick, I propel us forward. The heavy feel of the slick rock above disappears. I pull Ry's limp body up with me as my head breaks through the surface.

My first gasp of air is all pain; my lungs seem to have forgotten how to work. I'm dimly aware of Dayne coughing and gasping beside me. I turn Ry over, and she starts to retch up river water. When two Zeroes swim out to meet us, neither Ry nor Dayne fights them as they're pulled the rest of the way onto the rock ledge.

Vlaz, who seems to be the only one who made the swim without incident, shakes out his shaggy coat, spraying everyone already on the rocks. There's just enough room for him to fit on the ledge so long as everyone else stays huddled together. Vlaz's yellow eyes are dull, and I feel a pang of guilt for his wounds that are still leaking blood.

"We'll get you fixed up," I promise him.

Vlaz whines and gives my face a gentle lick.

My father stares down at me as I pull myself all the way onto the slippery rock. "Welcome to the Lair."

CHAPTER 26

My father and his Zeroes leave to get bandages for Vlaz and dry clothes for us, giving us a few minutes to ourselves.

Dayne, Ry, and I huddle together on the wet rocks, with Dellin standing a few paces away.

"Here." I toss the rope binding Fake Hendrix's wrists to Dellin. "You can hold him." Every time I look at the man, I see my aunt's body crumpling on the ground at Crowe's feet.

"Shouldn't we blindfold him?" Dellin asks, catching the rope.

Ry laughs. "I don't think he's going to be rushing back to Malarusk to report on what he's seen." She turns to Fake Hendrix. "What do you think?"

The Dusker hasn't said much since we dragged him all the way here, but he meets Ry's gaze with a defiant look. "When the darkness comes, I'll be rewarded."

Ry scoffs. "Duskers and their darkness."

"Soon," Fake Hendrix says, and it's the first word he's said that hasn't been twisted with humor or mockery. It reminds me of the way the Dusker woman said the same thing back in Tanguro. It wasn't the words themselves—a prophecy I've heard all my life—but the way they were said. It wasn't a hope for the darkness. It was a promise.

We all look at the man. The water has washed all of his white paint away. His eyes have lost all hint of the dazzling green and have returned to their natural murky-brown color.

"I think we should blindfold him anyway," Dellin says.

When no one responds, she tears a piece of cloth from her shirt and ties it around Fake Hendrix's eyes. I notice she stands behind him the whole time, making sure he doesn't see her face.

Paranoid coward.

Ekil and Brogut are holding their own hushed conference as far from the rest of us as they can get. Vlaz, looking miserable, sits next to me with his head drooping.

"What do we do now?" I ask.

"We've got no leverage," Ry scowls in Fake Hendrix's direction, "so this cursed mission was all for nothing."

"If the Banished surrender to the Duskers," Dayne says, "it's all over for the Solguards."

"Then we have to find a way to keep the Banished from surrendering," I say.

"How?" Ry demands. "Give them Fake Hendrix? Re-paint his eyes and skin?"

"We don't know which dyes they used," Dayne says. "And Valior knows Hendrix, so he wouldn't be fooled by anything of inferior quality."

"We need to stall them," I decide. "The Banished leaders gave us a week. That means we still have four days to figure out something else we can give them, something that will make them think we're strong enough to be worth fighting for."

"And that would be exactly what?" Ry asks. "In case you haven't noticed, we're more or less your father's prisoners at the moment. *Again.*"

"I may have a solution to your problem."

We all startle at the sight of Zeidan coming down the dimly lit path toward us.

"Like you'd help us," Ry scoffs. "Are we supposed to believe you've become a philanthropist in your old age?"

"There's no need for charity when our interests are aligned," my father replies.

"They are?" My brother's loathing is undisguised.

"You need a show of strength that will give you authority over the Banished, and the ability to withstand an attack from Malarusk," he says.

"And what do you need?" I ask. "Like Ry said, we all know you well enough to know you don't make an offer unless it's to your benefit."

My father studies me for a moment. "I want what I have always wanted—a world where you belong. A place where your strength is valued, rather than feared. A world where there are more like you."

Ry and Dayne are muttering, but my father ignores them.

"You need me," he says, looking only at me. "You need what I'm offering."

Brogut, bored with all of the words he doesn't understand, prods me with his elbow and then points a fleshy finger at my father. "We kill now?"

I bite my lip, knowing I'll probably regret what I say next. "Not yet."

I look at Dayne and Ry. My brother looks sick with disgust. Ry just looks beaten. Even her curls have lost their vitality and are flattened to her head. And then I look up at my father. My father, who, just weeks ago, I would have given anything to track down and kill.

But everything is different now. Aunt Jadem is dead, and the Solguards are facing a massacre. Wade and Wokee and all the rest of the Solguards' lives are at stake.

We can play your game, too, I think as I meet my father's stare.

"What are you offering?" I ask him.

My father gives me a knowing smile. "An army."

✳ ✳ ✳

While the others change into dry clothes, Dayne works on bandaging Vlaz. The two Halves scour the riverbank for driftwood they can fashion into another spear for Brogut.

After a short argument, I convince Dayne and the others to stay behind with Vlaz, who won't be able to fit through the narrower passages inside the mountain, while I go see whatever my father wants to show me. I tell them it's because the Zeroes are less likely to be aggressive if it's just one of us with their master. The real reason is that if I have to see my own agony reflected on Dayne and Ry's faces for another second, I'll fall apart.

"Bring the Dusker," my father tells me. "I have just the place for him."

"Be careful, Hemera," Dayne warns, turning away from Vlaz to pin me with his gaze. "Zeidan's got a poisonous tongue. He'll kill us the moment we're no longer useful to him."

"Let him try," I say.

I'm not the same girl who wandered into Tanguro all those months ago searching for her lost boyfriend.

My father crosses his arms. "I would not have rescued you from certain death if I wanted you destroyed."

I look at my father, dressed in the same sand-colored cloak he wore when he was Captain of Subterrane Harkibel. His long beard is no longer salt-and-pepper, but completely white. But the intelligent, scheming look is still bright in his eyes. I know better than to trust a word he says.

I give Fake Hendrix a vicious tug. He squishes up the path behind me, still in his sopping wet clothes. I reach back and pull off the ridiculous blindfold Dellin insisted on. Fake Hendrix seems resigned to whatever fate he's been dealt, and he doesn't try to struggle as I pull him along.

I follow my father as the path turns up and away from the water. Steps are cut into the stone and lead up into the mountain.

Although it's as dark in here as it was in Subterrane Harkibel, it doesn't feel like the ceiling might cave in at any moment. There is no packed dirt or wooden beams that shift under too much pressure. In here, it's just stone and more stone. Instead of going down, deeper into the ground, we walk up and into the mountain.

Lanterns hanging from iron rods nailed into the rock give off small beams of light. The main path is wide and tall, maybe even enough for Vlaz to fit. I feel a pang of guilt at the thought of Vlaz, injured and huddled on that cold rock ledge. At least he can swim back into the sunlight whenever he pleases.

It's still hard to believe we're *inside* Darkness Peak.

"How did you build all of this?" I ask, my voice echoing off the high ceilings.

My father turns back to look at me. "I didn't. The Zeroes did."

The blades of the Zeroes' scythes bob ahead, glimmering in the lantern light.

"They're unnatural," I say. My voice echoes off the lofty ceiling, making it sound like I shouted the words.

My father gives me a knowing look.

My cheeks heat with shame. Those words…they're the ones the Dwellers used as their excuse for abandoning a ten-year-old girl in a cave collapse…the ones that have always been used to isolate and humiliate me.

I swallow hard. I don't want to think about the fact that I have more in common with these Zeroes than with either Halves or humans.

When we reach what looks to be the end of the path, one of my father's Zeroes bends to unwind a thick chain wrapped around a door's handle. The Zero tosses the chains to the side and pushes the door open. I pause.

"More catacombs?" I had meant to sound sarcastic, rather than high-pitched and nervous.

"In a sense," my father replies.

I'm grateful Dayne isn't with me now. Ekil and Brogut, too. They're still haunted by what happened in the catacombs, and the torture they—and so many others—suffered in my father's experiments to create the Zeroes. I steel myself and follow my father inside, pulling Fake Hendrix with me.

I don't know what I expected, but it wasn't this.

We're inside a huge chamber. The air is thick with oily smoke rising from a stubby branch of candles perched on the floor. At first, I think the stench is coming from the candles, but a closer look reveals the people chained all the way around the room's perimeter. Not just any people—Duskers. Lots of them. Their gray cloaks are filthy, but I still recognize these prisoners for who they are. The room smells like sour air and unbathed bodies.

The Duskers strain against iron chains binding them in a line along the wall. Their eyes are slitted against the brightness of the lantern my father holds. Many of the prisoners are emitting strange, muffled sounds. When I look closer, I realize they're gagged.

"There are eighty-nine of them, plus the ten I made after leaving Tanguro," my father says. He takes the rope from my hand and loops it through an iron hook on the wall, binding Fake Hendrix along with the others. "He makes one-hundred."

"How?" my voice is small.

"There are more benefits to the Lair besides the fact it's impossible for humans to reach," my father replies.

At the puzzled look I give him, he explains, "Every month, the new recruits have their initiation ritual—"

"—on Darkness Peak," I finish.

My father nods. "It's taken longer than I wanted, but I couldn't risk my Zeroes taking too many at once, or the Supreme would have suspected something more than the regular hyenair and Burn vulture attacks."

"We'll never fight on your side," Fake Hendrix spits, his voice hoarse from disuse. "Long live the Dusker Supreme!"

"You may find you don't have a choice in the matter," my father tells the Dusker.

"I don't understand." I shake my head. "You said you had an army."

Fake Hendrix was right about one thing. My father might have them chained to a wall, but the Duskers would never change their allegiance, no matter what they were threatened with.

My father looks at me. "I don't have an army _yet_. That's where you come in."

"I don't believe it." Anger pulses in my chest. "You're just the same liar who ran away from Tanguro with his tail between his legs."

"Careful, daughter." His expression darkens. "I said you could have your army. One that will give you your best chance against the Duskers. I'm offering you full control of that army." He waits while I get my breathing under control. "But if you want all that, you will need to help create it."

"How?" I ask, barely managing to get the word out through the hatred searing my insides. "How do I create an army from _this_?"

"You've seen the strength of ten Zeroes, and they were made with diluted blood." His eyes take on a faraway look. "Think of what you could do with a hundred of them made with pure blood."

"I'm not a monster like you," I spit. "I'm not going to torture humans and Halves like you did."

My father gives me a pitying look, which only makes me madder. "We are more alike than you might think, daughter. We are both leaders. And leaders have the responsibility of taking action, even when there might be consequences.”

“*Might* be consequences?” My laughter is harsh. The sound makes the chained Duskers restless. “You tortured Halves. You killed people. You almost killed my brother!”

“And because of their sacrifices,” my father continues in his calm, cool voice, “I possess the formula for making the transition from human to Zero. No one else needs to die.”

“Except them,” I gesture at the prisoners.

“Are you really defending the killers of your friends at Tanguro?” my father asks, a hint of disbelief in his otherwise calm demeanor. “The killers of your aunt?”

For the first time, I can’t come up with a reason to disagree with him. He’s right. The Duskers have taken so much from me. They’re the reason I might lose the rest.

Would it be so bad to give them a taste of their own medicine? To make them the hunted rather than the hunters?

“Hemera, listen to me. You have more strength than any living being in this world. Stop waiting for someone else to come up with a solution to your problems.”

“I’m not—”

“Of course you are!” My father’s face is flushed now, his careful control slipping away. “Turn your grief into something more.” He takes a deep breath. “This war is coming. You alone have the power to decide its outcome. You can condemn us. Or you can save us all.”

My aunt said the same thing…right before she walked into Malarusk for the last time.

I think about Aunt Jadem.

What was it she said before? *There is nothing more powerful than a willing sacrifice.* Something tells me she didn’t have an alliance with my father in mind when she spoke those words, but if helping my father was all that stood between the Solguards and annihilation…?

My aunt’s last moments have played over and over in my mind. I just stood there and watched, as useless as I was when my mother was killed.

I'm a Bisecter, stronger than humans and Halves, and yet I couldn't save either of the people I loved so much.

What's the point of being this way if I can't even protect the people I love?

My father is right about one thing. Since the battle at Tanguro, I've been drowning in grief, too caught up in my failures to do anything except hide in shame.

Not anymore.

"I want to do to Crowe what she's done to me. I want to destroy her and everything she's built."

CHAPTER 27

I step into the small, circular room my father has given to our company. There are enough bedrolls for Ry, Dellin, Dayne, and me, as well as Ekil and Brogut. On the far side of the room is a cloth screen blocking a small copper tub and water spigot. A crudely built wooden table topped with clay bowls is pushed up against the wall. A branch of candles throws wild shadows along the wall. The space is small, with no natural light, of course. It makes me long for the high ceilings of the buildings at Tanguro and the sunlight-warmed Solguard fortress.

But Tanguro is destroyed, and Solis is soon to follow.

Ry and Dellin are asleep on their bedrolls. Dayne is sitting cross-legged on the hard floor. One hand is grasped around nothing, like he's holding the phantom of his lute. When he sees me, he rises to his feet in a fluid motion.

"What does the bad man say?" Ekil asks.

Before I can answer, Dellin starts to moan.

"No, no, no." She writhes on her bedroll.

Ry jolts awake, looks around like she doesn't remember where she is, and then turns to Dellin.

"I don't want to—" Dellin's face is streaming with sweat and tears as she clutches at the side of the bedroll.

"Dell?" Ry leans over the girl. When she doesn't wake up, Ry shakes her. "Dellin, you're dreaming."

"I don't want to remember!" The power of her shriek stuns Ry, so when Dellin punches her across the jaw, Ry doesn't even try to deflect it.

I cross the room in two strides and wrench Dellin's hands down to her sides. I loosen my grip when I realize the other girl is crying. Her shoulders shake with great, heaving sobs. Tears track down her perpetually dirty face.

"Shh." Ry motions for me to let go, and she cradles Dellin. "It was just a dream." She rocks Dellin like a child.

I have trouble feeling sympathy for Dellin after she abandoned us outside Malarusk. I want to tell Ry to stop treating her like a baby. But instead, I wait awkwardly beside Dayne and the Halves for Dellin to calm down.

When she stops crying, Dellin looks at me. "I didn't run away from the fight because I was scared."

For a moment, I think I must have spoken my thoughts out loud. But then I decide she must just be reading the emotion on my face.

"But you don't understand," she continues. "If the Duskers had seen me—if they had found me—"

Her chest heaves, and Ry gathers her into her arms again, murmuring softly.

"It's fine," I say, just wanting to put an end to this bizarre conversation. "There may be a way for you to make it up to us."

Dellin looks up at me, her gray eyes glistening.

"Someone needs to go back to Solis. Wade needs to know what happened—"

I imagine the look on Wade's face when he finds out Jadem is dead. Just the thought steals my breath away.

Wade knew Jadem long before I met her. She rescued him from the Duskers and gave him a home with the Solguards. She was like family to him. After the death of Sal, his mentor and adopted father, Jadem was the only parent figure he had. It makes my heart ache to know I won't be there when he finds out she's gone.

And Wokee…Wokee used to follow Aunt Jadem around her orchards for hours on end while she answered his questions about the plants and animals she raised. She helped Wokee train Vlaz. Wokee lost his mother, too, and loves Aunt Jadem the same way I do. And now she's gone.

I swallow before turning my attention back to Dellin, the only person I can look at without falling apart.

"Wade has to keep the Banished leaders from surrendering. Tell him to do whatever is needed to stall them."

"What's the point of staving off the inevitable?" Dayne asks, his voice tired. "We don't have Hendrix. We're never going to get Hendrix." He scrubs a hand across his face. "It was all just a sickening waste."

"Because," I bite my lip, knowing they're not going to like this part, "we're going to offer them something different—something better."

* * *

We all go to the bottom level of the Lair, where the rock meets the dark water, to see Dellin and Vlaz off.

My father assured us the Duskers who chased us here wouldn't have lingered to see if we'd return, especially since so many of their recruits have disappeared from around this area. Still, just to be safe, I tell Dellin to get in the air as soon as they're on the riverbank and to fly high enough that the Duskers won't be able to shoot Vlaz again.

Two of my father's Zeroes are standing on the rock ledge, their black eyes staring straight ahead at the dark water. As Vlaz walks past them, he snarls. It's not the warning or hunting snarls I've heard from him before. All of Vlaz's fur stands on end, and his black lips quiver over his exposed fangs. He looks monstrous.

The Zeroes don't pay any attention to him. They just stand there, black eyes staring into nothing.

"Easy boy," Dayne says, as he checks the hyenair's bandages and guides him to the water's edge. "No ripping out throats. At least, not today."

"How do we know the Duskers aren't going to attack the fortress before we get back?" Ry asks. "It's a miracle they haven't already destroyed it."

"We don't know," I say through gritted teeth. "But there's no point in going back unless we have something that can actually be of use to the Solguards."

If we went back now, it would mean admitting failure to the Banished leaders. It would mean the ruin of Solis and the death of all the Solguards. It would mean Aunt Jadem's death was meaningless.

"Then we have to get something useful, and fast," Ry says, her voice laced with panic.

I nod. *I'm working on it.*

As I rub Vlaz's flopped ear and Dayne adjusts the bandage on his neck one last time, Ry and Dellin walk to the other side of the ledge overlooking the river. With the rush of the water, I can't hear their words, but I see the way they embrace.

A sharp stab of jealousy cuts through me. *It doesn't matter*, I tell myself. Ry can have other friends…*even if those friends are secret-keeping cowards who hate me.*

When Ry wipes a tear off Dellin's cheek with her finger, I roll my eyes.

"Remember," I say to Dellin. "Tell Wade to do whatever he has to in order to stall them."

If the Banished leaders surrender before we return with the Zero army, this will all have been for nothing. Aunt Jadem's death will have been for nothing. And I won't let that happen.

Dellin nods and climbs onto Vlaz.

"And don't pull his feathers," I tell her, more harshly than needed.

To Vlaz, I whisper, "Take care of Wokee."

And then he's diving into the water with Dellin clinging to his back.

✳ ✳ ✳

Once we're back in our chamber with the door shut, and it's just Dayne, Ry, the Halves, and me, I'm ready to tell them my plan.

Ry might trust Dellin, but I don't. Having kept plenty of my own secrets through the years, I know when someone is hiding something. And Dellin is definitely hiding something.

"Now that she's gone," I begin, but Ry cuts me off.

"She's a good person, Mer."

I scoff. "At best she's a filthy—and I mean that literally—coward." I give Ry a challenging stare. "But I'd be willing to bet she's something worse."

"If you're implying that she's—"

"A Dusker spy?" I ask. "Yeah, I am."

We look at each other, and I know we're thinking of the same person. *Gorgoran.*

"She isn't," Ry says, venom in her voice. "She wouldn't."

"Can we get back on point?" Dayne demands. "Hemera, what happened with Zeidan?"

I take a deep breath to compose myself. And then, I tell them about my father's offer. As expected, they don't take it well.

Brogut and Ekil roar. Dayne almost matches their fury.

"Absolutely not," my brother snarls.

"This isn't like last time," I argue.

"Halves refuse to give blood." Ekil crosses his arms.

"Refuse," Brogut echoes.

I force out a breath, trying to stay calm. "An army of Zeroes would give us the strength we need to fight the Duskers. If we defeat them, we can get your river back. You won't have to fight the Banished anymore. You'll *survive.*"

"Zeroes are evil," Ekil says.

"They're the only way I can help you get what you want," I reply.

A wave of guilt washes over me. The Zeroes are the reason why the Halves were my father's slaves for years, and now I'm asking them to make more. But I spoke the truth; there's nothing else I can think of to help them.

Ekil and Brogut exchange a glace, and then I see Ekil's posture droop just a little. I steel myself against the onslaught of regret.

"This will work," I tell Ry and Dayne with a confidence I don't feel. "A hundred Duskers will be changed into Zeroes. Zeidan has figured out the right combination of Halve and Bisecter blood—"

Dayne makes a disgusted sound in the back of his throat.

"The Zeroes are monsters," Ry protests. "You know that better than anyone. And now you're suggesting making more of them?"

"They'll follow my command. I don't know how it works exactly, but with my blood in them, I'll control them."

And without Hendrix, it's our only option…to fight monsters with monsters.

"And you think he's telling the truth?" Ry asks.

Almost at the same time, Ekil asks, "You trust?"

I falter. Of course I don't trust my father. He's done nothing but scheme, and betray, and kill.

But then I remember Aunt Jadem's body crumpled on the ground, and the ruined courtyard at Tanguro. I have to do *something.*

"He's our enemy, and that's not going to change." I repeat these words for the Halves, as well. "But he wants the same thing we do…for now."

"And what happens when we don't want the same thing anymore?" Dayne clenches and unclenches his hands, seeming not to know what to do with them without his lute.

I meet my brother's gaze and feel a sharp pang at the anguish on his face. I know it's even worse for him to be around my father than it is for me.

"We kill him," I promise. "Just like we said we would, just like he deserves."

Dayne heaves a deep sigh. "Nothing good can come of helping Zeidan." He pauses, and the air around him seems weighted with meaning. "But I'm with you, little sis. If this is what you want."

"Me too." Ry slings a hand across my shoulders and gives me a peck on the cheek. "I'm with you."

"Halves will give their blood one last time," Ekil says, but the words cost him. He sags against the wall in defeat.

Brogut just lets out a growl.

I look at my friends, overcome with emotion. The fact that they're willing to support this—support *me*—after everything they've been through….

"Thank you." The words aren't nearly enough to carry the weight of everything I feel, but everyone nods like they understand, anyway.

CHAPTER 28

After a fitful sleep, Ekil, Brogut, and I walk up the path to the Duskers' chamber. The Halves are both silent, their heads bowed. It feels like a death march. When we reach the door, my father and his Zeroes are already waiting for us.

My father appraises me.

"Are you ready to change the world, daughter?"

"Let's just get this over with," I mutter, pushing past him.

Unlike the silence I was greeted with the last time my father brought me in here, this time, everything is in chaos.

It takes less than moment to discover Fake Hendrix somehow managed to loosen his and some of the other prisoners' gags. They're shouting themselves hoarse. When he sees me, Fake Hendrix snarls and rattles his chains.

"You monster," he rasps. "The Dark God will kill you and every other abomination in this filthy place!" He pulls back his head and hurls a gob of mucousy spit in my face.

I wipe a sleeve across my face.

I turn away, but then I remember…this man is the reason why we're here now. He's the reason we have nothing to offer the Banished leaders. He's the reason why Crowe could kill Aunt Jadem without consequences. And afterward, why her death meant nothing.

I turn back to Fake Hendrix and reach forward, yanking him to me by the collar of his cloak.

"You want to see a real monster?" I ask. "I'm going to turn you into one."

"Do your worst," he replies. "The darkness will come and swallow you whole. You'll be—"

"Shh," my father puts a finger to Fake Hendrix's lips. At the same time, he lifts a dagger and makes a long, narrow cut in Fake Hendrix's skin, just above his collarbone.

Fake Hendrix's words cut off. Tears stream down his cheeks as he writhes against his chains.

"Halve blood first." My father motions Ekil forward.

One of the Zeroes lowers its scythe, dangerously close to Ekil's arm. Brogut snarls and leaps forward, wrapping his enormous hands around the Zero's neck. Without missing a beat, the Zero swats at Brogut as one would a pesky insect. Brogut goes crashing into the opposite wall, toppling several of the Duskers with him.

"What the hell?" I demand.

"There is no cause for alarm." My father's calm is infuriating. "My Zero simply meant to open up a vein."

"We do it ourselves," Ekil growls, shaking his fist in my father's face.

I translate Ekil's words.

Shrugging, my father motions to one of the Zeroes, who places a dagger at the Halves' feet. Ekil bends to pick it up, but Brogut grabs it first.

"Let the blood flow until the precise moment I say to stop," my father tells me. He waits until I've translated the instructions before demonstrating how Brogut should hold his dripping arm over Fake Hendrix's wound.

Fake Hendrix's feet scrabble against the stone floor as he tries to shift away. Brogut holds his bloodied arm over the Dusker's open wound. With the first drop of Halve blood, Fake Hendrix begins to writhe.

My father's Zeroes are ready. One grips Fake Hendrix's shoulders on each side, holding the Dusker still while my father motions for Brogut to keep letting his blood flow. An ugly dark substance begins to bubble out of Fake Hendrix's wound.

The Dusker's screams reach a fever pitch. He bucks and strains against his captors, reaching his hands up as far as the Zeroes' grip will allow him, like he's trying to claw off his own skin.

Watching his suffering makes me want to either throw up or tear my eyes out just so I won't have to witness it for another second.

"Stop, I can't take it—"

My father silences me with a wave of his hand. He is intent on Fake Hendrix, his lips moving like he's counting. My father straightens up at the same time that Fake Hendrix's body goes rigid. The Dusker's screams cut off as he falls prostrate on the ground, his eyes rolling back into his head. In the absence of his screaming, all I can hear is my own ragged breathing and heartbeat as it pummels my ribs.

"It's time, Hemera."

I want to tell him no, that this was a terrible idea, that I don't want to torture anyone. But then I remember my aunt's broken body. I remember one of the last things she said to me. *You will save us all.*

Before I can change my mind, I close my hand around the dagger my father offers and yank the blade across my palm. Pain blossoms as blood warms my skin. The gash leaks a thick, brownish blood.

"Press your palm right against the gash and let your blood flow into him," my father instructs.

I stand motionless, mesmerized by the trail of ugly blisters rising from the wound on Fake Hendrix's flesh. My throat has gone dry.

"Quickly now, before the Halve blood kills him." My father points to the wound on my palm that is already beginning to seal itself off.

I grit my teeth and stretch out my palm over the opening on the Dusker's neck. With one quick motion, I squeeze my bleeding palm against the gaping cut. The moment my blood touches his flesh, there is a sizzling sound like meat frying in a pan.

Pain, like a thousand needles, rushes from the palm of my hand all the way up my arm. I grit my teeth to keep from crying out as my limbs fill with the fiery heat.

When it passes, I'm left with only a dull throb and a sense that my own limbs are weighed down by invisible chains.

An inhuman shriek, the likes of which I have never heard and which raises the hair on the back of my neck, fills the chamber. It's coming from Fake Hendrix.

"Keep your hand still," my father commands.

A pain worse than any I have ever felt races across my scalp, making my head feel like it might split in two. I double over and close my eyes. I grit my teeth and force myself to stay on my feet.

Slowly, the pain in my head begins to ease.

Bloody froth wells up and dribbles between the narrow space between my hand and Fake Hendrix's flesh. The Dusker, awake again, writhes as a white foam bubbles from his mouth. His entire body convulses. Purple veins cover his face and neck. It looks like the poison of my blood is going to make his insides burst apart.

"Help him." My voice is barely audible over the screams that threaten to drive me insane. I pull my hand away from the wound. "Help him!"

Before my father can say anything, the shrieks end. Fake Hendrix's body begins to jerk and twitch.

"He is passing into the second stage," my father observes. "I believe enough of your blood entered the wound for a successful transformation, but we shall see."

Fake Hendrix's sprawled legs begin to lengthen before my eyes. His neck swells, black veins spreading across his pale flesh like tree roots. A ripping sound fills the chamber as the gray cloak, which had hung loosely on the Dusker, is stretched until the material tears at its seams.

His neck spasms, and with every jerk of his head, clumps of hair come free from his scalp.

I back away until I'm pressed against the wall. My teeth are chattering even though sweat is rolling down my face.

This is wrong, a voice screams in my head. *Aunt Jadem is dead because of him*, another voice argues.

With a last jerk, Fake Hendrix's eyes roll back in his head. I gasp as the whites of his eyes seem to fill with fluid until all the color, all the white, has been replaced by inky black. His body crumples into a ball and stills.

"Is he dead?" My voice is unnaturally high.

"Not at all." My father nudges the Dusker's still body with his boot. "His body is adjusting to the new blood."

I flex my hand, allowing blood and feeling to rush back into my fingers.

Exhaustion still makes my limbs feel like lead, but there's something else, too. A new, unfamiliar strength fills my veins. It's like whatever happened to me when I touched the Dusker's skin took away my energy but replaced it with something else. I close my eyes and allow myself just to feel.

When I open my eyes, the man huddled in a heap on the floor is no more. In his place towers a black-eyed Zero. If it weren't for the ratty gray cloak stretched across its chest, I wouldn't recognize this creature for what it used to be.

Muscles that couldn't exist on any human stand out on the Zero's flesh, bulging and rippling with every movement. Even though the chamber ceiling must be eight feet high, the Zero has to hunch its shoulders to keep from scraping its now-bald head.

The Zero bears some resemblance to the ones surrounding my father, but it's also different. This Zero is just *more*. It's taller and more muscular, and its whole body quivers with untapped energy. Even Brogut looks insignificant and flabby by comparison.

"Magnificent," my father breathes.

The Zero lifts up its head. It sniffs, two long inhales as it sucks air through the slits of its nose. Its black eyes swivel on me.

As its eyes find mine and the silent connection is formed, a rush of power flows through me. The very air seems to thrum with it. There is a burning deep inside of me I don't recognize. A strength I've never known envelops me like a blanket. *I feel dangerous.*

"Even I can feel it," my father says.

"Feel what?"

He motions toward the Zero. "Its new strength is in part your own." He stares thoughtfully at me for a moment. "When you test yourself, my guess is you may find your own strength enhanced."

I'm…stronger?

"There are no others like you, Hemera." My father's voice carries a note of pride. "Your powers can be limitless, if only you reach out and take them."

My father's words light the hunger that has been growing inside me since I first pressed my palm to Fake Hendrix's flesh.

"Does it know what I did?"

My father shakes his head. "What you witnessed earlier was not just a physical transformation." He regards the new Zero. "The new blood destroyed the Dusker's mind. This creature before you recalls nothing of its past life."

"It doesn't remember who it was five minutes ago?" I ask, swaying on my feet. Ekil puts a hand on my arm to steady me.

"Any memory tied to emotions disappears, as the creature itself no longer has any capacity for emotion. Fortunately," he stares up at the Zero, "they are instinctive creatures. They retain knowledge about how to survive, which makes them excellent soldiers."

My father's eyes flick to me for a fraction of a second before returning to the Zero. "Your blood runs through its veins. And so it is under your command."

I think I detect a hint of wistfulness in his voice.

The Zero sniffs the air again. It takes a step closer to me.

"Think of it like a young animal scenting its mother," my father explains.

The analogy is almost laughable.

"Could Brogut control the Zero, since it carries his blood, too?" I ask. For some reason I can't explain, I want my father's answer to be *no*.

"No," my father says, and I let out a sigh of relief. "There is far more of your blood inside it than the Halve's, and thus it is you the Zero scents most strongly."

A black stripe marks the spot just above the Zero's collarbone where my blood and the Halve's entered the Dusker's flesh. Without knowing why, I reach a hand up to touch the spot.

I expect the Zero to flinch away, but it doesn't move. The Zero's skin is rougher than a human's, but not as scaly as the Halves'. Its black eyes stare straight ahead as my hand moves to the pulse at the Zero's throat. A strange ripple of energy passes through the Zero's flesh into the place where my fingers are pressed against its pulse.

"You want to protect your people." My father's voice is hushed, reverent. "This is the way."

This…creature…is made of flesh and bone. It breathes in and out like any other living being. The Zero's corded muscles press against the surface of its skin as if they're about to burst out. This terrible, beautiful creation standing before me didn't exist minutes ago. *I* created it.

Strength flows into my hand, and I can't tell whether it's coming from me or from the Zero's pulse where my fingers still rest. A heady rush passes through me again, but this time, I recognize it for what it is. It's the sheer, raw power of having made something stronger than any other creature alive. And it answers to me. Terror and elation war within me.

My father huffs impatiently. "Go on, give it an order. It is at your command."

The black depths of the Zero's pitiless eyes swivel on me, sensing my gaze. Hesitation fills me at the sight of this hulking brute. I wipe the sweat from my brow, feeling the sliminess of blood that still rests atop my freshly healed hand.

Wokee once told me hyenair can sense fear, which makes them think of prey. He said any hesitation is seen as submission, which makes the animals see you as food. He said the key to not becoming Vlaz's lunch was to pretend to be bigger and stronger.

While I doubt the Zero would try to eat me, I think the same principle must apply. I straighten up to my full height, forcing myself to look into the Zero's unblinking stare.

"Can you break free?" My eyes move to the shackles squeezing around the flesh of its muscled torso.

"I've found orders to be most effective when combined with hand gestures," my father says.

I point at the chains, miming the act of ripping them off. It feels incredibly stupid.

The Zero's black eyes swivel onto the manacles. Twisting its great shoulders, the Zero snaps the iron links wound around its middle. The iron pieces fall to the ground and skitter across the stones.

The Zero bends down, picks up a piece of the chain, and offers it to me.

"Marvelous." My father claps his hands together.

The Zero stares unblinking at me, the chain still gripped in its enormous hands.

"You are making history, daughter. You are bringing in the new age."

"And what age is that?" My voice is unsteady.

"The age of the Bisecter, of course."

CHAPTER 29

Even though there is only a small mark on my palm from the one-hundred times I slashed it with the knife, the fire running through my veins hasn't receded. It's not unpleasant, exactly, just different.

I feel both less and more, somehow. A part of me went into each transformation, and I'm not sure if I'll ever get those pieces back. Still, these hundred Zeroes standing before me, their black eyes trained on me, infuse me with a strength that is twice, three times more than whatever I lost.

I feel more powerful than before.

Ekil and Brogut are both slumped against the wall, exhausted and weak from blood loss. Even though they gave less blood than me, and their skin didn't directly touch the Duskers', they are slower to recover than I am. By the end, they were both shuffling from prisoner to prisoner as though their ankles were weighed down with bricks.

"Time to rest," my father announces, nodding to Ekil and Brogut.

My father leaves the door open as we file out. The Zeroes are no longer chained, and there's nothing to stop them from walking right out of this place. Somehow, though, I know they won't.

My father disappears down the path, saying something about getting a tonic that will help renew the Halves' strength. I stand with the two Halves outside the chamber. Ekil slumps to the ground.

"Thank you," I say. "I know that wasn't easy—"

Brogut, teeth bared, takes a step toward me. His balled fist makes a weak swipe at my throat. I block it. Brogut darts his head forward like a serpent, his jaws snapping shut on the air just past my ear. I push him against the wall, pinning his arms to his sides.

"Were you trying to bite me?" I ask the Halve, bemused.

"You trick us."

"That's not an answer." I release Brogut, putting my hands on my hips.

"Make Halves weak," Brogut says, motioning at Ekil.

"I'm trying to help you," I say, feeling my anger rise. "What do you expect from me?"

"Making monsters is bad," Brogut snarls.

"We'll see if you still say that when we've defeated the Duskers and you get your river back."

"Sleep now," Ekil says, gesturing for us to help him to his feet.

"This will help the Halves," my father says as he climbs back up the steps to us. There are two small vials in his hand.

I take the vials from my father and give them to Ekil. After translating my father's instructions for how much of the liquid to swallow, I wave the Halves on. "I'll be there soon," I tell them, before turning back to my father.

"So, how do you feel?" he asks as soon as it's just us and the Zeroes.

How do I feel? *Alive.* Alive in a way I've never felt before.

"It's the blood bond," he says, regarding me.

"The what?" I look up from where I'm observing the scar across my palm. Even though the wound has healed, the black slash remains. *Strange.*

"When you created the Zeroes," my father clarifies. "It made you stronger."

Blood bond. So that's what I felt with every transformation.

"Show me," my father says. "Don't hold back."

My father's words light the hunger that has been growing inside me since I turned Fake Hendrix. Taking a deep breath, I let the need inside me swell.

The rush of strength as my fist cuts through the air is like nothing I've ever felt. I close my eyes, bracing myself for the pain of my bones cracking as my fist slams through the thick stone wall of the chamber.

I hear—rather than feel—the jarring of my bones. There's no pain. Stone crumbles into dust as the entire section of wall dissipates into a puff of smoke. It's like it never existed. A rumbling follows. A huge chunk of rock cracks away from the ceiling.

The rock falls toward us. A part of me is aware of my father throwing himself to the ground behind his Zeroes. Thrusting one fist into the air, I punch straight through the stone. The entire slab of stone disintegrates before it reaches the ground.

Dust fills the air and blinds me, but I hardly notice. The Zeroes don't try to shield themselves or even flinch as debris rains down around them.

I'm barely winded. Raw, unbridled power pumps through my veins. I feel like I could take down the entire mountain if I wanted.

I was strong before. But this…this shouldn't even be possible. My fist is bloodied, but the bones and flesh have already knit back together. There is none of the pain or exhaustion I felt using my strength in the past. I'm left only with a single thought. *More.*

My throbbing pulse begins to slow and my vision clears. The wave of power recedes somewhat, and I feel more like myself again.

"You amaze me, daughter." My father's voice is hoarse from the rock dust clouding the air.

I turn to face him.

"Don't talk to me like that…like we're suddenly okay." I'm breathing hard, but not from the exertion of destroying a wall of stone.

"I don't understand—"

"I know you only saved us because you needed me for this." I flail my hand at the Zeroes. "It doesn't change everything else you've done."

"I did what I had to," my father replies, his voice an infuriating calm. "Without the experiments, this," he mimics my hand gesture, "would never have been possible. Sometimes, the sacrifice of a few is needed for the greater good."

"That's your excuse for everything," I say, my voice rising.

"It's the truth," he replies.

"What about my mother?" I explode. "Did you have her killed because you thought it was *necessary?*"

At that, my father seems to grow smaller.

"I never meant for them to kill her," he says. "The Halves were not as controlled as I thought. It was an accident."

"Like I'm supposed to believe that," I snarl.

"I loved her."

The words are so foreign coming from his lips I'm dumbstruck. I don't think I've ever heard him say *love* in my life.

My father shakes his head. The faraway look has been replaced by the intelligent gleam I'm familiar with. "You understand what it's like, don't you?"

My breath catches. I didn't think he knew what happened to Brice, but his shrewd look tells me he knows exactly what happened.

He nods at whatever he reads on my face.

"This changes nothing," I tell him.

"If you want the world to change, your understanding of it must change, as well."

His words follow me as I stalk back down the path.

I go down to the river instead of up to the sleeping chamber I share with the rest of my companions. My mind is too jumbled, my anger too hot. I don't want to admit that any part of what my father said could be true.

As I plunge into the water, my fury cools. Some part of me knows my father's cruel experiments have given the Solguards their last ray of hope. I'm not grateful for it, and it certainly doesn't erase his crimes, but it's something.

The thought comforts me.

And then there's part of me, the part I've been ignoring since my father and his Zeroes appeared to rescue us, that's relieved to be on the same side as my father. Creating the Zeroes with him felt a little like when we were in the Subterrane, before I knew about everything he'd done.

I'm still trying to puzzle my way through these thoughts when I head back up the path into the mountain.

Whatever I expected to find when I opened the door of our small chamber, it certainly wasn't Dayne holding a knife to my father's throat. And yet, that's exactly what I find.

CHAPTER 30

I won't let you," Dayne is saying. "I'll kill you before you can corrupt her."

My father, for once without his Zeroes, stands calmly, his face blank of all emotion.

"Thank the sun," Ry says as soon as I step into the room. "Hemera, do something before your brother gets himself hurt."

"I'm the one with the knife," Dayne growls.

"Yeah, and he's the one with the Zeroes," Ry retorts.

"Dayne?"

I put a hand on his arm and feel the way it trembles with his contained fury. "Dayne, it's okay," I say, tugging his arm down. "I'm okay."

Dayne gives my father a murderous look. My father simply hands me a vial, telling me to give it to the Halves after they finish the ones from earlier, and strides out of the room.

"What was that about?" I ask my brother.

"He's slippery," Dayne says, breathing hard, "and I won't let him manipulate you for his own ends."

"Dayne, we've been through this." I rub my eyes, feeling tiredness descend. "We both want the same thing for now. Nothing else has changed."

"I know what he's like," Dayne persists. "Hemera, I can't protect you from him."

The way Dayne's face sags in defeat at this admission should make me feel pity. It doesn't.

"I don't need your protection," I say.

"No good can come from an alliance with him," Dayne persists. "No good can come from these Zeroes."

"So you've said." My voice takes on a sarcastic edge. "And yet, no one else is doing anything."

"Sometimes it's wiser not to act," Dayne says.

"I tried that." My voice is rising. "Do you remember what happened to Jadem? She's dead because I didn't do anything!"

"Hemera—"

"Don't say it," I warn.

It's not your fault. The words echo like a chorus meant to torture me.

Dayne stares at me for a long moment.

"I'm taking a walk," he mutters.

When the door closes behind him, the room is left in silence.

"We go to hunt," Ekil says, breaking the stillness.

He and Brogut take the vials and stalk out of the room, leaving Ry and I alone. Deflating with their absence, I sink down onto my bedroll and bury my face in my hands.

"Oh Mer." Ry comes to sit beside me.

"I didn't mean to yell at him like that," I say, my voice muffled from behind my hands.

"Dayne will be back," Ry says. "He just needs to cool off. You know how men can be with their grudges." She rolls her eyes, which gets a small smile out of me.

"What if he's right?" I ask.

Ry gives me an appraising look. "I never told you this, but when Jadem found me in the ruins of my settlement, I was about as full of regrets as you can get." Her voice is flippant, but there's a hardness underneath. "Jadem told me something that's stuck with me. She said I was a Solguard now, and Solguards don't have time for regrets. She said the difference between a Solguard and the Banished is choosing to go forward, even when it seems hopeless."

That's exactly the sort of thing Aunt Jadem would say. My heart squeezes.

"So, you think I did the right thing?" I ask.

Do you think Aunt Jadem would have thought I'm doing the right thing?

My hand fumbles for the silver key dangling at my throat. *What would you have wanted me to do?* I want to ask my mother. The answer comes as quickly as if she'd whispered it in my ear.

Be brave, Mer.

My mother wouldn't want me to be afraid. She'd want me to do whatever I had to in order to spare innocent lives. Isn't that what she did herself all those years ago?

"Yes, I think you did the right thing." Ry gives me an encouraging smile. "Whatever the outcome, I believe your aunt was right. You're going to save us all." She laughs. "But no pressure or anything."

A half-sniffle, half-laugh escapes me. Ry winks at me.

"Ry," I say, sitting up. "I need to apologize to you."

"Apologize? For what?"

"When you walked in on Wade and me." I swallow. "I swear I didn't know you felt that way about him."

A burst of laughter leaps out of Ry's mouth, startling me. I give her a questioning look.

"Dellin was right," Ry says, looking amazed. "You really don't know."

"Know what?" I ask, feeling defensive at the mere mention of the other girl's name.

"Do you love him?" Ry asks, rather than answering my question.

"I don't know." I shake my head, all the confusion and pain rushing back. "I think so, especially when I'm with him. But then I think about it, and I can't help but feel…guilty."

"Guilty?" Ry asks, like the word surprises here. And then, after a moment, understanding dawns on her face. "Oh, because of Brice?"

I nod, trying not to think about how even the mention of his name feels like a weight on my heart.

"Hemera, he was a selfish bastard," Ry says. "There's nothing to feel guilty about."

My harsh laugh fills the room. "He died saving my life. I'm pretty sure that should earn me a lifetime of guilt."

"You made a choice, Mer." Ry moves closer to me, rubbing soothing circles on my back. "Just like you did today. You *chose* to do something, and right or wrong, that means something."

"What does it mean?" I ask, relaxing into her touch.

"It means you're brave. That you're willing to do what no one else can for the sake of something bigger, something more."

For some reason, her words strike me in a way that no amount of reassurance from Dayne or Aunt Jadem ever could.

"Let the guilt go, Mer," Ry says, still rubbing circles on my back. "Just let it go."

And just like that, I feel a weight being lifted off my chest. A small sigh escapes me. I feel myself being lulled into a heavy-lidded state of relaxation.

"What was Dellin right about?" I ask Ry.

Her hand falters on my back.

Ry clears her throat. "Mer." She shifts away from me, turning her head so I can't see her face. "That high day, when I walked in on you and Wade...." She trails off. The tips of her ears have turned crimson.

I've never seen Ry like this before.

"If I had known you felt that way about him," I say, trying to make her feel less embarrassed, "I would have talked to you first."

Ry screws up her face. "I'm not in *love* with Wade." She says it like she can't imagine anything more disgusting. "For sun's sake, Hemera, he's like a brother to me."

"Then why did you seem so upset?"

Ry laughs again, the redness spreading from her ears all the way down her neck. "Dellin said you had no idea, but I didn't believe her. I thought it was just so *obvious*." Ry reaches up and strokes her thumb across my cheek.

"What's obvious?" There's a strange fluttering in my stomach. I have no idea what Ry is working up to telling me.

"It was you I was after." Her voice has gone low and sultry, and for some reason, that makes my blood flow a little faster.

"Me?" I ask, a little breathless now.

Instead of saying anything else, Ry leans forward, closing the space between us. Ry cups my neck with her hand. And then her lips are touching mine.

I'm so startled I can't react at first.

Ry pulls back just enough for me to see the desire and question in her eyes. When she leans forward, I don't pull away.

Her lips are on mine again, but firmer this time, like the silent question that was asked has been answered.

"Hemera," Ry murmurs against my partly-open lips.

I squirm at the realization of Ry's tongue doing…things…to the inside of my mouth. I don't pull away. I can hardly breathe.

Tingles go up my spine as she tugs gently on my lower lip with her teeth. Alarm bells ring in my head. There is a reason why this is wrong, completely wrong, but I can't remember what that reason might be. My limbs turn to liquid as I melt into her embrace. When one of Ry's hands glides up and brushes over my chest, a shudder goes through me.

"Ry," I squeak, but she silences me with another caress of her hand, another tug on my lip. A small sound rumbles deep from somewhere inside me as she presses me down onto the ground. There are stones digging into my back, but I barely feel them.

Ry's lips move down, tracing a line across my throat. Sensations light my insides as her hand sweeps lower, finding its way beneath the hem of my shirt.

"My strong, sexy, Bisecter." Ry says the words between kisses.

I'm not sure what makes me do it…maybe it's the fire still coursing through my blood from changing the Zeroes. But instead of being embarrassed, instead of pulling back, I wrap my arms around Ry and submit to her caresses.

"That's right." Ry slides her tongue along my skin, leaving a trail of goosebumps in its wake.

I don't notice the sound of the door opening and footsteps moving inside until Ry has already rolled off me.

Ekil and Brogut shuffle into the room, Brogut with a new tree trunk spear and Ekil with the remains of two partly-devoured fish.

My blood pounds in my ears. When I steal a glance at Ry, she winks at me. Her face is flushed, but nothing else about her reveals…*that* just happened.

I don't even know what that *was.*

"I think we should all get some sleep," Ry announces. She gives me a wicked grin before flopping down onto her bedroll. I don't know how she could sleep after what we just did, but in minutes, she's breathing deeply.

When the sound of Brogut's snores are so loud I'll either go crazy or punch something, I make my way from the room, closing the door behind me. As soon as I'm alone on the path, I press my back against the wall, breathing in the stillness.

Wade. The image of his face fills my mind in the absence of other sights and sounds, even as the ghost of Ry's lips and hands still play across my body.

How could I betray him like that? Wade is the one who is in my dreams. He's the one who—in the absence of my guilt for Brice—I know I want.

So why did I do…*that*…with Ry?

It didn't feel the same as when I kiss Wade. When I kiss Wade, it's more like I'm trying to show him everything I'm thinking and feeling through our touch. But this…this felt easy, without the weight of expectations or unspoken promises. This felt exciting, dangerous. Like how I feel with the Zeroes. A small shiver runs down my spine.

I can feel the weight of Wade's Solguard pendant at my throat. For once, though, it doesn't comfort me.

"Hemera? What are you doing out here?"

I almost jump out of my skin at the sound of my brother's voice.

"Nothing," I answer, too quickly.

Dayne sighs. "I'm sorry, little sis." His gaze slides to our mother's silver key hanging around my neck. "It's just, being in this place…being around *him*." Dayne sighs again. "After everything that happened with our mother," he shakes his head. "I just promised myself I wouldn't leave you alone to deal with him again."

I know it still plagues my brother that he was in Malarusk when my mother was killed. That so many years passed before he learned I was still alive.

"I'm sorry, too," I tell him. "I shouldn't have talked to you like that."

"We have to look out for each other," Dayne says, and I know he's thinking about Aunt Jadem. "It's just us now, Mer."

For some reason, I think of the Zeroes.

CHAPTER 31

Voices rouse me from the depths of sleep. Loud voices. I crack open my eyes.

"Well, if it isn't my favorite Bisecter!"

It takes me a confusing moment for me to place the familiar voice.

"Jarosh?" I croak. "What are you doing here?"

"Looking for you, of course," Jarosh replies.

I look up to see my friend smiling down at me. Except it's not the Jarosh I remember.

"You look amazing," I say, rubbing my eyes.

Jarosh waggles his eyebrows. "Didn't know it was like that between us." He leans closer to me like he's going to tell me a secret. "It's fine with me, but have you ever seen your boyfriend pissed off?"

I give him a playful shove, and then hurry to steady him as he stumbles backward.

"Oops, sorry." I grin as Jarosh winces and rubs his side. "But seriously," I prod. "What happened to you?"

Jarosh's skin is glowing with health. His muscled frame gives off no evidence of his recent near-death. Before, his hair had been pulled into a perpetual knot at the base of his skull; now, it now hangs in glossy waves down his back. Colorful feathers and wooden beads are braided among the strands. He looks somehow taller and more filled out.

Jarosh grins and shrugs. "Life with the Halves has been good to me."

Standing behind Jarosh, one hand on his shoulder, is the female Halve that healed him.

"Camike, right?" I ask.

She steps out from behind Jarosh and gives me a shy smile.

"No way," Ry says. She's standing in the doorway, her eyes narrowed, as Jarosh wraps his arms around Camike and kisses her. "Please tell me you're not dating a Halve."

"I dated a healer once," Dayne says, looking amused. "Good with their hands."

"List of things I didn't need to know about my brother—"

"Blech," Ry says, pretending to gag.

"Halves don't date," Jarosh informs us with a roll of his eyes. "They are far more refined than humans in that regard."

Ry and I exchange a look.

Camike, noticing my attention, points to Jarosh and says, "My mate." I could almost swear the rough skin of Camike's cheeks have turned pink.

I blink at her in surprise. Her words are crisply articulated in the human language.

"My mate." Jarosh confirms, winding an arm through Camike's and smiling at her in a way that pulls at my heart.

"But you can't even speak her language," I point out.

"It's a work in progress." He makes a strange grunting noise that has absolutely no meaning in any language, followed up with equally senseless hand gestures and a caress to Camike's cheek. Camike beams.

There's a goofy grin on Jarosh's face I've never seen before. And it's all for Camike.

"Well if that smile isn't the most disgusting thing I've ever seen, then it's not sunny outside," Ry announces.

Jarosh only grins wider.

"How did you find us?" Dayne asks.

Jarosh explains how they had been searching for us when they found Vlaz. The hyenair led them to the river, and then Camike *in her infinite brilliance and slightly emasculating strength* swam them into the Lair.

Ekil and Brogut clasp arms with Camike, greeting her in the Halve language. She repeats Jarosh's story for their sake. Ekil doesn't react, but Brogut's already-fearsome face goes stormy with anger.

"Humans bad," he says, before retiring to his bedroll to sulk.

Jarosh looks me up and down, his smile dissolving. "You're looking all hollowed out." He glares around the room. "What's your father done to you?"

I shake my head, too grateful to see my friend to worry about anything else just yet.

"If I find out he's pulled some more of his—"

He breaks off as Camike makes a cooing noise and strokes his stubbled chin. Jarosh relaxes under her touch, seeming to have forgotten whatever threat he was about to make.

"Hey," Jarosh's expression turns serious. "We heard about Jadem." He swallows. "Is it true?"

The silent chamber is the only answer he needs. Jarosh nods slowly. "She was a good leader." His eyes meet mine. "A good person."

Tears burn the back of my throat.

The ground underfoot trembles, and then I hear a whimper of excitement as Vlaz comes bounding up to the chamber. He stops short when he realizes he won't be able to fit his entire body through the door.

"Hey buddy." Dayne reaches overhead to give his flopped ear a rub. "How's your neck feeling?"

Vlaz drools contentedly as Dayne continues to pet him.

I go to greet the hyenair, but as soon as I stretch out my hand to scratch him like I always do, Vlaz's body goes rigid. His black lips quiver, and a quiet growl escapes his parted fangs. I step back, uncertain.

"Vlaz…it's me."

At the sound of my voice, Vlaz's ears prick in my direction and he wiggles his body in greeting. I take another step toward him, and this time, he lowers his head so I can better reach his ear.

"Well, that was weird," Ry comments.

Dayne doesn't say anything, but his brow is furrowed.

"It's pretty dark in here," I say with a shrug. "Maybe he thought I was someone else."

"Jarosh, Camike," Dayne gives her a polite nod, "while we appreciate the visit, I'm assuming you're here with news from Wade?"

Wade. I can't even look at Ry at the mention of his name.

"Indeed we do." Jarosh clears his throat. "Wade says, and I'm summarizing now, mind you, but he says to get your asses back to the fortress…yesterday."

When we all just stare at him, Jarosh sighs. "Okay, those weren't his exact words. But he did have to tell the Banished that the mission was successful and you got Hendrix." He clears his throat. "So, congratulations on that, I guess."

"He what?!" Dayne, Ry, and I say at once.

"He had to." Jarosh shrugs. "The Banished leaders practically have one foot out of the fortress, and he's doing everything he can aside from imprisoning them to keep them from surrendering to the Duskers."

"Then we have to get back there," Ry says. "Now."

"Not without some kind of leverage, you're not," Jarosh says. "There'd be no point."

"We have leverage," I tell him. "Zeroes."

"Zeroes?" Jarosh looks hard at me. "You mean the creatures that almost killed you back in Tanguro? The reason your father tried to squeeze us dry?"

"You didn't get squeezed at all," I point out, irritated now.

"My mate did!" He jabs a finger at my chest.

"If you have any better ideas for saving us all, then please share them," I shoot back. "Because as far as I can tell, without the Zeroes, we may as well surrender to the Duskers ourselves." Even saying those words makes me feel sick.

I force myself to take a breath. "Look, I don't like it either. But the Zeroes are the only things strong enough to give us a chance against the Duskers."

"And you know this how?" Jarosh asks. "Because Daddy Psycho told you?"

I flush. "I can prove it to you."

Jarosh raises an eyebrow. "Well, by all means, convince me." He folds his arms.

"It's a good idea, daughter."

"Why do you always have to sneak up on us?" Ry demands, clutching at her chest. "Is it part of the grand plan? Give all of Hemera's friends heart attacks and remove them from the equation?"

My father ignores her. "Let your friend see the Zeroes for himself," he tells me. "It will give you a chance to see their strength in action." A gleam of something…victory, perhaps, flashes across his eyes. It vanishes just as quickly.

My father leads the way as we wind our way up the path to the Zeroes' chamber.

The closer we get, the more I feel the pressure inside me ease. It's almost like there's a taut cord linking me to the Zeroes, and with each step that brings me nearer to them, the cord slackens. I hadn't even realized the pressure was there until it loosens and I can breathe easily again.

We all stand in the doorway as my friends get their first look at the army. *My* army.

"What have you done to them?" I ask, stepping inside the room.

The Zeroes are no longer clad in the shredded remains of the Duskers' cloaks. They're wearing armor—tiny, interlocking loops of metal that cover everything below their necks and above their knees. Iron-plated boots are fitted to their large feet. It's much more intricate than the simple metal skirts my father's original ten Zeroes wear.

"I thought these clothes more befitting of creatures of their strength and stamina," my father says. "The armor makes a statement, as do the creatures who wear it."

These outfits are ones only the Zeroes could wear. Even without touching it, I know the metal would be far too heavy for any human to fight in. It would also fry any human the second he stepped onto the Outside.

Each Zero grips its own scythe.

"Where did you get all these…uniforms from?" I manage to ask.

"My Zeroes made them months ago," my father replies.

Months ago?

"How did you know I'd agree to change them?" I ask. "You could have been stuck with all these clothes and no bodies to fill them."

"Because I know what I would choose if I was in your place." My father smiles. "And regardless of whatever you've convinced yourself, you and I are not so different."

I want to retort, but all of my attention is on the Zeroes.

The room pulses with their power combined with my own. I don't know if the others can feel it, but it thrums inside me like a second heartbeat.

"You know," my father murmurs in a voice too low for the others to hear, "I believe we are only a few more generations of Zeroes away from creating true Bisecters."

"No." The loudness of my voice startles us both.

These creatures might have some of me in them, but they are not me.

"No," I say again.

My father only shrugs.

The others all stare transfixed at the Zeroes, but the Zeroes don't pay any attention to them. They only look at me. A small shiver of satisfaction ripples through me. A tension I hadn't even knew I was feeling melts away at the sight of my creations.

Brogut gnashes his teeth as he clutches his tree trunk spear, although he isn't foolish enough to raise it. If he were an animal, his hackles would be raised.

Vlaz's hackles *are* raised. He's growling, and it takes a stern command from Dayne to keep him from lunging inside and tearing the Zeroes to shreds…or getting torn to shreds himself.

"I'll be damned." Jarosh lets out a low whistle as he moves his body in front of Camike, blocking her from the Zeroes' sight. He turns to face my father. "You're a real bastard, you know that?"

"Jarosh." I put a hand on his arm.

"And you." He rounds on me. "Letting your father lure you into a trap, just to use you? *Again?*"

My face heats. "It's how we're going to defeat the Duskers."

"They will get our river back," Ekil tells Camike.

Camike looks at me, her black eyes all trust. "If Halve saver says so, then I believe."

I manage a small smile, even as I feel the weight of her faith settle onto my shoulders.

"I don't like it," Jarosh says.

Camike lays one of her hands on his cheek. She leans forward, and for a brief moment, their foreheads touch. It's a private moment, and when they pull apart, the murderous look is gone from Jarosh's face.

"What's done is done," Dayne says. His words have an ominous ring to them. "But I don't like the idea of bringing them back to the fortress, especially when we have only Zeidan's word they will follow Hemera's command."

A fair point.

"Don't take my word for it," my father says. "See for yourselves."

The rest of us look at each other.

"The Dusker initiates are making their way down the mountain as we speak," my father explains. "You could order the Zeroes to attack them."

"We don't have time," I say, feeling my anxiety rise. "The Banished are going to surrender. And then Solis—"

We're running out of time.

"Me and Brogut away for too long," Ekil says. "Need to get back to our Halves."

I nod in agreement.

"Perhaps if the Zeroes kill the recruits, it will delay the attack on Solis," my father argues.

I know what my father says is true, but I can't help the hesitation I feel. Even if the Zeroes can kill the recruits without any trouble like my father seems to think, and that's a big *if*, we'd be ambushing the newest Duskers, the ones who haven't yet become killers. They're not innocent, and I know they'd kill us if our positions were reversed. Still, could I really consider killing them all, just for the sake of proving the Zeroes' worth?

"You'll have to kill them eventually," my father says, correctly reading whatever expression is on my face. "May as well do it on our terms instead of theirs."

I nod. I don't like it, but I know he's right. It'll be better to kill them now before they can do more damage to the Solguards later.

"That's an awful lot of recruits," Dayne points out. "Aren't there usually hundreds of them?"

Hundreds? I swallow.

"Yes," my father replies, "which means we'll likely need about twenty of the Zeroes to dispatch them."

Ry's mouth falls open.

"Twenty Zeroes to take out hundreds of Duskers?" Dayne asks. "Are you out of your mind?"

I don't say anything. I saw the Zeroes' strength at Tanguro for myself…felt their strength when I fought them.

"That's being conservative," my father replies evenly. "Five of them would likely do the job just fine."

I listen to the others argue back and forth until we're out of time.

"Hemera?" Dayne asks. He gives my father one final glare before fixing his gaze on me. "What do you want to do?"

I look into his steady blue eyes, and for a moment, I can almost pretend it's our mother staring back.

It isn't fair to have such a big decision resting on your shoulders, my mother would say if she were here now, *but I know you will make the right choice.*

With the echo of her voice still in my mind, I'm gripped by the memory of the battle at Tanguro. I think about all the men and women I tried to protect…all the people who died defending the fortress.

Every one of them was killed by a Dusker.

I look at my father. "Let's see if these Zeroes are the army we need."

CHAPTER 32

As we make our way down the pathway, the Zeroes follow behind us. Their armor clinks with every step.

"Why do they make that sniffing noise?" Ry complains. "It makes them seem even more…" she grasps for the word, "beastly."

"They are scenting for the blood of the one who made them," my father answers.

"And the others?" Dayne points at the ten that surround my father. "Those don't seem to be following Hemera."

We all stop to look at the Zeroes my father made from blood he took by force. I shudder at the memory of the tube hooked into my vein, carrying my brown blood from my body.

"Hemera was not here when they awoke," my father says after a pause. "I was all they saw."

"So, they think you're their mother," Jarosh says with a straight face. "That makes sense."

Ry and Dayne snicker.

"Blood is stronger than any of that," my father says, ignoring the gibe. "They will follow Hemera as soon as she claims them."

"And what about the first ones you made?" I ask. "What happened to the ones from Tanguro that I didn't kill?"

My father shrugs. "Once I made these ones with your blood, I had no need for their inferior prequels."

I see the meaning behind my father's words. "So, you just killed your own creations?"

My father says something in response, but it's lost to the sound of rushing water. The path ends at the ledge overhanging the Darkness River.

"Well," my father says, when I just stand there, "give them an order."

"Get in the water," I say, and then, remembering my father's instructions from before, point at the water and make a paddling motion.

I feel ridiculous doing it, especially with the others watching, but the Zeroes understand. They jump in, barely making a splash. They treat water as they await my next order.

Emboldened, I direct the Zeroes to help my friends through the water. Ekil and Brogut refuse to be helped, and Jarosh will only go with Camike. Dayne and Ry submit to being carried with only some grumbling.

I wait for the others to disappear into the swirling black water. And then I jump in.

The current drags at me. Still, I barely feel any resistance. The swim is easy. *Too easy.*

The Zeroes bobbing in the water beside me are kicking up enough bubbles for me to know my muscles should be straining against the water's pull. And yet, this swim is no more difficult for me than if I were making my way through a still pond.

In only a few moments, I'm swimming out of the darkness and into blinding sunlight. I crash through the water and heave a great breath.

Ry, Jarosh, and Dayne are pulling themselves from the water, straining against their sodden cloaks. I'm grateful once again that I'll never have to wear one again.

My father directs us to the opposite riverbank, the one closest to Malarusk.

"Aren't we a bit exposed?" Ry asks, looking at the barren landscape.

"The Zeroes' instincts are best provoked when their master faces a true threat." Zeidan squeezes out the hem of his cloak. The water droplets hit the ground and are immediately swallowed up by the parched earth.

"What's that supposed to mean?" Dayne demands.

"That a true battle is the best way to demonstrate their strength."

"I can appreciate the irony," Jarosh says, "of Duskers returning from a meeting with their precious Dark God and running into these monsters."

"This is a terrible idea," Dayne says.

"These Duskers won't be expecting a fight," my father says in his Captain Harkibel voice. "There is almost no risk." He looks at me. "Just be sure the Zeroes slay them all. We don't want any of the Duskers to be able to report back to Crowe about what they saw."

We all stare into the distance where a small cloud of dust is just becoming visible from the approach of many pairs of feet.

No survivors.

Seeing my hesitation, my father says, "Consider what these soldiers have done to earn them a place among the Duskers."

"I think you should do it," Ry tells me. "Give them a taste of their own bitter medicine."

The Halves nod at me, silently telling me to go ahead. Only Dayne shakes his head.

"But what if the Zeroes…go crazy, or something? What if they refuse to obey me? What if—"

"No better time than the present to find out," my father says. "But I see no reason why they won't follow your every order."

"Should I—" I begin, but my father cuts me off with a wave of his hand.

"Trust the strength of your bond. Trust them."

"You certainly do know a lot about these creatures," Dayne says, his eyes slitted in suspicion.

"I made it my business to know," my father snaps back.

Focus, I tell myself. *This isn't your first battle.* I don't let myself think about what happened the last time I led an attack.

"You," I point to a group of Zeroes. They step aside from the rest. "Hide in the gulley and wait for my signal." I point and flap my hands in a way I hope communicates whatever meaning is lost in my words. "You," I point to another group. "Go around behind those boulders."

The Zeroes move off in the directions I indicated without hesitation. Heaving a sigh of relief, I give more orders. Soon, only my father's Zeroes remain. I look at him, like I'm asking for permission, and then inwardly scowl at myself.

"You," I point to them. "Go far enough around that you won't be seen, and approach from behind. Make sure none escape."

For a second, I think they'll stay with my father. But then, slowly, they move away from him to follow my orders.

I feel the tethered connection with them, but it's weaker than the one I feel with the Zeroes I created myself. My connection with these ones feels like a frayed rope that might snap.

All of the Zeroes move into position. The sun glinting off their metal clothes and the blades of their scythes gives them an other-worldly appearance. My friends stand on the riverbank watching. Ekil has a hand on Brogut's shoulder, and I think it's to prevent him from joining in the fight himself. Jarosh and Ry are bantering while Camike smiles. My brother stands apart. His eyes aren't tracking the Zeroes; they're fixed on my father.

Zeidan watches the Zeroes move off with a thoughtful gaze. As the Captain of Subterrane Harkibel, I expected him to have criticisms and suggestions in abundance. But to my surprise, he doesn't say anything. He looks smaller without the ring of Zeroes surrounding him. He looks more like my father now than he has in a long time.

I shake off the sense of nostalgia as the dust cloud materializes into Duskers.

"Fifty, sixty?" I muse, shielding my eyes as I try to pick out the individual bodies amid the swirl of dust and gray cloaks.

"Closer to eighty, I should think," my father replies. "A poor test of the Zeroes' strength, but I suppose it will have to do."

I push down my rising unease as the Duskers begin to shout to each other and draw steel. They've seen the Zeroes.

They spread out, forming a wide semi-circle to corner our small group with the river at our backs.

Please, I silently beg the Zeroes.

Someone shouts a command, and the Duskers stop in perfect alignment.

"How dare you desecrate this hallowed ground," one of them calls. "Prepare to die."

The Dusker waves his hand. *Such a casual motion.* Like Crowe, at the moment she looked down at my aunt, kneeling and bloody, and broke her neck.

The Duskers surge forward.

"Attack!" I shout.

For a moment, nothing happens. There are a few scattered chuckles from the Duskers. I feel the blood drain from my face.

And then the Zeroes begin to pour from the gulley.

As they merge with the soldiers in gray, the laughter turns to screams.

"Demons!"

"Monsters!"

It's not a battle. It's a massacre.

The Duskers don't even have a chance to lift their blades before the Zeroes' scythes are slashing them in half. My army disposes of the enemy with brutal efficiency.

When a Dusker gets close to me, the Zeroes converge on him. The Zero that reaches him first takes the Dusker's head and smashes it between its hands like an overripe fruit. I bite down on the inside of my cheek, the metallic taste of blood filling my mouth. Blood and bone fragments splatter the Zero's face, but it doesn't even blink.

There's no emotion in their relentless slaughter.

And when it's done, mere minutes later, there's no celebration…no excited whoops or screams. The Zeroes simply go still. Their scythes are slack at their sides, blood still dripping from the curved blades.

Men in gray cloaks are splayed out across the blood-stained earth. My army is untouched.

I look from the dead bodies strewn across the ground to the creatures that brought their destruction. I should be glad to see my enemies lying dead. After all, they would have killed me without a moment's hesitation. They would have killed my brother and my friends.

These Zeroes are the answer to my aunt's last wish, to save everyone.

But something about the brutal, mindless slaughter makes a feeling of dread curdle my insides.

My head snaps up as movement in the distance catches my eye. A Dusker who had been at the rear of the company rises as if from the dead and is now running.

Something about the soldier is wrong. He's too small to be a Dusker. I squint harder.

Is that a...."

"Child! Hemera—" Dayne starts forward.

A wisp of brown hair trails out of the gray hood and a small gloved hand reaches up to push it back into place. He looks about the same age as Wokee, all angles and knobby limbs. A supply pack, nearly as big as the kid himself, bounces with the frantic pace. I push through the line of Zeroes.

What were the Duskers thinking, bringing a little kid to Darkness Peak?

Go ahead and report back on what you saw, I think as I watch the child run. He's a kid; no one's going to believe him.

A shadow falls across the child's path. And then another.

Moving with such speed their profiles are blurred are ...Zeroes. *My* Zeroes. The ones I sent to keep any of the soldiers from escaping the battle.

CHAPTER 33

What had I told them? *Make sure none escape.*

"Stop!" I scream, running. "Leave him alone."

But the Zeroes are already in motion. I don't even know if they've heard me.

"Stop! Stop! Stop!"

I'm still screaming the word long after the Zeroes have gone motionless and the child is curled on the ground. Dead.

My legs give out as I fall to my knees beside the tiny, broken body. I gently pull back the hood of his cloak, barely registering that *he* is in fact a *she*, and that her neck flops backward like a fish when I clutch her to my chest.

I beg her, plead with her, but it's useless. She's dead. Because I ordered it. I ordered the Zeroes to do this.

Choking, gasping sounds escape me. It's a tortured sound I don't even really register as my own until I cover my face with my hands. The child's face, perfectly white like all the Duskers, is already starting to blister from the sun. Her eyes, a strange, beautiful gray like the color of her cloak, stare unseeing at the sky. One of her arms is stretched out on the ground. The other is curled around something. When I pull it out of her lifeless grip, a sob escapes me.

It's a doll.

The toy is covered in dirt and there's a smear of blood across its torn cloth dress. One of its thread eyes has come detached, making it look like yet another casualty of my doing.

I'm only dimly aware of Dayne crouching down beside me, and then the others. Brogut stoops to pat the child's head with such gentleness it shatters my heart.

"Hemera." Dayne says my name, and nothing more.

He was right. He knew something like this would happen. But I can't find the words to tell him.

"It could have been Wokee." The words rasp out of me, and with them, I'm struck with the full weight of what I've done.

"Hemera, come away from here."

I look up through blurred vision to see my father.

"You." Dayne rounds on my father. "I knew no good could come from any of this. I knew you would hurt my sister. And now, look…." My brother's voice hitches. He turns away in disgust.

"I didn't know they would have a child with them." Zeidan's voice is gruff as he kneels beside me. Carefully, gently, he closes the child's eyes.

"Come back to the Lair now."

Standing, my father reaches a hand down to me. It stays extended in the air for several moments before I allow my father to pull me to my feet. He puts a steadying arm around me as my legs give way beneath me.

"Get your hands off her," Dayne growls, but I wave him away.

My good, kind brother. I can't stand the thought of having him be near me right now, not after what I've just done.

I'm dimly aware of Ry brushing tears from her eyes, and Jarosh holding Camike against his chest as if to shield her from the gruesome sight.

"The Zeroes will bury her," my father is saying. "There's nothing else to be done." His arm wrapped around my shoulders steers me; I have no will to try to stop him.

I don't bother to wipe away the tears leaking from my black eyes.

One of the Zeroes sniffs the air and moves a step closer to me. A shudder runs through my body. The tug of energy I feel toward it is both repulsive and irresistible.

"I'm a monster," I whisper.

"She was a Dusker child," my father says. "She may have been cut down before you could see her grow into a cold-blooded killer, but that's what she would have been." He swallows, looking almost as nauseated as I feel. "It is cruel, I know."

We walk in silence until we reach the riverbank.

"But the test was successful," he says.

"Successful?" I bark out a bitter laugh.

My father nods. "The Zeroes followed your every order."

My order. There's no one to blame for the death of that girl except me.

"You should not hesitate to bring them back to Solis now," he continues. "Show the Banished leaders what they can do."

I just shake my head, unable to speak. Every time I blink, I see Wokee's face plastered on the body of the dead girl.

"Hemera," my father sighs. "Crowe will not give you time to mourn. As soon as she figures out her recruits aren't returning, what do you think her next move will be?"

His question jolts me out of my stupor.

"They'll have no reason to wait any longer. They'll attack Solis."

My father nods. "I expect within a day or two the Dusker Supreme will know about the massacre, if not its cause. It will only take a few more days for them to mobilize and reach Solis."

I measure the angle of my shadow. "We leave at low day," I hear myself say. I turn to the others without really seeing them. "Gather your things."

* * *

An hour later, we sit around an untouched pile of Sustum bricks. My father's invention, one he came up with for the scouts of Subterrane Harkibel, contains enough nutrients to keep a person going for a long stretch. But their gritty consistency and bitter taste make them anything but satisfying. Ry picks up one of the greenish squares, takes a small bite, and grimaces.

The scraping sound as Dayne sharpens his knife against a stone sets my nerves on edge.

Ever since he had to leave his lute in the clearing outside Malarusk, he hasn't seemed to know what to do with his hands. More than once, I've seen his fingers stray to the spot where the instrument used to hang around his neck. And now, after everything that's happened, he seems even more jittery and unsure of how to occupy himself.

Jarosh picks up one of the Sustum bricks and shoves the entire thing into his mouth. He chews once, twice, and then promptly spits the contents of his mouth onto the ground. "What in the hell is that? River cabbage and dead fish?"

"Yes," Dayne and I say in unison.

My brother quirks his lip at me in the smallest of smiles.

Jarosh wipes his mouth on the sleeve of his cloak. "And people say Halve food is disgusting."

"Raw stag is disgusting," Ry points out.

"Mmm, stag." Jarosh licks his lips.

Camike gives Jarosh a disapproving cluck before picking up a Sustum brick. "Don't waste." She takes a delicate bite, before spitting it out herself. Jarosh grins.

For some reason, an intense loneliness washes over me at the sight of Jarosh and Camike.

In the end, Brogut and Ekil devour the rest of the Sustum bricks. Brogut even licks the crumbs.

"We have to take my father with us," I say, nodding in the direction of the door. "We can't leave him here."

I don't know what to think of my father anymore, but I know we can't leave him here to do who-knows-what.

Ry wrinkles her nose. "He's not riding on Vlaz behind me, that's for sure. Probably stab me right in the back."

Dayne sighs. "You're probably right about bringing him with us. At least until we decide what to do with him, we shouldn't let him out of our sight."

"What are we going to do?" The words are out of my mouth before I can stop them. Hopelessness threatens to close in around me.

Dayne's face softens. He reaches out a hand and touches Sal's rebel sun hanging from my neck, and then he gestures to the curling rays of the sun marking both of our hands. "We're Solguards. We fight for a better future; that's what we do."

I swallow hard.

Dayne gives my shoulder a squeeze. "I'm here with you, little sis."

"And me." Ry drapes an arm over my shoulders.

"Us too." Jarosh holds up his and Camike's interlocking hands.

Ekil and Brogut take a step closer and hold their hands out to me.

I'm unprepared for the rush of emotion that floods me at the sight of our little group. *You don't deserve their loyalty*, a voice whispers in the back of my mind. But the trust in their eyes as they stare into mine is unwavering.

✳ ✳ ✳

I don't think I'll be able to sleep. But as soon as I lie back on my bedroll, my eyes close.

My dreams are filled with images of Aunt Jadem's fortress. Soft linens and plush feather mattresses. Kynthia birds flitting in and out of every chamber. Sunlight reflected in Wade's golden eyes....

But all of those images fade as enormous beasts come clomping down the stone tunnels of the fortress, scattering the sunlight and the birds. Zeroes, hundreds of them, wave their scythes back and forth across the men and women who are trying to flee. Wade tries to stand in front of me, and he's cut down with all the rest. Blood sprays through the air, wetting my face and clinging to my hair.

"Stop!" I scream, but it's too late.

Wade, Wokee, and countless others lie stretched out on the ground at my feet. Every one of them is dead.

My eyes fly open.

My surroundings come into focus. Panting, I look around the dimly-lit room. Ry is lying on her back next to me. My thin blanket lies in a heap on the far side of the cave; I must have thrown it while fighting my imaginary foes.

I lie still as I wait for my harsh breathing to return to normal. I tell myself it was just a dream, but the image of all those dead Solguards lingers in my mind.

Have I made a huge mistake? The Zeroes are too strong, too wild. *What if Dayne was right?*

But then I think about Wokee and Wade and all the rest of the rebels. Not as they appeared in my dream, but as they actually are. They are the reason why I created the Zeroes.

I swipe a hand across my eyes. *You will save us all.*

CHAPTER 34

I expected my father to resist coming with us. Instead, he relents after only a brief argument. I suspect it's because he doesn't want the Zeroes to be far from his sight. Inwardly, I'm relieved. He's the only other person who really understands the Zeroes. If we're going to mount any kind of reasonable defense against the Duskers, I have a feeling I'm going to need his help.

I had feared my father wouldn't want to give up control of the ten Zeroes he made before bringing me to the Lair. But for some reason I don't dare question, he seems content just to observe them, even if he isn't the one commanding them anymore.

After much grumbling from Ry and Jarosh, and a quiet sort of angry resignation from Dayne, it's agreed that Zeidan will ride Vlaz with them.

The Halves, Zeroes, and I will cover the distance on foot. Jarosh doesn't want to let Camike out of his sight, but Vlaz is still recovering from his injury, and Camike is strong and fast enough to make the run. It's only when she murmurs to him and places a soft kiss on his forehead that Jarosh relents.

I take off with the Zeroes first to get them away from Vlaz. Every time the hyenair gets a whiff of them, he becomes wild, snapping his fangs and lunging like a beast possessed.

The Halves follow, although they aren't as fast as the Zeroes.

It feels good to run, especially now that we're running to the fortress rather than away from Malarusk. It feels good to be doing *something*.

We keep to the trees for as long as we can, going out of our way to avoid Malarusk. I look up when Vlaz's shadow crosses overhead, and then I pick up my pace until it's almost like I'm flying myself.

Even though the air is stifling, my energy doesn't wane as I cross the distance on what feels like weightless feet. The clumsiness that's plagued me my whole life, the way my two legs never seemed to quite understand what the other was going to do, has disappeared. Rocks and roots littering my path don't get in my way. Every part of me just feels better…more fluid and more certain. Like I make sense now in a way I hadn't before.

My pace flags only when I crest a steep rise. The distance is growing between the Zeroes and Halves and me, so I stop to give them time to catch up. From where I'm standing, I can see the lines of Zeroes approaching, and the three Halves far behind them.

I wait, admiring the graceful movements of the Zeroes. Their legs pump across the uneven ground, their taut muscles flexing with every step. They don't stumble on the rocks or slow when they reach the hill. They aren't even breathing hard, in spite of all the extra weight their armor adds. As they come closer, their energy surrounds me like a hundred small suns.

I turn back in the direction we're headed. But before I can reorient myself, my attention catches on something else.

To the north, where I can just make out the iron gate marking the entrance to Malarusk, smoke is rising. For a second, my heart leaps. Maybe the citadel is on fire. Maybe the Duskers are under attack. But a prickling, sinking feeling tells me the smoke means something else. The smoke is too dense, too black, and I know instinctively that it means something far worse for us than for the Duskers.

There must be hundreds of fires burning to create so much smoke, even though I can't see any flames from here. As the billowing clouds meet with the sky overhead, the clear blue transforms to black. It looks like someone took a giant blackwood pencil and scratched out the normal color of the sky.

Could this smoke have something to do with the weapon the Banished leaders said the Duskers were building?

The wind shifts, and I catch a familiar, acrid scent. I shield my face inside the collar of my shirt and blink the gritty feel from my eyes. It takes only a moment to place the smell. It's the same scent that hovered over the dying Solguards in the healing cave. I remember Wade saying every Solguard who ventured near Malarusk came back covered in that foul-smelling black substance.

It's the same smell, I'm sure of it.

But whatever was covering those Solguards wasn't smoke. It was something sticky and tar-like.

I blink as the haze settles like a blanket between the hillock and the citadel. My lungs feel like weights in my chest. When the wind shifts, pulling the smoke away, I inhale a breath of clean air. The ache in my lungs starts to recede.

When I squint in the direction of Malarusk, I notice the empty land the smoke had just been overlaying looks different. The ground is no longer a sandy brown, but black as pitch. *The smoke stained the ground black, just like it did to the men in Solis.*

I once saw a place in the forest outside Subterrane Harkibel that had been ravaged by a cook fire that wasn't extinguished. The leaves were burned off the trees and everything was covered with gray ashes for days. But the ground never turned black.

A strange, eerie silence has blanketed the land, as though the smoke swept all life away with it.

I make a mental note to talk to Wade about it when I'm back at Solis. Maybe his scouts have discovered something more about what the Duskers are planning that will make all of this make sense. With a last glance, I turn my back on the smoke.

I don't slow again until the trees thicken and I have to follow a winding path through the underbrush. The Zeroes are behind me. Even though I can't see them through the dense foliage, I can feel their presence. The invisible tethers connecting me to each of them give me comfort. I know they feel it too, and are unwilling to test the limits of the bond between us.

I'm so lost in my thoughts I don't process the sound of twigs snapping. I step past the trunk of an enormous script tree and run straight into someone. Stumbling from the force of the collision, I distantly register the glint of sunlight on a sword's blade. Before I can regain my footing, hard steel crashes into the bare skin at my neck.

CHAPTER 35

*C*rack.

A sliver of pain darts across my neck just as two shards of metal fall to the ground on either side of me. I look down, too stunned and confused to do anything else. *A sword's blade…broke…on me.*

"Hemera!"

What's left of the sword's hilt clatters onto the stone ground as arms fold me into an embrace that robs me of breath. His voice, his smell, the familiar shelter of his arms, enfold me. *Wade.*

"I could have killed you." He pulls back to look at me, sheer amazement reflected in his eyes. "I should have killed you—" his voice hitches. He lets go of me and presses a hand to the trunk of a tree, steadying himself.

Wade's honey-colored eyes, boring into me and making me feel stripped bare, make my heart lurch into my throat.

"I think I did more damage to your sword than it did to me," I point out, making an attempt at levity.

"But that doesn't make any sense." Wade stares at the shards of steel on the ground. "Even you're not that strong."

I shrug, even though I know the explanation lies in my link with the Zeroes. What had my father called it? *Blood bond.*

"Tell me Zeidan hasn't been…doing experiments on you." Wade looks me up and down, his face darkening with rage. "Has he hurt you?"

"Wade, no one can hurt me." I gesture at the broken sword for emphasis.

"But," Wade shakes his head. "How is this possible?"

I let out a shaky breath. There's nothing I want more than to bury my face in his chest and breathe him in. I want to stare at his beautiful face and forget about everything else.

"It's complicated," I say. And then, after a pause, "What are you doing out here by yourself?"

"I was coming to get you."

"Me?" A thousand questions rush to the surface, but Wade anticipates them.

"The Duskers haven't come yet. My scouts report they haven't left the citadel."

"Oh." I swallow. "Then, why—"

"The Banished leaders," Wade says. "They said you had your week to return with Hendrix, and they refuse to wait any longer. They've sent messengers ahead to their settlements. Hemera, they're surrendering."

"When?"

"They leave next low day."

"They can't." I'm already striding ahead.

"What happened in Malarusk?" Wade practically has to jog to keep up with me.

When I don't answer, he puts a hand on my shoulder and spins me around to face him. "What happened with Hendrix?"

While I try to find a way to explain what's happened, his next question knocks the breath from me.

"Hemera, is Jadem really dead?"

I look at Wade and let him read the answer in my expression.

He hangs his head.

When Wade meets my gaze, I notice the hollowed-out look to his cheeks, the shadows darkening the planes of his face. Seeing the grief in his eyes is almost like watching Crowe kill Aunt Jadem all over again.

"Hemera, I—"

The ground trembles from the pounding of many sets of heavy boots. Wade looks down at his fallen sword, before seeming to remember why it's in pieces, and then draws a dagger from his belt. As the Zeroes come into view, the sound of their sniffing fills the air. They stop a short way from me.

Wade snarls like a cornered beast. He pushes me behind him, shielding me, even though he must know there's nothing he or his dagger could do to cause the Zeroes even the slightest bit of harm. The Zeroes' black eyes are trained on me.

"We couldn't get Hendrix," I say, putting my hand over Wade's and lowering the dagger. "But I have something else." I swallow. "Something better."

I don't know where to begin, so I just start talking. Wade stands completely still as I tell him about the Dusker prisoners, and how I used my blood and the Halves' to change them.

I stop just short of the battle with the Dusker recruits. My throat is dry from talking, and my memory of the little Dusker girl is still too raw.

After a pause I'm afraid will stretch into forever, Wade rakes a hand through his hair. "So, these Zeroes…you control them?"

I nod, grateful he hasn't turned around and run from me. *At least, not yet.*

He's quiet as he regards the Zeroes, with their metal clothes and scythes. "Okay. I can't believe I'm going to say this. But this might just work." His eyes sweep over the Zeroes.

"Really?"

He nods. "There are thousands of soldiers in Malarusk already, and more Banished are joining them every day." Wade wipes sweat from his forehead with the back of his glove. "We just don't have the numbers. I have no idea what else to do to keep everyone alive."

I can see on Wade's face what this admission has cost him.

He looks so vulnerable just standing there. I wind my arms around him and lean my head against his chest. I feel, rather than hear, his sigh as he pulls me closer.

"If you can convince the Banished to fight with us, and these Zeroes are as strong as you say, we might have a chance." Wade kisses the top of my head. "Not that I won't still strangle your father the first chance I get." He laughs without humor.

I drop my arms and step back, unable to meet the intensity of his gaze.

"I did something." I swallow. "Something horrible."

Before I can say anything else, a ground-shuddering thump announces the arrival of Vlaz.

"Wade!" Ry slides off Vlaz's sweat-lathered back and throws herself at him.

A confusing wave of emotions flashes through me.

Don't be stupid, I tell myself. After all that's happened…after all that is going to happen…there are far more important things to be worrying about. *Like how to save the entire Solguard fortress.*

Ry catches my eye as she hugs Wade. She looks at me in a way that makes my face heat.

"Where's Camike?" Jarosh demands, his eyes moving restlessly over the trees.

"Behind us," I motion in the direction. "They weren't as fast, but they'll be here."

Without a word, Jarosh is stomping off, back in the direction we came from.

"Jarosh has a girlfriend," Ry says in answer to Wade's raised eyebrows.

"A mate," Dayne corrects, sliding to the ground and shaking the hand Wade extends to him.

My father is the last one to join our circle. His eyes flick to the ground, where Wade's sword still lies in pieces. His gaze passes between the shards of steel to me, recognition spreading across his face.

"Interesting," is all he says. He holds my gaze for another second before turning his attention to Wade.

"Wade, is it?"

Wade's jaw tightens. "How do you know my name?"

My father stares at him without emotion. "What kind of parent would I be if I didn't know about the man pursuing my daughter?"

Wade lets out a harsh laugh. "What kind of parent tries to kill his own daughter?"

My father meets Wade's accusatory gaze without batting an eye. "Hemera needed to understand her own strength. There is no room in this world for the weak." He gives Wade a sidelong look, as if to ask, *Are* you *weak?*

Wade bristles, but before either of them can say anything more, Jarosh and the Halves come into view. We all look at Jarosh, who has his arm wrapped around Camike's waist.

Wade, for his part, manages to keep a straight face as Jarosh makes introductions.

"Nice to, uh, meet you." Wade holds out his hand to Camike, who takes it in her larger hand and offers him a shy smile.

"The Zeroes need to be fed," my father says, either oblivious—or more likely, indifferent—to our party's reunion.

"What do they eat?" I ask, feeling guilty for not having thought of their needs before.

"You must be eager to speak with the Banished leaders," my father tells me. "If you will find a place in the fortress for them to stay, I can take care of the rest."

"That's awfully generous of you." Dayne gives him a suspicious glare.

Zeidan sighs. "You are the ones who insisted I come with you. I can't imagine you would rather have me idle?"

"Feeding the Zeroes would be great," I tell my father.

I give Dayne a pleading look. *Now isn't the time.*

We make our way back to the fortress. The easy chatter that usually flows between us has turned into a weighted silence.

When we come into view of the Solguard archers ringing the caves' entrance, Wade exchanges words with them to make sure neither the Zeroes nor the Halves are attacked as we enter. Jarosh holds Camike close, daring the soldiers with his eyes to even think about coming near her.

"Hemera! Dayne!"

My heart lightens at the sight of Wokee emerging from the fortress. Hardly aware of what I'm doing, I shift my body so I'm standing between Wokee and the Zeroes.

Wokee's curls are plastered to his forehead from the waterfall. He throws himself at me, and then, before I can wrap my arms around him, he's tackling Dayne.

When it's Jarosh's turn, he slaps Wokee's hand in some complicated pattern that is lost on the rest of us. When Wokee catches sight of Camike, her hand wrapped around Jarosh's waist, his jaw drops.

"Wokee," Jarosh announces. "Meet my mate and the love of my life."

Ry rolls her eyes. "Laying it on a little thick, don't you think?"

"She's not ugly, I guess." Wokee wrinkles his nose. "But she's still a girl."

"Indeed she is." Jarosh winks. "And so much more."

Wokee giggles. "You're gross." His gaze moves to the Zeroes, and his eyes go wide. "Those are the monsters that tried to kill you at Tanguro, aren't they?"

Wokee pulls out his small dagger, which looks like a toy compared to the Zeroes' scythes.

Seeing Wokee standing next to the Zeroes makes my blood run cold. For a moment, it's not him, but the little Dusker girl. My heart stalls in my chest.

Wokee continues to fire questions at me, but I can't make my mouth form the words to answer them.

Dayne steps in when I stay silent. "Yes, they're going to help us defeat the Duskers, no they aren't as strong as Hemera, no you can't fight with them."

And then Wokee asks the question that snaps me back to reality.

"Is Jadem really dead?"

When I don't say anything—can't say anything—Dayne crouches to the ground in front of Wokee.

"She is."

Wokee's chin wobbles. "The Duskers killed her, didn't they?"

Dayne nods.

"Are the Duskers going to kill us, too?"

"No." I clench and unclench my fists. "I'll never let them hurt you. I swear by the sun." There is a fierceness in my voice I don't recognize. "I couldn't save Jadem, but I'll never let them touch you."

Wokee's lower lip is still trembling. Dayne leans in and whispers something to him. When he stands back up, Wokee sniffles and wipes his sleeve across his eyes.

"Hemera," Dayne looks at me. "It's time."

I nod, taking a shuddering breath. "Wade, get the Banished leaders. I'm convening the council."

CHAPTER 36

Ry breaks off from our party first, saying she needs to talk with the archers. I know she's really going to find Dellin. It irks me, even though I have plenty of more important issues to be worrying about.

Jarosh, Camike, and Brogut go to check on the rest of the Halves.

I tell Dayne, Ekil, and Wade that I'll meet them at the council. My connection with the Zeroes tugs at me, and I know I won't be able to focus on anything else until I know they're taken care of.

I open the door to the chamber set far into the recesses of the fortress where we agreed to keep the Zeroes. Their heads are bent over the remains of whatever animal my father fed them. My father stands in the center of the room, observing their every move with undisguised fascination.

"Do I want to know what they're eating?" I ask, stepping into the room.

Scenting me, the Zeroes lift their heads. I push down a shudder at the sight of their blood-stained teeth.

"We all need to eat," my father replies.

"What happened to your arm?"

We both look at the bandage wrapped around his forearm.

"Just a scratch," he replies.

"I need you to keep an eye on them during the council meeting," I say. "I want you to wait outside the meeting chamber and bring them in when I call for them."

From the last council meeting, I know these Banished leaders have a taste for the dramatic. If I'm going to keep them from running off to Malarusk at low day, I'll need all the drama I can conjure.

My father nods. "You'll have to command them to follow me, of course."

I look at the Zeroes nearest to me. "When he comes to find me," I make an exaggerated gesture at my father. "Follow him."

The Zeroes' only reply is their sniffing.

My father and I watch the Zeroes in silence for several minutes.

"What if the Banished leaders don't think they're enough?" I blurt out.

My father gives me an amused look.

"It's just, Aunt Jadem was always able to convince them, but…."

"With her gone, you don't think they'll be as receptive?" my father offers.

I nod.

"You don't need to convince them," he says. "You show them."

"How?"

"If I were you," my father gives me a sly look, "I'd do it like the festival."

"But how do I—"

"*Think*, daughter."

The Dark God festival. It was a yearly celebration in the Subterrane territory required by the Duskers. There was extra food, costumes, and special dances. But the best part was the competition. The strongest Dwellers competed in events, and the winner was always recognized in a special ceremony attended by a Dusker Captain.

The most popular event was the wrestling.

I look at my father. He nods, seeing my understanding.

My mind turns over what I'm going to say…what I'm going to do…as I lead my father and a dozen of the Zeroes down the thousand steps—it seemed easier than trying to explain to them how to use the glide.

I line them up just outside the meeting chamber, where they won't be seen until I'm ready.

"Wait until I call for you," I tell my father.

He nods.

"And keep any Solguards from coming this way. I don't want anyone panicking and trying to attack them."

My father nods again.

I step past the two men guarding the entrance to the meeting chamber, and then turn back. I surprise myself when I say, "Thanks for…you know…."

My father looks at me. "It's my pleasure."

As soon as I step into my aunt's meeting chamber, my eyes go to the chair at the head of the long wooden table—Aunt Jadem's seat. It's empty.

I thought I knew what to expect when I returned to the fortress, but nothing could prepare me for the grief that crashes over me like a wave. My knees wobble.

You didn't die for nothing, I think. *I won't let you have died for nothing.*

With a force of will, I look away from the empty chair and take my seat at the table.

"Well, now that the Bisecter is here, can we get this over with?" Tut, the gold threads in his goatee gleaming in the candlelight, makes an impatient motion with his hands. "Where's Hendrix?"

Valior, perched on his cushions with his flask cradled between his hands, cranes his head to see through the doorway like he expects Hendrix to magically appear.

"He's not coming," Dayne says.

"You do have him, though?" Liglette asks, fingering the beads in her long braid.

When no one says anything, Tut lets out a roar. "Lying Solguards!" He turns to Valior and Liglette. "I told you it was a waste of time staying here. I told you, didn't I?"

"Just a minute," I try to say, but they don't even hear me.

Tut scrapes back his chair and rises. "If you're done wasting our time, I have to finish packing."

"Sit down."

Wade's voice is even, barely raised, and yet a stillness falls over the room. I feel a fierce pride at the way all eyes turn to him.

"Young man." Valior points a gnarled finger at the empty chair. "The Solguards are leaderless now. We aren't bound to the council anymore. There is no council."

"Jadem appointed me as the Solguard leader in her absence," Wade says without missing a beat. "And I'm telling you," he meets the eyes of Tut, Valior, and Liglette, "to give us an hour of your time."

When no one argues, Wade nods. "Sit down."

Tut sits.

My insides flood with feeling…gratitude, pride, and something else I can't name. Something that makes my heart beat a little faster.

"Hemera," Wade says. "Tell them."

I swallow. "We went to get Hendrix because you needed proof the Solguards could stand up to the Dusker army." I look at my brother, who gives me an encouraging nod. "We don't have Hendrix, but we have something else. Something better."

Liglette raises her index finger. "I'm afraid we've already made our choice. We will send messengers announcing our surrender to Crowe as soon as it's low day. Meanwhile, we will return to our settlements. We, and our people, will seek refuge in Malarusk."

"Whatever *proof* you've dredged up," Tut says, "we're not going to wait around for the Duskers to annihilate us with their weapon."

I remember the black smoke billowing up from the citadel, and I can't think of a response.

"Unless you dug up a thousand or two new soldiers we haven't heard about before…." Valior says with a chuckle, which turns into choking as he takes a sip from his flask.

"That's exactly what we have," I say.

That gets their attention.

"We have something that has the strength of a thousand soldiers," I modify.

"You aren't yanking our chains again, are you, girl?" Valior asks before his words dissolve into coughing.

"I can prove it to you," I reply.

"Well, this I gotta see." Tut gives me a gold-toothed grin.

"Guards," I call.

When the two men poke their heads into the room, I say, "Tell the Captain we're ready."

For a moment, nothing happens. And then my father enters the chamber, followed by a dozen of the Zeroes. The links of their metal armor clink together as the Zeroes file in, their right hands holding their scythes.

Liglette gasps. Tut's eyes flit around the room like he's looking for an escape. Valior grips the edge of the table as he wobbles on his cushions.

The Zeroes look even bigger standing in this confined space. A little thrill passes through me at the thought that I, and I alone, control them. I feel the tug of our connection, like an invisible rope tethering me to each of them.

"The Duskers might have a weapon," I say, breaking the silence, "but so do we."

"How many?" Valior asks.

At my answer, Tut scoffs. "That's a drop in the bucket."

"The Duskers have ten-thousand strong," Valior agrees.

"Each Zero has the strength of ten, even twenty soldiers," I argue. "They are part Halve and part Bisecter. My blood, my strength, runs through their veins."

"With your thousands, and the Halves," Wade tells the Banished leaders, "we'll be strong enough to rival the Duskers."

I confer with Ekil, and he bobs his head. "The Halves will help destroy gray cloaks," he says.

"Hell of a lot better than Hendrix," Wade says. "Wouldn't you all agree?"

"If what you're saying about these—" Valior taps a finger against the side of his flask as he searches for the right word "—creatures is true, if they're really as strong as you say, it might be enough."

My heart surges.

"But," he wags a finger.

My hope plummets.

"You lied to us about Hendrix." He peers at me through watery eyes. "And I'm not going to make the mistake of taking you at your word again."

Tut and Liglette nod in agreement.

"For all we know," Tut lets out a deep-throated laugh. "You're just blowing steam up our asses."

"Don't take my word for it," I say, ignoring Tut's smirk. "You can see how strong they are for yourselves."

"What are you proposing?" Liglette asks.

Wade and I exchange a glance.

"What I propose," I say, "is a demonstration."

Liglette shakes her head. "I fear there is nothing you can say or do to sway me at this point. For my part, my decision is made."

Wade leans forward, resting his elbows on the table. His golden eyes pierce each of the leaders in turn. "You're not going anywhere. Not until you've seen what the Zeroes can do."

The three Banished leaders exchange a look.

"Very well," Valior says. "We will give you an hour of our time in the low day, and not a minute more."

Wade and I exchange a relieved look. I want to jump up and punch the air in victory, but I force myself to stay seated.

"If we don't like what we see," Tut warns, and then he shakes his head. "If we don't *love* what we see…."

"We're out of here," Valior finishes.

"And our surrender to the Duskers will be final," Liglette adds.

"Low day it is," Wade says. "We'll be ready."

CHAPTER 37

I close the Zeroes inside their chamber. When I step into the tunnel, Wokee barrels into me. Vlaz, who is trotting behind him, comes to a skidding stop. The hyenair looks even bigger than usual. I take a step back before thinking, and then I feel stupid for being afraid of Vlaz.

"I brought you this," Wokee says, putting something sticky into my hands.

I look down to see a mostly-crushed berry tart, the purple juices staining Wokee's hands and now mine.

"Um, thanks?"

"Come on," he takes my hand. "You too, Dayne. There's something I want to show you."

Dayne raises his eyebrows, but he follows as Wokee tugs me deeper into the fortress. Vlaz trots after us, making the ground tremble with his every footfall. His giant tongue snakes out and, before I can react, the remains of the decrepit tart have disappeared.

I remember the way Vlaz growled at me in the Lair, but it seems like he's back to himself now. It must have been the combination of his injury and the unfamiliar place. I decide not to tell Wokee about it.

Everyone we pass flattens themselves against the sides of the path to avoid Vlaz.

Wokee takes us to a part of the fortress I've never been to before. I can tell from the smell of earth and growing things we're approaching the orchards. But instead of taking us to fruit-bearing trees or a root garden, Wokee stops in front of a small cave. Unlike the tunnels, which are cavernous enough to let in sunlight without it filtering all the way down, this cave is lit only by candles. Vlaz, who is too big for the space, waits on the path as Dayne and I follow Wokee inside.

Stretched across the entire wall is what looks like a quilt. On closer inspection, I realize it's not made from wool or cloth, but living flowers. The blooms are Solguard blue, and they're woven in the shape of the rebel sun.

"I did it for Jadem," Wokee says. "You know, to honor her."

"Wokee," I breathe, tears springing to my eyes.

"They'll keep growing," Wokee says. He points to where the flowers' delicate vines are burrowing into the crevices of the stone wall.

"It's perfect," I tell him.

"Jadem's the only one who could ever figure out how to make things grow underground," Wokee says, studying the flowers.

"Not the only one," Dayne corrects. He rests a hand on Wokee's head.

"We're like family, aren't we?" Wokee asks, looking from Dayne to me.

"We *are* family." Dayne says. "The three of us."

"Vlaz, too," Wokee adds.

Vlaz, hearing his name, pokes his head into the doorway and gives a happy wiggle of his body.

"The four of us," Dayne amends.

"And nothing's gonna happen to you, right?" Wokee asks.

The look in his eyes squeezes my heart.

"We're all going to protect each other," Dayne says, wrapping an arm around Wokee.

"Well, we do have Hemera on our side. Who's going to mess with a Bisecter?" Wokee sniffles, laughs. "I bet she's stronger than a thousand Duskers."

"Two thousand!" Dayne counters, ruffling Wokee's curls.

My hand goes to the silver key at my throat as I look at Dayne and Wokee. I feel stronger than ever, but it's not because of the Zeroes. It's because of the two people standing beside me. *My family.*

✳ ✳ ✳

After Wokee has run off, saying something about needing to water the spicy brittlebush—Dayne and I are left alone, staring at Wokee's living tribute to Aunt Jadem.

"Are you sure about this demonstration?" Dayne asks me. "Zeroes fighting Duskers is one thing, but letting the Solguards fight them?"

"It's the only way to convince everyone of how strong they are," I say. "The Zeroes won't have weapons, and I'll tell them to disarm, not hurt."

Dayne's frown deepens. "What happens when someone holds a dagger to their throat? We don't really know anything about their true nature."

"Obeying me *is* their nature," I counter. "My blood runs through their veins. They have no choice but to do as I command."

Dayne's face looks pained.

"It won't last long," I say, trying to ease some of his worries. "It'll only take a few minutes for everyone to see no human is a match for the Zeroes."

"I wish I had some alternative to offer," Dayne sighs. "But I don't."

"It's going to be fine," I tell him.

We stand in silence for a few more minutes, each lost in our own thoughts.

"I'm going to find the musicians," Dayne says. He turns back to the tunnel. "There's gotta be someone on this sinking ship with a lute to spare."

Dayne and I split off at the glide. I'm so focused on everything that needs to be done, I don't even notice where my feet are taking me until I'm standing outside the door to Wade's chamber. As soon as I realize where I am, my face heats, and I turn to double back the way I came.

Before I take a step, the door opens and Wade is standing there, shirtless.

"Hello." His golden eyes sparkle as they follow the direction of my gaze. I realize I'm devouring him with my eyes. I force myself to look back up to his face.

"Hi," I manage.

There are so many things I need to say to Wade. A thousand unspoken words hang between us. But right now, I don't care about a single one of them.

I leap forward, and Wade barely has time to wrap his arms around me before I catapult us backward into his room. His deep, husky laugh tickles my ear as he shuts the door behind us.

Whatever it was that made me pause the last time I was here is gone, replaced with something frenzied and wild. I don't just want Wade, I *need* him.

"Hemera," Wade laughs again. "What's gotten into you?"

"I have no idea," I answer as I trace a line of kisses across his stubbled jaw.

He takes my face in his hands, making me still, and meets my black eyes with his honey ones. His brow is furrowed in concern.

"Don't get me wrong, I'll go along with this plan in a second." Wade searches my face. "But there's something…different."

I know Wade is just trying to protect me, to keep me safe from doing something I might regret. But those words sting.

After I rescued Brice in Tanguro, he told me I had changed. As much as I had wanted to fall back into our old patterns the moment we were reunited, those words hung between us, and we were never the same.

"Not like it's a bad thing," Wade says. "Just, you're not yourself. I can tell."

"You don't know everything about me," I snap.

"I'd like to." His eyes rake over me, making me feel warm.

My anger vanishes.

"You're right," I say. "I guess it's just been…a lot."

A lot doesn't even come close to covering it, but Wade nods in understanding.

"When was the last time you slept?" he asks.

"I—" I pause, thinking about it. "I don't remember."

Wade takes my hand and leads me over to his bed. My blood stirs and I reach for him, but Wade shakes his head.

"You need sleep, love."

He seats me on the edge of the bed and pulls off my boots. Then, he undoes the tie of my cloak and pulls the hood back, letting his fingers linger at the nape of my neck. It feels so good I reach for him again, but he steps back, chuckling.

"You'll be the death of me, Hemera."

Wade presses me back against the pillow and pulls the thin blanket up to my chin, tucking me in like I'm a child. Then, he climbs onto the bed and molds his body to mine.

"Sleep, love." He kisses my hair and wraps his arms around me.

Sleep is the last thing I want right now, but with the warmth of Wade's body and the steady rhythm of his heartbeat, it's exactly what I do.

CHAPTER 38

I can't breathe. Darkness presses in on me on all sides. And then, out of nowhere, I'm blinded by light. A raging fire surrounds me.

There are people. I see their shadowy figures as they try to claw their way through the roaring flames. They call out to me, begging for help. I throw myself into the fire to reach them. But no matter how far I push into the inferno, I never get any closer.

Voices cry out to me from every direction.

"Where are you?" I yell.

With every step I take, the flames grow hotter. My clothes and hair disintegrate. My skin is burning too fast to heal itself. Smoke and heat fill my lungs until I can't breathe.

They're dying, all of them, and there's nothing I can do.

A form rises out of the fire. It's the Dusker girl, her face covered in black scars. Flames pour from her eyes and mouth.

"Hemera, wake up."

Someone is screaming. My entire body is convulsing. I tear free from the arms holding me back.

"I have to save her." My voice is raspy from the smoke. To the little girl, I shout, "Where are you?"

"Shh, love. It's just a dream."

"Let go. I have to go. I have to save her!"

"Open your eyes, Mer. Come back to me."

That voice. The smoke begins to clear.

Wade. My eyes flick over the dimly-lit room, and I remember where I am. My face still feels hot, like the flames really were erupting all around me. I look down, expecting to see scorch marks on my skin and clothes…expecting to see the charred remains of the little girl.

"I gave the order," I whisper. "It's my fault."

Wade draws me against him. "What order? What's your fault?"

The feel of his arms around me helps the fire still raging in my mind begin to recede.

"Wade, something happened with the Zeroes. Something I made them do."

I force myself to tell Wade about the Zeroes' first battle. I speak quickly, trying to get it all out before I lose my nerve.

When I tell him about the Dusker child, Wade's face goes ashen.

"It was my fault," I say, unable to look at him. "If it hadn't been for me—"

"Hemera." Wade's voice is husky. "I know what it's like, believe me." He bends so I'm forced to meet his gaze. "I can't close my eyes without seeing all the scouts I've sent out, only to have their burned remains brought back to me."

His golden eyes slide away from me. "If Sal had been here, those soldiers would probably still be alive." He laughs bitterly. "I couldn't even convince the Banished to choose us over the Duskers."

"You're an amazing leader," I choke out, overcome by the addition of his pain and regret to my own. "Sal and Jadem would be proud of you. I know it."

The intensity of Wade's gaze as it meets mine is almost overwhelming. Even though it's the last thing I should be thinking about, my eyes are drawn to the perfect curve of his lips. He reaches out and touches the metal rays of the pendant dangling next to my mother's key around my neck.

"How can you even stand to be near me, after everything I've done?" I ask, my voice unsteady.

Wade stops tracing the pattern of the necklace and looks at me. "More easily than you can possibly imagine." His lips graze my forehead, my hair, the tip of my nose.

"We only have a couple hours until low day," I force myself to say. My internal clock, honed from so much time spent underground, is almost as accurate as my shadow in the sunlight. "I have to check on the Zeroes, and I'm sure you have a million things to do before the demonstration."

Sighing, Wade rolls over me, making me laugh for the first time since the Dusker girl was killed. He lands on his feet and holds out a hand to me.

We dress quickly and head up to the second level of the fortress. My mind is already going through a mental checklist of everything I have to do, but Wade isn't finished with me yet. Before we reach the main tunnel, he pulls me behind a column.

"Just in case you had any illusions that I wasn't interested...." Emotion flickers in the gold of his eyes. Wade bends his head until our lips meet.

I should pull away. Anyone coming down the tunnel could see us. But I can't bring myself to care. I wrap my arms around Wade's neck, parting my lips. A soft moan escapes him, the vibrations thrumming against my skin. Warmth turns to fire as he deepens the kiss.

"You know, I'll give the humans one thing." Jarosh, Camike in tow, saunters toward us. "They sure know how to feather a mattress." He leans against the wall next to us, either oblivious to—or not caring about—the fact that Wade and I are wrapped in each other's arms.

"You don't say," Wade deadpans, stepping back from me.

Ry and Dellin are behind them, followed by Ekil and Brogut. Dellin doesn't say a word to me, but my attention goes straight to her anyway. She has her hand resting on Ry's waist...like she owns her. When Ry sees me looking, she gives a pointed stare at Wade, and then quirks her lips into a half-smile. She runs her tongue over her top lip, keeping eye contact with me the whole time, before leaning in to whisper something to Dellin.

I look at Wade, but he doesn't seem to have noticed the exchange. Annoyance and guilt war within me.

Jarosh yawns. "Nothing like a good high day's sleep before I beat up a bunch of Zeroes."

"Wait." Ry puts up her hand. "You're going to try and fight the Zeroes?"

Jarosh shrugs. "I am the strongest soldier in the fortress." His smile grows as Camike turns her attention on him. "You know, after Hemera, of course." He stands on his toes to kiss Camike on the cheek. "It will be my responsibility to throw my hat into the challenge, so to speak."

"Brogut fight too," the Halve says. He is busy sharpening his nails on the pointed end of his new tree trunk. He hasn't even bothered to cut off the roots, which are dribbling a trail of dirt in his wake.

"Better get the healers ready," Ry mutters.

I want to tell Jarosh not to fight them, to wait until they've been tested more, but I know how that would seem. If I don't believe in my ability to control the Zeroes, then no one will, and the Banished leaders will leave without ever having seen what they can do. So, I swallow all the warnings that want to leap out of my mouth and just nod.

We move in a group up the thousand steps. Even though Jarosh and Camike are chatting—loudly—in some language that is neither human nor Halve, a strange quiet surrounds our company.

Something about the fortress seems different. I look around, trying to place it. The waterfalls still burble along the rock walls. There are Solguards coming and going. It's even more crowded than usual with the Halves being here. Even so, there is a distinct absence of…*something*.

"The kynthia birds are gone."

Wade stops walking, one foot hovering over the next step.

"They all just dropped dead one day." He looks up, like he expects to see them still fluttering overhead. "They fell out of the air by the dozens. It was awful."

"When Crowe killed Aunt Jadem?" I ask in a whisper. "How could they have known?"

"It's said they recognize each other by the sound of their heartbeats," Dellin says.

I give her a look that says *I don't think anyone asked for your opinion.*

Wade nods. "I have no idea how they knew, but…." He trails off, unable to finish.

I take Wade's hand, not caring who sees. He laces his fingers through mine and gives it a squeeze.

As soon as we reach the top step, we're immediately surrounded by scouts and soldiers all looking for Wade. He manages a quick smile in my direction before he's swallowed up by everyone who needs a piece of him.

Hearing footsteps behind me, I turn to see Ekil.

"You give your word about protecting Halves if we help you?" Ekil asks.

"I promise I'll do everything I can to get your river back," I tell him. "If we can defeat the Duskers, the Banished will leave you alone. I'll make sure the Halves aren't bothered anymore."

That satisfies Ekil, but worry gnaws at me. Is this just going to be another Tanguro? Am I just leading them to their deaths?

Even if the Banished agree to join us, and even if we can somehow reconstruct Solis to be defendable, people are still going to die. Lots of them.

Ekil and the others have already lost so much.

There's nothing else I can do, but it still feels flimsy to promise to help them only after my enemy is defeated. It doesn't matter that the Halves share the same enemy…it still feels wrong somehow.

One thought—the image of my aunt's body decomposing somewhere behind the iron gate—is all it takes to remind me. I'm doing this for her…for everyone who died at Tanguro.

You will save us all.

CHAPTER 39

There you are."

My father, seated on the ground in the center of the Zeroes' chamber, rolls up the script tree bark he was writing on. He adjusts the bandage on his arm and stands up.

The Zeroes, which had been standing still as statues, begin their sniffing as soon as they sense my presence. All of their heads turn to me at once, their black eyes boring into me. As though they're one creature, they heave a deep sigh.

I feel it, too.

It's like I'm where I am supposed to be. With the Zeroes so close, I'm whole again. Raw power flows down the tether between us.

My body feels tight, like a coiled spring that has been packed into too small a space. For the first time, my aunt's words seem less like a hopeless wish and more like a promise. With this army, I can save everyone. I *will*.

"Are you ready?" My father regards me.

I nod.

"Good, because you'll have to be explicit with your instructions if you want to avoid any more...accidents.

With those few words, all of my confidence vanishes and the old doubts come crashing back.

"Will you be there, just in case?" I ask, hating the note of uncertainty that my voice betrays.

"If you wish." My father scratches at the bandage on his arm. "But they're your Zeroes."

I notice there's fresh blood seeping through the bandage. "You should probably get that stitched up," I tell him.

"Careful daughter," the Captain replies, raising an eyebrow, "or I might start to think you care about me."

* * *

The entire fortress has turned out to see the Zeroes. All of the reactions—the gasps and whispers and open-mouthed stares—follow at a respectful distance as we make our way to the Outside.

We follow the path to the clearing where the demonstration will be held. When I step through the trees and into the open space, it feels like a hive of insects has exploded inside my stomach.

An enormous arena has been set up, marked off by wooden logs stacked four high all the way around. Various weapons are piled outside the arena's entrance for anyone who challenges the Zeroes.

Surrounding the arena on all sides are people and Halves. The noise they're making as the Zeroes step into the clearing is deafening. Some are blowing on small noisemakers, others are waving flags. All of them are waiting for us.

A long sheaf of script tree bark is tacked to a post beside the ring's entrance. A Solguard stands beside it, writing odds and the order of the fights with the nub of a blackwood pencil. Coins change hands as names are added onto the script tree scroll.

It's almost like this really is the Dark God festival…except with far higher stakes.

It should encourage me to see how many people turned out to see the Zeroes. Such a show of strength and numbers is what we need to convince the Banished to join us. But all I can think about are the ways this could all fall apart.

"Maybe Dayne was right," I tell my father. "What if I can't stop them? What if they kill someone?"

I'm ready for him to laugh or to make some snide comment, but he doesn't.

"It would be foolish not to maintain a healthy respect for something so powerful," my father says, his gaze sliding to me. "That's a lesson it took me too much time to learn."

I try not to show my surprise. If I didn't know him better, I would think there was remorse behind my father's words.

"Trust in the strength of your connection with them, daughter. So long as you are there with them, there can be no more or less bloodshed than you desire."

I take a deep breath and nod.

The crowd parts for the Zeroes. Fear and excitement fill the air in equal measures. I motion for the Zeroes to line up within view of the three Banished leaders who are sitting on wooden stools at the arena's edge.

"Hemera! There you are." Ry's curly red hair marks my friend in the crowd as she pushes her way to me. "Can you believe what's going on out here?"

"Someone's going to get killed," Dellin muses as she looks at the arena.

Fighters are already lining up. They look miniature next to the Zeroes; even the Halves look unthreatening in comparison.

"No one's getting killed," I say. And then, more quietly to Ry, I ask, "Can you have a few archers ready, just in case…?" I'm unable to finish the request that will lay bare my fears about the Zeroes.

Ry and Dellin exchange a swift look. Ry nods.

I incline my head toward the tall, leafy trees at the edge of the clearing. "I think it would be best for appearances' sake if you weren't too obvious about what you're doing."

"That shouldn't be a problem," Ry says. "We can stay far enough back that no one will even be able to see us from here." She winks at Dellin, and it makes me want to punch something.

"Good," I say, already walking away.

"Hey!" Ry jogs to catch up with me. "It's going to be great. You're great." She bends and kisses me on the cheek. And then she's running back to Dellin before I can react.

There's a roar from the crowd as the first competitor enters the arena. A quick flash of anger goes through me when I see it's Jarosh. *Why couldn't he let someone else go first?*

I tell myself I don't want him in the arena because he's still recovering, not because I doubt the Zeroes or my ability to control them.

Jarosh pumps his fists in the air, riling up the people who surround the arena. He shouts out suggestions for raising the bets. He kisses the hands of the women he passes, flashing his toothy smile and generally making an idiot of himself.

He steps up to the weapons piled outside of the arena. Jarosh makes a show of picking up each one, offering it to the crowd, and putting it back when their reaction isn't to his liking. When he selects a heavy, spiked ball and chain, the crowd roars in approval.

Jarosh gives the weapon a swing. There's a *crack* as a branch on a nearby tree snaps away at first contact with the spiked ball. Everyone applauds. A woman, one of Ry's archer friends, shouts, "I'll have your babies!"

Shaking my head, I turn my attention to the Zeroes, which stand stoically and await my orders.

"Disarm him and lay him on the ground," I tell the Zero that will be Jarosh's opponent. "Do not hurt him."

I look to my father for approval, and he nods.

I step back until I'm just outside the ring. I gnaw on my nails while I wait to see how the Zero will react to Jarosh's attack.

The crowd hushes as the two opponents make their way into the arena.

"You said each one of them was as strong as ten, even twenty, humans," Tut calls in the midst of the silence.

"I did," I reply, trying to keep my voice even.

"Then let nineteen more opponents enter the ring!"

His cry is met with a cheer of approval from the crowd.

I bite my lip. *Not for the first round,* I want to argue. There will be too much going on, too much out of my control. But if I say anything, it will seem like I don't think the Zero is strong enough.

"Trust your connection."

I hadn't even realized my father was standing right beside me until his voice is in my ear.

When I give a short nod, there is another roar from the spectators as the man taking bets selects the rest of the challengers. Most of the men are big and muscled and unfamiliar to me. But when Ekil, Brogut, and four other Halves enter the arena, the crowd goes wild.

Brogut raises his sharpened tree trunk above his head, shaking it the way Jarosh had with his weapon. But instead of cheers and applause, the crowd boos.

The Solguards tolerated the Halves' presence, first on Aunt Jadem's orders and now on Wade's. But that doesn't mean they don't want to see the Halves bleed. Many of the Solguards had family who were killed by Halves. Some of them still have relatives in the Banished lands who are battling the Halves for their lives. The Solguards want to see them defeated.

I scan the tree line looking for Ry and Dellin but see no sign of them.

At my command, the Zero steps into the arena. It's wearing its armor, but its scythe is on the ground at my feet. As the twenty men and Halves make a circle around the Zero, their weapons gripped in their hands, a heavy fear sinks into my bones. Whether my fear is for the opponents or the Zero, or some combination, I'm not sure.

The opponents are crouched low, prowling. The Zero, weaponless and towering over all of them, stands motionless. The crowd quiets in anticipation of the fight. I look to make sure the three Banished leaders have their attention fixed on the ring, and then I give the signal.

The man taking bets blows a short blast on his horn.

One of the Halves lunges. In a motion too fast to see, the Zero has disarmed him. The Halve is on his back, hands and feet flailing like an overturned bug, mouth open in a grunt of surprise that is drowned out by the yelling spectators.

A Solguard is next. He lets out a frustrated roar as his axe goes flying from his hands, and his sword is wrested from his grip with an imperceptible flick of the Zero's wrist. When the man rushes to tackle the Zero head-on, the Zero steps to the side a hair's breadth, causing the guard to launch himself into open air. The crowd roars with raucous laughter as the man collapses in the dirt.

One of the other men has picked up the fallen sword and is trying to come up behind the Zero, unobserved. For the briefest moment it seems his stealth might have paid off. And then the Zero spins around and grips the sword's naked blade in its bare hands. With an imperceptible tug, the Zero takes possession of the sword. To everyone's delight, the Zero raises the sword and brings it down on its bent knee. The blade cracks into pieces.

Jarosh signals to Ekil and Brogut, and the three of them attack together.

Jarosh moves like he's going to hit the Zero head-on, but at the last moment, he ducks left. The Zero is off balance for the briefest moment, but it's enough for Brogut to tackle the Zero from behind.

Jarosh scrambles to get out of the way as Brogut and the Zero roll on the ground, fighting for the dominant position. Brogut's hand searches for his fallen tree trunk, but when it rolls out of his grasp, Brogut reaches for the Zero's neck with his bare hands.

My breath catches when the dust settles and Brogut is seated on the Zero's chest. But before the crowd can react, the Zero bucks, throwing Brogut off. It doesn't even blink as it reaches up a hand and wraps it around the chain of Jarosh's weapon, which comes within striking distance of the Zero's shoulder. With a flick of the Zero's arm, the ball and chain are soaring out of the arena and into the trees. When Jarosh tries to tackle it, the Zero wraps its arms around Jarosh's middle, near to his old injury.

If the Zero re-opens Jarosh' wound, I'll never hear the end of it.

"Stop!" I yell.

The Zero goes motionless. Jarosh ducks under its grip.

Camike, who ran into the arena as soon as Jarosh lost his weapon, is pulling at Jarosh's hand, trying to get him to leave the ring. Jarosh is saying something to the spectators at the arena's edge that is making them hoot and whistle. Jarosh sweeps a hand behind Camike, dips her over his arm, and kisses her.

There is wild applause, boos, and jeers.

Wade is shouting at Jarosh to get the hell out of the arena. Someone trying to place a bet pushes past me, and I lose my balance. I'm still righting myself when I hear my father curse.

"Hemera—"

Brogut is running straight for the Zero, the sharpened edge of his tree trunk aimed at the Zero's stomach. The Zero isn't moving to defend itself. It doesn't turn its body to make itself a smaller target…it's just standing there.

"Hemera, your command," my father says, his voice urgent.

By the time I figure out what he means…that the Zero isn't defending itself because I ordered it to stop…it's too late.

A spray of black blood arcs through the air. There are screams as onlookers duck away from the poisonous blood.

It's the last thing I see before I collapse.

CHAPTER 40

Hemera. What's wrong? What's happened?"

My brother's face swims in and out of view.

"I'm bleeding...."

I hold my hand to the wound, trying to keep the torn flesh together. I've never known pain like this before. It's constant, unrelenting.

"What happened to her?" someone asks.

"It's not healing," I groan. *Why isn't it healing?*

"Hemera—"

"It hurts!" *Please, make it stop.*

"Hemera." Dayne is holding my face, forcing me to look at him. "Where are you hurt?"

"My stomach!" I scream.

"Get her cloak off," Dayne yells. "I can't see the wound."

"Hemera." My father's voice is calm. "You aren't injured."

Pain rushes through the wound anew, and I want to claw my father's calm right off his face.

"My stomach," I cry. Blood loss is making everything unfocused. I can feel the slickness where my hand is pressed to the wound.

They would all have to be blind not to see....

"You are not injured," my father says again. "Your Zero is."

With those words, my mind clears and my vision sharpens.

I hold up my hand, turning it over. Even though I swear I can feel the blood congealing on my palm, there's not a single drop. I brace myself, and then I look down at my stomach. Where there should be torn flesh, blood, and innards leaking, there's nothing. Not even a scratch.

But the pain is still there.

"It's your bond with them," my father says, shaking his head in fascination. "Their life force is tied to you, and in a way, so must yours be to them. It's a more powerful connection than I imagined."

"My sister isn't one of your experiments," Dayne snarls.

"Someone help that Zero!" I shriek, my voice sounding wild even to my own ears.

Doubled over, I limp into the arena. My father and Dayne follow, still arguing. Zeidan presses a bandage to the Zero's wound and begins to wrap it. I feel the pain in my own stomach ease just a bit.

"Did you know this would happen?" Dayne is asking.

"The nature of these things is that I don't have all the answers," my father replies.

Another agonizing shock of pain goes through my stomach. I grind my teeth as I wait for it to subside.

It's not real, I tell myself. I look down at my stomach, trying to prove it to my brain, but my mind is unconvinced. The pain is as real as the blood streaming from the wound in the Zero's stomach.

"What will happen to her if one of them is killed?" Dayne demands, his voice rising.

My father shrugs, but there are faint lines of worry creasing his brow. "That remains to be seen."

My attention goes to the bloodied tree trunk lying on the ground beside the Zero. *My* Zero. My gaze scans the crowd until I find who I'm looking for.

Brogut.

He hurt my Zero…tried to kill it. My feet are moving before my mind can form a coherent thought.

My fist meets with bone, and a whoosh of air goes out of Brogut as he thumps to the ground at my feet. I crouch over him, one knee on his chest, and wrap my hands around his neck. A choking sound comes from Brogut's throat as he strains for breath.

I squeeze harder.

There are shouts around me, but they all blend together. All that seems real is the pain in my stomach and Brogut's flesh yielding to my grip.

"You don't want to do this." One voice cuts through the annoying buzz of all the rest.

I look up from Brogut's purpling face, and my eyes meet Wade's.

"Yes, I do," I snarl in a voice that doesn't sound at all like my own.

"You don't want to do this," Wade says again. "I know you, Hemera."

Wade wraps his arms around me. "Come on, love," he says in my ear. "Come back to me."

Slowly, I release Brogut and let Wade pull me into his arms.

Brogut coughs and heaves in a shuddering breath. He gives me a murderous glare before slinking off to join the other Halves on the far side of the arena.

My body starts to shake. *What did I almost just do?*

"It's okay," Wade says. "You're okay."

"What if you weren't here?" Panic tightens my chest at the thought of what I almost just did. What I wanted to do.

"I'll always be here, love."

CHAPTER 41

You proved your worth today, young lady." Valior, perched on his cushioned chair in the meeting chamber, gives me a missing-toothed smile. "These Zeroes will be our salvation."

"Or our doom," Dayne mutters.

"Be that as it may, you earned the support of the Eastern settlement." Valior's grin widens.

"I'll admit," Tut says, "I didn't think there was anything you could do to convince me." He exchanges a look with Liglette. "But the North is with you, too."

"I am pleased to be able to tell you," Liglette says in her melodic voice, "the Western settlement will join with the Solguards."

I just nod, too exhausted to try to come up with the right thing to say.

"These creatures have gotta be better than whatever they're cooking up in Malarusk," Valior chuckles. "The Duskers won't know what's coming for them."

"Good." Wade's tone is business-like, but I can tell how relieved he is.

"So, what's next?" Tut asks.

"The Halves and Solguards are already here," Wade says. "How soon can the rest of your people arrive?"

"If they spread out, the messengers can probably get to all the settlements in a little under a week." Valior rubs at the stubble on his chin. "Our people are starving and weak, so it will take them longer to get here. Probably two weeks."

No one speaks for a moment, but we're all sharing the same thought. The Duskers will have come and gone before the Banished even get here.

A wave of fury sweeps through me like wildfire. If the Banished leaders hadn't been such cowards, if they'd sent for their people sooner, we'd have a chance now.

Tut interrupts my dark thoughts. "We're still avoiding the real problem here."

"Which is?" Wade asks, his teeth clenched.

"Jadem, in all her wisdom, didn't build this place to withstand a real fight. It was supposed to stay hidden."

"Well, it's not hidden anymore," Wade snaps. "We'll need to reconstruct the fortress as much as possible before the Duskers attack." He turns to me. "Will the Halves help us set up defenses?"

I translate the question for Ekil. After a long pause, during which Ekil stares at me in a way I'm not sure what to make of, the Halve nods.

"I'll send weapons and provisions and a handful of guards with the messengers," Wade tells the Banished leaders. "Your people will be the rear defense. We'll box the Duskers in."

"You don't *box in* ten thousand soldiers, my boy," Valior says. "But I do admire your spirit."

"You haven't left us with many options," Wade shoots back.

"The Duskers are soldiers from birth. They are trained and disciplined, and their weapons are forged from iron." Liglette swallows. "Our soldiers are made by necessity. Our weapons are wood and stone. We have heart, but we're hardly a match for the regimented troops that will be attacking."

"The Zeroes will make up for whatever your people lack," Wade argues. "We should be focusing on our strengths rather than weaknesses."

Something about Wade's words makes a new possibility occur to me. I turn it over while the others argue.

"What if we didn't defend the fortress?"

Everyone stops talking and looks at me.

"If being prepared gives the Duskers the advantage," I press on, "then let's not give them time to prepare."

"Are you suggesting…." Tut's words trail off. He looks at the other two Banished leaders. "Is she insane?"

"They'll never expect us to attack them first, in their own territory."

"Yes," Valior says, "because that would not only be insane, it would be impossible."

Even Dayne and Wade are looking at me like I've lost my mind.

"It used to be impossible," I correct. "But things are different now. We have the Zeroes."

The room goes quiet while everyone absorbs what I'm suggesting.

"You think they could break down the iron gate," Wade says.

I nod.

"There's nowhere to hide out there." Dayne grips his new lute in his hands so hard I'm afraid he might break it. "The Dusker archers have clear shots from the mountain lookouts."

"But the Zeroes are fast, aren't they?" Wade asks, looking at me. "Could they make the run from the forest to the gate without being shot down?"

"Yes," I say without hesitation. "And they'll be able to break down the gate in under a minute, which wouldn't give the Duskers many shots."

"With those metal outfits of theirs," Tut says, warming to the idea, "they won't sustain heavy injuries as long as they're quick on their feet."

"They are," I assure him.

"And since the Duskers don't know about the Zeroes," Liglette adds, "we'll have the element of surprise."

"We could get Ry and Dellin on Vlaz and have them pick off some of the Dusker archers from the air," Wade says, and I can tell he likes the plan.

Wade gets up from his seat and walks to the door. "Get Rylin," he tells the guard standing by.

When he comes back to the table, he says, "She'll be able to tell us the exact positions of the Duskers' archers and the best approach for the Zeroes and our foot soldiers."

"The Easterners have some experience with explosives," Valior muses. "If the Zeroes could give us cover, my people could take care of sealing up some of the citadel's exits."

"That would let us funnel those gray bastards up through just a few tunnels." Tut grins, his gold teeth flashing. "We could pick them off one at a time."

"It wouldn't matter that they have better soldiers than us if we cut off their ability to use their entire force against us at once." Valior rubs his hands along the metal surface of his flask. He raises it to his lips, and then, changing his mind, puts it on the table without drinking.

"Halves can go in behind Zeroes," Ekil offers once I've outlined the plan's beginnings for him. "Kill the ones on the Outside."

"I think Wokee has some cammamoss growing down in his orchards," Dayne says. "It might be enough to help us surprise them."

A sharp pang goes through my heart. I first learned about cammamoss in Tanguro, back when Brice and everyone else in the fortress was still alive. We covered our soldiers with it, and it made them next to invisible.

"I like this plan," Liglette announces. "It is very bold. The Duskers will not expect it."

No, they won't. I allow myself a moment to imagine the look on Crowe's face when we march through the tunnels of her citadel, not as her prisoners, but as conquerors.

This is for my aunt, I'll say. Right before I cut her throat.

"I'll grant you the plan has spirit." Valior sits back, steepling his fingers on the table in front of him. "It'll save time, too. We'll send the messengers to the Banished lands as planned, but we'll have the rest of the Solguards following behind. Once we're all convened, we'll go straight on to Malarusk together."

"It needs some finesse," Dayne says, "but it's a good plan."

"Then it's decided," Valior declares. "Make your preparations. We should leave as soon as everyone can be readied."

"The sooner we get to Malarusk, the better our chances will be," Wade agrees.

"There's something else," I say, just remembering. "When I was passing through the Dusker territory on my way here, I saw this smoke…."

There's a soft knock at the door, and then a guard walks in.

"Begging your pardon." The guard's face is bright red as he addresses Wade. "We have a problem, Sir."

"You may speak freely here." Wade motions for the guard to come forward.

"You asked for Rylin, but the thing is," the guard clears his throat, "she's gone."

"Find Dellin," Wade says. "Either Ry will be with her, or she'll know where to find her."

I stifle my irritation.

"That's just the thing." The guard shifts on his feet. "Dellin's gone, too."

Wade, Dayne, and I look at each other.

"Perhaps they went for a walk?" Liglette asks.

"They were seen flying out on the hyenair." The guard shakes his head. "I'm sorry, Sir. We just assumed, I mean, I just thought…." He clears his throat again, his face turning an even deeper shade of red. "No one thought to stop them."

"Not your fault." Wade waves a hand. "I'm sure there's an explanation."

When the guard continues to stand in the doorway, shifting uncomfortably, Wade raises his eyebrows.

"Anything else?" he asks.

I can't help but notice the way authority seems to roll off Wade.

It's so different from the boy I first met…the one who talked too much, who always had a smile and a joke ready, who trained me how to fight. When I look at Wade now, that boy is gone, replaced with someone hardened by loss and responsibility. There's something tragic about it, and it makes me hate the Duskers even more.

"The boy, Wokee."

At the mention of Wokee's name, my attention shifts back to the conversation.

The guard looks at Wade. "I believe he knows where they've gone."

CHAPTER 42

Dayne, Wade, and I find Wokee in Vlaz's empty nest. He's sitting on a mound of straw, fingering the embroidered blue ribbon he's been carrying around since the feast. As soon as he sees us, he balls it up and shoves it in his pocket.

"What are the Crystal Caves?" Wokee asks without preamble.

It takes me a moment to remember where I've heard of them before. Aunt Jadem said those words when I mentioned the story my mother used to tell me about a clear river and beautiful caves.

At first, I'm surprised Wokee has heard the story, too. But then I remember my mother got most of her tales from traders who passed through the Subterrane territory. Some of those traders likely would have gone to the settlements in the Banished lands, as well. It makes sense that the Dwellers and Banished would share some of the same stories.

"Just a legend," I tell Wokee.

Dayne gives me a strange look. "The Crystal Caves are quite real."

I start. "But Aunt Jadem said it was just a story our mother made up."

Dayne raises an eyebrow. "I happen to know it was where our mother used to meet with my father, before she married the Captain."

"Our mother?"

Dayne nods.

I shake my head, trying to process what this means. "But if the Crystal Caves are a real place, then why did Aunt Jadem say it was just a story?"

"I haven't the faintest idea." Dayne shrugs. "She must have known they were real."

I think back to my conversation with my aunt. I remember the strange looks and the forced smiles. I hadn't understood them at the time.

"Why would she have lied?" I ask.

Saying those words, implying my aunt deceived me, hurts.

"What does any of this have to do with Ry's disappearance?" Wade asks. He glances at the doorway where guards and scouts are lining up to speak with him.

"I was coming to check on Vlaz," Wokee explains. "Ry and Dellin were inside and they were whispering, so I stayed outside and listened." He gives us an apologetic look. "I know eavesdropping is rude, but they were acting weird."

"What did you overhear?" Dayne asks.

"Ry had something Jadem had given her. I didn't get a good look," Wokee wrinkles his nose in concentration, "but I think it was a key."

I remember when Aunt Jadem gave Ry something at the feast, and I thought it might be a key. It must have been the same one Wokee saw today.

"And the Crystal Caves?" Dayne presses. "What were they saying about the Crystal Caves?"

"I think Jadem left Ry some kind of note before she died that said to go there." Wokee's voice hitches on the word *died*.

"And Dellin went with her?" Wade asks.

Wokee nods. "The strangest part is that when I came into the cave, they both acted like they didn't want me to know what they were up to."

Wade lets out a breath.

"They know how to steer Vlaz?" Dayne asks.

Wokee nods. "I should have stopped them, but it was Ry, so I didn't think—" he breaks off and looks at me. "Am I in trouble?"

"Of course not," I tell him.

"Why wouldn't she tell us she was leaving?" Wade's brow furrows.

"If Dellin is some kind of spy," Dayne begins, but Wade cuts him off.

"I know Ry, and she's not a traitor."

"Maybe Dellin tricked her somehow," I say. "Or forced her."

"Ry isn't stupid or helpless," Wade replies. "If she's with Dellin, it's because she wants to be."

I feel a quick stab of annoyance. How could Wade be so sure of her? In the smallest part of my mind, I wonder if he would have defended me the same way if it had been me who disappeared.

Of course, he would have, the rational part of my brain says. *And it's an irrelevant thought, anyway.*

"She told me not to tell any of you she was leaving," Wokee says. "I don't think she wanted you to follow her."

"That much is clear," Dayne says. "The question is why?"

"And why would she bring Dellin with her instead of us?" I add.

We're all silent for a moment.

"We have to go after her," I decide. No matter how much everyone wants to trust Dellin, Ry might still be in trouble.

"The Crystal Caves are far from here, farther than any of the other territories," Dayne says. "It would take weeks to get there."

"I'm sure they'll be back soon," Wade says without much confidence. "We're probably worrying for nothing."

Dayne nods. "The Crystal Caves were abandoned years ago when Burn vultures started to nest nearby. Whatever she's hoping to find, I guarantee it's not there."

"In and out," Wade says. "With Vlaz, they'll be back in no more than a day."

"Don't even think about it," Dayne tells me, reading my thoughts. "You can't go running off to a place none of us has ever been with a hundred Zeroes trailing you."

"We can't run the risk of a Dusker seeing the Zeroes," Wade agrees. "And I don't want the Banished leaders thinking anything is wrong. They're skittish enough as it is."

I don't say anything and neither does Wokee. His eyes are fixed on the spot in the room where all of the supply packs made specially for hooking around Vlaz's harness usually rest. They're all gone.

✳ ✳ ✳

High day comes, and Ry and Dellin are still missing. Either they've made it to their destination, or they're holed up in a travel cave somewhere along the way.

I leave the note I hastily scribbled for Wade with my father, since he's the only one in the fortress who doesn't see Wade as his leader. He's also the only one who won't try to stop me.

Wade and Dayne will be furious with me for leaving without them, but by the time they find out I'm gone, they won't be able to do anything about it.

When I told him where I was going, my father offered to lead the Zeroes to the Eastern settlement. I bit back a comment about never trusting him enough for that, considering how he's done nothing but help me since rescuing us from the Duskers. I asked him instead to keep feeding the Zeroes while I was gone. He'd done it from the beginning, and I had no interest in hunting the mystery meat my father always had for them.

My father was right about the Zeroes needing to follow someone in my absence, though. The only person I could bear to have authority over them was my brother. So, before I left, I commanded the Zeroes to follow Dayne when the Solguards left the fortress.

I asked Liglette if she knew where to find the Crystal Caves. As the leader of the Western Banished—a people who survived by following the stag herds across territories and digging crude caves where they stayed for only a few months at a time—I figured she would have come across the place in her travels.

Part of me hoped Liglette would wrinkle her brow and tell me the Crystal Caves were a myth, just like Aunt Jadem had said. But she didn't. She just told me the straightest path to find them.

It's easy to steal out of the fortress without anyone looking twice at me. Solguards and Halves are throwing supplies into packs, sharpening weapons, and planning routes. No one even glances at me as I make my way up the thousand steps and through the archway that leads to the Outside.

It's high day, and I'm alone. Even though the air is stifling, I feel free in a way I never do during low day. No one else can survive more than a few minutes in this sun's intensity. And so, for the next twelve hours, the Outside is mine, and mine alone.

"I'm coming for you, Ry," I say.

And you, Dellin. Because no matter what everyone else thinks, I know she's behind whatever's happened to Ry. And if Dellin is a Dusker spy like I'm sure she is, then it will make it all the easier to kill her along with Crowe.

I curl my right hand, the one emblazoned with the Solguard tattoo, over my heart as I look back at the fortress.

And then I'm running.

THE END

* * *

Because reviews are so important for a book to be successful, please considering **leaving a brief review** at your favorite online bookseller if you enjoyed *Halve Human*. Many thanks!

* * *

Book 3 in the Bisecter series, ***Dusker Dark***, is now available!

* * *

Stephanie Fazio's e-Newsletter

Sign up for **Stephanie Fazio's e-Newsletter** to learn about upcoming books at: https://stephaniefazio.com/subscribe/

Acknowledgements

It seems like I just finished writing my acknowledgements for *Bisecter*, but now, here we are with Book 2 in the series. I couldn't be more thrilled, and I have so many people to thank for the way it has turned out.

First and foremost, to my incredible husband, Andrew. Thank you for the late-night brainstorming sessions, endless mugs of tea, and for filling my every day with so much laughter and love. Especially love. There is no one I would rather share this amazing journey with.

To my parents. Thank you for believing in me long before I believed in myself.

Thank you, Rachel, for being the best sister anyone could ever ask for. And thank you, Julie, for being my bestie. I love you both.

To my amazing team, who helped bring my dream to life. Huge thanks to Ellen Schaeffer, Whitney Dorr, Teodora Chinde, and Sebastian Lacle. You all made the process, and not just the outcome, so much fun. Your creativity is truly inspiring.

For my earliest readers, who made incredible suggestions that brought the book to new and exciting places. Special thanks to Bob Brodsky and the rest of my ARC team. Thank you for your patience and belief in this work.

And thank you to my readers, for your support and enthusiasm. You all inspire me to strive for better with each book.

About the Author:

Stephanie Fazio is a fantasy author. She grew up in Syracuse, New York, and prior to writing full time, she worked in the fields of journalism, secondary education, and higher education. She has an undergraduate degree in English from Colgate University and a Master's degree in Reading, Writing, and Literacy from the University of Pennsylvania. Stephanie lives in Austin with her husband and crazy rescue dog. When she isn't writing, she's getting lost in parks, hosting taco nights, or ironically and miserably losing at word games, but having fun while she does it.

Connect with Stephanie Fazio

Visit her Website: https://www.stephaniefazio.com
Sign up for her newsletter: https://stephaniefazio.com/subscribe/

Discover other books by Stephanie Fazio

Continue the saga with *Dusker Dark*, Book 3 in the Bisecter series.

Available to order now!

StephanieFazio.com